Odd One Out

ALSO BY NIC STONE

Dear Martin

Odd One Out

NIC STONE

Crown
New York

Text copyright © 2018 by Andrea Livingstone
Jacket photograph copyright © 2018 by Nigel Livingstone

All rights reserved. Published in the United States by Crown Books for Young Readers, an imprint of Random House Children's Books, a division of Penguin Random House LLC, New York.

Crown and the colophon are registered trademarks of Penguin Random House LLC.

Visit us on the Web! GetUnderlined.com

Educators and librarians, for a variety of teaching tools, visit us at RHTeachersLibrarians.com

Library of Congress Cataloging-in-Publication Data is available upon request.
ISBN 978-1-101-93953-6 (trade) — ISBN 978-1-101-93954-3 (lib. bdg.) —
ISBN 978-1-101-93955-0 (ebook)

Printed in the United States of America
10 9 8 7 6 5 4 3 2 1
First Edition

Random House Children's Books supports the First Amendment and celebrates the right to read.

For all the people who just don't know

Book One

The Game Plan

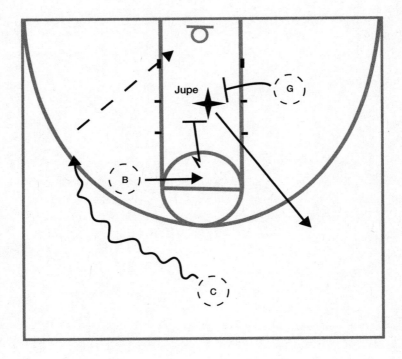

1

I, Courtney Aloysius Cooper IV, Should Be a Very Sad Dude

I should be devastated or pissed or deflated as I let myself into the house next door and climb the stairs to my best friend's bedroom. I should be crushed that less than a month into my junior year of high school, my latest girlfriend kicked me to the curb like a pair of too-small shoes.

It's ridiculous that I have to stop outside the door to get my act together so Best Friend won't get suspicious, isn't it? Rubbing my eyes so the whites look a little red, slumping my shoulders, hanging my head, and poking my bottom lip out just the slightest bit so I *look* sad . . .

Best Friend doesn't even look up from her phone when I open the door. Normally I'd be offended since I did all this work pretending sadness, but right now it's a good thing she keeps her eyes fixed to the little screen. She's sitting at her desk, laptop open, in one of those thin-strapped tank tops—nothing underneath, mind you, and she's got a good bit more going on up there than most girls our age. She's also wearing *really* small shorts, and she's not small down bottom, either. In the words of her papi: "All *chichis* and *culo*, that girl . . ."

And I can't *not* notice. Been trying to ignore her *assets* since they started blooming, if you will, in seventh grade. Largely because I know *she* would kick me to the curb if she knew I thought of her . . . that way. But anyway, when I see her sitting there with her light brown skin on display like sun-kissed sand and her hair plopped on top of her head in a messy-bun thing, my devastated-dumped-dude act drops like a bad habit.

I close my eyes. The image has already seared itself into my memory, but I need to pull myself back together. With my eyes still closed, I cross the room I know better than my own and drop down into the old La-Z-Boy that belonged to my dad.

Despite the squeak of the springs in this chair, she doesn't say a word.

I crack one eye: no earbuds. There's no way she doesn't realize I'm in here. . . . She smiles at something on her phone, tap-tap-tap-tap-taps around, and after literally two seconds, there's the *ping* of an incoming text. She L's-O-L.

I sigh. Loudly. Like, *overly* loudly.

Tap-tap-tap-tap-tap-tap. "You're back early," she says without looking up.

"You should put some clothes on, Jupe."

"Pffft. Last I checked, you're in *my* domain, peon."

Typical. "I need to talk to you," I say.

"So talk."

Ping! She reads. Chuckles.

Who the hell is she even talking to?

I take a deep breath. Wrangle a leash onto the green-eyed monster bastard raging within. "I can't."

She glares over her shoulder at me. "Don't be difficult." God.

Even the stank-face is a sight to behold. "You're the one being difficult," I say.

"Oh, well, excuse me for feeling *any* opposition to you waltzing into my room without knocking and suggesting that *I* adapt to your uninvited presence." She sets her phone down—thank God—faces her computer, and mutters, "Friggin' patriarchy, I swear."

I smile and glance around the room: the unmade bed and piles of clothes—dirty stuff on the floor near the closet, clean in a basket at the foot of the bed; the old TV and VHS player she keeps for my sake since she never uses them when I'm not here, or so she says; the photo on the dresser of me, her, my mom, and her dads on vacation in Jamaica six years ago; the small tower of community service and public speaking certificates and plaques stacked in the corner that she "just hasn't gotten around" to hanging on the white walls.

I'll never forget my first time being in here ten years ago: she was six, and I was seven, and a week after Mama and I moved in next door, Jupe dragged me into this "domain" of hers because she wanted "to know more about my sadness." She knew we'd moved because my dad died—I told her *that* the day we met. But *this* was the day I hit her with the details: he was killed in a car crash and he'd been out of town and I hadn't gotten to say goodbye.

Still hate talking about this.

I cried and cried on her bed, and Jupe wrapped her skinny arms around me and told me everything would be okay. She said she knew all about death because her bunny Migsy "got *uterined cancers* and the vet couldn't save her." And she told me that after a while it wouldn't "hurt so bad," but "I'll be your friend when it hurts the most, Courtney."

And there she is: Jupiter Charity-Sanchez at her computer, with her grass-green fingernails, three studs in each ear, and a hoop through her right nostril, likely organizing some community event to bring "sustenance and smiles" to the local homeless or a boycott of some major retailer in protest of sweatshop conditions in Sri Lanka.

Jupe—my very, very best friend in the universe. Force, firebrand, future leader of America, I'm sure.

This is home. *She* is home.

"Did you pull together a donation for the Carl's Closet clothing drive like I asked you to, loser?" she says.

See?

"I forgot," I reply.

She shakes her head. "So unreliab—"

Ping!

She snorts when she reads this time.

"Who are you texting?" I ask as she taps out her response.

"If you *must* know, her name is Rae."

"Rae?"

"Rae. She's new. Just moved here."

"Why don't I know her?"

"She's technically a sophomore."

"So why do *you* know her?"

4

"What's with the third degree, Coop?" She turns back to her computer.

I grab a pair of balled socks from the clean-clothes basket and lob it at her head.

Bingo.

"Excuse you!" She spins her chair to face me fully. Which I assure you is a blessing *and* a curse. She's cold. Needless to say, my mind is no longer on this *Rae* person. In fact, quite thankful for the blanket Jupe keeps draped over the back of the La-Z-Boy. Down over my lap it goes.

Thanks for nothing, basketball shorts.

I lean my head back and close my eyes. *So, so cold, good Lord.* "Please put some clothes on, Jupiter."

"I absolutely will not," she says. "If you'd knocked, I would've had the *chance* to put some clothes on. But you didn't. So suck it up."

I open my eyes to scowl at her. Phone's to the side, and she's typing away on the laptop with her nose in the air.

So this is war, apparently.

"You're refusing?"

"My room, asshole."

"Fine." I move the blanket. "You don't wanna put clothes on, you'll have to deal with me sitting here with a tent in my shorts."

"What?" She looks at me.

I point to my lap.

"OHMYGOD!" She leaps from the chair, bumps the desk, phone falls to the floor—bonus!—and runs into her closet.

Winner, winner, chicken dinner.

"I hate you," Jupe says, poking her head out the door while she finishes dressing.

I laugh.

"No, for real." She reappears in ratty sweatpants and the baggiest sweater I've ever seen, plops down in her desk chair, and shoots knives at me from her honey-colored eyes. "I really, for *real*, hate you. . . . I can't believe you just wielded your *wand*."

"Pure biology, Jupe," I say. "It's nothing personal." Which is true for the most part.

"You're such an ass."

"Nah." I tuck my hands behind my head.

Have I mentioned I love winning? Just hope that phone doesn't ping again. No clue who this "Rae" is, but I'm not okay with some *girl* distracting my best friend while I'm sitting right here.

"God, what I wouldn't give to knock that shit-eating grin off your face," she says.

"Admit it, Jupiter: your love for me runs as wide and as deep as all the oceans combined."

"Oh my God." Another eye roll. "What are you doing here again?"

"Huh?"

"Here," she says. "Why are you *here*? Aren't you supposed to be on a date?"

Oh. Right. That.

Deep sigh for effect, and then: "Jupe, I need the Jam."

The Jam is this song-and-dance ritual Jupe and I do every time I get dumped. Which happens more often than I care to admit.

"You're not even serious right now," she says.

"The Jam, Jupiter."

"Coop, it hasn't even been a month! What the hell happened?"

"Cue the Jaaaaaam!"

She shakes her head and reaches for the laptop. "You're unbelievable," she says, shifting her fingers around on the touchpad and clicking a few times before looking over at me. "You ready for verse two?"

"Oh, I will be."

As the opening bass solo kicks off, I have a brief flashback to my first time in this exact position: Sadie McGrady had broken up with me, and back then—a full two years ago—I was actually upset about it. I came to Jupe, and to make me feel better, she played the song now thumping against my eardrums. Jupe's been obsessed with Queen since we were little—the only thing she *does* have on display in her room is a poster of Freddie Mercury on her closet door, in fact—so I'd heard the song a thousand times but hadn't thought of it as a heartbreak jam until that moment.

First chorus: *(dun . . . dun . . . dun . . .)* ♩ *Anotha one bites the dust* ♩ . . .

After the last "another one bites the dust," I leap up from the La-Z-Boy as Jupe leaps up from her desk chair, and we land side by side for our verse-two dance break:

Arms thrown wide, head thrown back, cross arms over chest, then drop into a squat . . . look left, then right, then left, then right, jump up, cross the feet, and spin to face the back . . . right hand on right butt cheek, left hand on left butt cheek, bend at the waist and shake, shake, shake . . . right foot forward, pivot

7

*to the front, make a gun with your finger, shoot a shot, high
five.*

As the chorus plays again, I wrap an arm around Jupe's
waist and pull her down into the chair with me. I squeeze
her tight, set my chin on her shoulder, and sigh. She's always so . . . cozy.

And there's the *ping!*

She tries to get up.

Not happenin'. "Yeah, no." I hold on for dear life. "I'm in
distress. *Rae* can wait."

She sighs and relaxes.

"Thank you," I say.

"So what happened?" She lays her arms on top of mine.

I could stay like this forever, side note.

"You," I say.

"Me?"

"You. Again."

"Un-frickin'-believable." She moves my arms so she can
get up, and I let her this time. "What is *with* these girls?"

"They just can't get past you, Jupe." Neither can I, obviously. But of course I don't say that.

"It's ludicrous." She sits back at her laptop. "They do
know I'd rather sleep with them than you, right?"

So that stings. It shouldn't, of course—the only closet
Jupe's ever been in is the one where she just changed her
clothes—but it does.

Hope she's not planning to sleep with this *Rae* . . .

I clear my throat. "Doesn't seem to matter, Jupe. They
feel threatened."

She shakes her head. "So what did this one say?"

8

"Something to the effect of *'There's obviously something going on between you two and it's disgusting.'*"

"Wait . . ." She spins in her chair again and cocks her head. "How exactly would that be 'disgusting'? Heteronormative is still very much—"

"*Normative*. I know," because she says that *all the time* even though it's redundant. "I'm sure she was trying to make herself feel better. What can I say, Jupes? Despite your preferences, these girls can't seem to handle the fact that I have a gorgeous female best friend."

"Don't call me gorgeous, Coop. It's weird."

It's true. "Sorry."

"Well, sorry it didn't work out," she says. "This one was pretty hot, too. Amazing waist-to-hip ratio."

"True."

"Did you two . . ." She makes a sound like a popping cork with her lips.

So crude. "No, Jupiter."

"Still saving it for me, huh?" With a wink.

About that: I pledged my virginity to Jupe when we were in seventh grade after having real sex ed for the first time. Her response? "Eww, Coopie, *gross.*"

And no. I haven't broken said pledge despite the fact that Jupe's only ever been into girls and it will likely never happen.

Notice I said *likely*.

Yes, I'm an idiot.

Guessing she can see the idiocy on my face or something because she's laughing. Which makes my stomach hurt. And now I feel like a punk-ass.

Do I realize it's dumb to have secret feelings for my lady-loving best girl friend and to want said best girl friend to be my first sexual intercourse experience? Yes. But being reminded of the dumbness doesn't make me feel very good.

Where I was pretending to be sad before, there is genuine sadness now.

"This sucks, Jupe."

Of course *she* thinks I'm talking about the breakup.

She pokes her lip out, and then gets up and comes over to pull me out of the chair. "You need a cuddle, Courtney Cooper," she says. We walk over to her bed and I lie down on my back. She burrows underneath my arm, lays her head on my chest with her nose tucked right beneath my chin, and drapes an arm over my waist and a thigh over my thigh. "Better?" she asks.

This.

This is what I came here for. *This* is why when the girl whose name is already fading from my memory told me she was done with me, I breathed a sigh of relief. I've gone almost a month without *This*. Even if my best friend is gay, being all cuddled up with her while I have a girlfriend is obviously a no-go, but now that I'm free, I get to have *This* again.

I peek at her forgotten phone under the desk and exhale all my troubles away. Let her oh-so-Jupiter scent—which right now is all *mine*—carry me off. "Yes," I say. "Much better."

"It won't always be this way, Coopie," Jupe says. "One day, you'll meet the girl of your dreams, and the two of you will fit together like puzzle pieces. No more getting dumped."

I smile and kiss her forehead the exact same way I did when we lay like this for the first time nine years ago. Second grade: Jupe was seven and I was eight, and I came into her room one day and found her sobbing in her closet. When she told me what'd happened—some dickwad fifth grader had called her a "dumb dyke"—I asked if she needed a cuddle because, duh, cuddles ~~were~~ *are!* the supreme cure for all forms of malaise.

Fact: I was bigger than the mini-bigot—always been one of the biggest kids in school—so I kicked his ass the next day and totally got suspended. It was worth it considering Jupe hasn't heard a homophobic slur since.

The rest, as they say, is history.

"What can I say, Jupey?" I tell her. "You win some, you lose some."

2

The Scent of Jupe's Overpriced Curly-Hair Gunk in My Nostrils Always Marks the Start of a Perfect Morning

Screw coffee: when Papi knocks and yells, "Jupiter! Up!" at six-thirty, and I catch a whiff of Manuka Honey & Mafura Oil—ask me how many times I've been sent out to replace the stuff for her—I breathe in real deep and smile. A weight lifts from my chest and my left thigh, and then a light clicks on to my left. There's a reddish indentation on Jupe's cheek from where she was lying against a fold in my T-shirt, and her hair is all fuzzy.

"I'm taking first shower," she says with a yawn.

I suck my teeth, though I'm still smiling. "But you *always* get first shower."

"My house, jackass."

Considering how often Jupe and I have woken up with our limbs entangled over the past ten years—when we were younger, this could've involved a bed, couch, floor, pillow fort, "tent" made of beach towels, or stuffed-animal-filled

12

bathtub, and since everyone knows Jupe likes girls, the parents never made us stop sleeping together—we've probably had this exact exchange a couple thousand times.

Still smiling.

"Let Dad know you're here so he makes enough grits," she says. "Bottomless pit eating us out of house and home." She fake-scowls at me, then stretches and stands—incredible view, by the way. Grabs some stuff from the clean-laundry pile on her way out.

Thus commences my return to life as Decatur High's most eligible bachelor.

This is how the cycle goes: I'll be a free bird for a while—maybe a month, month and a half—and at first it's great because I get to spend all the time I want just living the Jupe-and-Coop life. Despite her I-run-the-universe schedule, Jupe always makes time for me: we do homework together, watch old movies, play one-on-one in my driveway, take aimless drives in the old BMW 5 Series we share, do volunteer work, play board/card games, practice my cheerleading lifts.

Did I mention I'm a cheerleader? Me and two of my basketball teammates are on the varsity football cheer squad. Keeps us in shape during football season, and it turns out girls around here really dig male cheerleaders. Jupe refuses to "publicly participate in an activity so subjected to the male gaze," but she lets me toss her around in the backyard. She's got a good fifteen pounds on our squad's heaviest flyer, so working out with her makes lifting *those* chicks easy as pie. Don't tell her I used the word *chicks*.

Basically, when I'm single, Jupe and I have fun together just being *us*.

But then sometime between the four- and six-week mark, she gets all "Coopie, you're too much of a catch to be spending so much time with me when there's a whole world of eligible straight girls out there."

It's a knife to the jugular every. single. time.

Again, I *know* she's into girls. *Everybody* knows Jupe's into girls. But it still crushes me *EVERY* damn time I hear "Coop, you need a girlfriend" come out of her mouth.

So I sulk for a couple of days, and then I buck up and find someone new to date. *This time will be different*, I tell myself going in.

Within a week or two, there's a new lady on my arm. No more Jupe-and-Coop. It's Coop-and-Johanna or Coop-and-Kaitlyn; Coop-and-Tamika or Coop-and-Quyen. And the girls are always great.

But compared to Jupe-and-Coop?

The thing nobody knows about me: despite being a six-foot-four, 210-pound combo guard—not to brag, but I'm ranked number two in the state, and started getting calls from college scouts in the eighth grade—I, Courtney Aloysius Cooper IV, am absolutely terrified of girls who aren't Jupiter Charity-Sanchez.

I have *no idea* how to be a good boyfriend. I've spent my whole life watching a successful romantic relationship between Jupe's two dads, who I totally consider my dads, too, but the only good hetero relationship I've ever seen was my parents'. And while it was clear Daddy loved Mama more than he loved anything, I was too busy playing with Legos and shit to pick up on the practicals.

I go after these girls I think I have a chance of developing real feelings for, but then they get all weird and googly-eyed and expectant. Next thing I know, I'm overwhelmed with anxious questions—*Is a kiss on the forehead too friendly? Should I hold her hand in public? What about posting couple-y pictures online? Should I go around to open her car door?* See, the girl I've spent the most time with would cut me if I tried to open a door for her. I have no grid for this shit.

I try to be all smooth and romantic like Humphrey Bogart—my dad's collection of Bogart VHS tapes, the VCR he used to play them on, and the La-Z-Boy where we used to sit and watch them play, all of which are now in Jupe's room, are the three things of Daddy's Mama let me keep—and there's been a time or two that I've watched Bogart movies *just* to study his characters' ways with the ladies . . .

But then I feel like a fraud and start to crave that place/ person where/with whom I can just be myself. My mind wanders while I'm on dates, or I get too touchy with Jupe at school, or I slip up and call whatever girl I'm with Jupiter.

Then the girlfriend dumps me.

My longest relationship lasted fifty-three days.

What do I do then?

Cue the Jam.

After cheer practice Monday afternoon, my boys and I hit the weight room. Jesse Cox, power forward—better known as Golly since he's a certifiable giant but *Goliath* is too hard to chant—is examining his stubble in the wall-wide mirror, and Britain Grier, starting point guard and the shorty at six foot even slash only white dude of our trio (though he doesn't "sound" like it) is spotting me on bench press.

I'm on my second set when Golly brings up the news of the day.

"So Coop, what happened with you and your girl, dawg? I thought things were good?"

"Yeah, brah." Lately, Britain's taken to referring to all his guy friends as a women's undergarment.

No clue.

"What can I say?" I tell them. "Guess I failed to meet her expectations."

Golly comes and stands next to Britain so they're both looking down at me as I do my last set. "Please tell us you smashed at least once," Britain says.

I rack the barbell. "She wasn't a beer can, fool."

"Aw, damn. Here we go with that feminism shit." Golly rolls his eyes as he adds a forty-five-pound plate to each end of the barbell. I rise, and he takes my place on the bench.

"What the hell kinda state-champ ballplayer says shit like that?" Britain says. "*'She wasn't a beer can'?*"

"You asked if I *smashed*—"

"We know what you meant." This from Golly. "It's just—" He shakes his head, then shoves the barbell into the air and begins his reps.

"It's just what?" I ask.

Golly finishes his first set and sits up and turns to face me. "Coop, you're in your *prime*, dawg! Chicks worship you."

"Right!" Britain says, moving to the squat rack. "You're like a deity and you don't even take advantage of that shit!"

"See, that's you guys' problem right there," I say. "Neither

16

of you have any appreciation for the inherent value of women as human beings."

"Coop, do you *hear yourself* right now?" Britain says.

Golly gets up to add more weight to the bar.

See? Goliath.

He lies back down for his second set. "You been hangin' with Jupiter *way* too much, homie."

"You assholes do realize that part of the reason girls like me is because they know I'll treat them with utmost respect, right?"

"Dawg, we not sayin' be *dis*respectful. But you can't tell me these girls don't offer you the goods. Your ass turns them *down!*"

"Right," from Britain. "And tell yourself they like that nice-guy shit if you want to, but these honeys ain't ignoring the fact that you're one of the top high school ballplayers in the state. Maybe even the nation."

"*And* you look like a less-swole, beardless version of that dude who guards the rainbow bridge in the Thor movies," Golly says. "With the brown skin and kinda lightish eyes? Women love that shit."

"It's not all about looks, Golly."

"He's hopeless, dawg." This from Britain. "This is what happens when a straight dude is raised by two gay men and has a feminist sister figure who doesn't like dudes."

"Wait, so my *valuing* of girls is a problem? And leave my 'sister figure' out of it—"

"Hmph," from Golly. "'Sister figure,' my ass." He sits up. "Coop, you think we don't know you're madly in love with Jupiter Sanchez, bro?"

"Can't say we blame you." Britain comes over and sits next to Golly on the weight bench. "Ya girl is fine as a well-aged wine."

So this is going to be a two-on-one, then.

"That she is, my friend," from Golly. "She's got that smile—"

"All that curly hair—"

"Them bright-ass eyes and luscious lips—"

"And booty for *daaaaaays*, brah—"

"HEY! You assholes watch your mouths *and* your minds!"

Golly starts cracking up. Which is always an interesting experience since he's six foot seven and 240 pounds of mahogany steel but has this high-pitched hyena giggle.

"Just admit it, Coop," Britain says. "You got a jones in your bones for your chick-diggin' stepsister."

"She's not my stepsister."

Golly laughs even harder. The guy's on the verge of tears. "Coop, how long have we known each other?"

I cross my arms and do the math. "Seven years."

"And in those seven years, how many times have we had a conversation about girls that didn't come back around to Jupiter?"

"How the hell would I know, Golly? Girls are pretty much *all* we talk about."

"And *every* time we talk about them—whether it's me getting laid, or you getting dumped, or Britain getting played—"

"Ey, shut yo big hyena-laughin' ass up, brah."

Golly giggles again. "My point is, no matter how/when/ why the conversation starts, it always ends with Coop

18

saying, 'Welp, guess it's a good thing I've got Jupe!' in his gee-golly-willikers voice."

Britain's barely visible blond eyebrows tug down. "You know what, you might be right!"

"I know I'm right," Golly says.

"Look, I know you guys are prolly jealous," I say, "but Jupiter Charity-Sanchez is my very best friend."

"You hear how he says her name?" Britain nudges Golly with his elbow.

Golly clasps his hands beneath his chin and bats his eyelashes. *"Jupiter Charity-Sanchez . . . sigh."*

Jackass.

"Hey, both of you can kiss my black ass."

"Well, we all know Jupe will never do it," Britain says.

"Brit, even if Jupe was straight, she wouldn't kiss Coop's black ass."

"Whatever," Brit says. "Y'all get my meaning."

Golly shakes his head but still says, "He's right, Coop. I know you still got some hope that Jupe'll wake up one morning craving that cobra in your trousers, but you gotta let that go, man."

"It's not even about tha—"

Golly lifts a hand the size of a baseball glove to cut me off. "Don't think we don't notice how you sabotage all your relationships so you can run back to Jupiter, Coop. You might have everybody else fooled with that sad-dumped-guy shit, but we know you."

"He's right," from Britain. "And seeing a strapping young chap of your stature and potential stuck on a girl you'll never have? It's hard to watch, man."

What the hell do I even say to that? Can't deny it, obviously. There's this poster in Dad's—as in Troy Charity's—office that says THE MOST IMPORTANT PERSON TO BE HONEST WITH IS YOURSELF. He says it's there to remind him of what his life was like before he came out, but it's definitely something I make an effort to put into practice.

It's just that *never* is really hard to swallow.

"I have no clue what to do, y'all." I drop my chin because I can feel prickles in the corners of my eyes. And while I grew up with men who stressed there's nothing wrong with a fella shedding a tear or two, weeping in the weight room in front of my boys is something I'd rather not do.

"All right, bring it in," Golly says. He and Britain stand and throw their arms around each other's shoulders, leaving a gap for me to join them in a three-man huddle.

Once I'm in, Golly says, "So what we need here is a game plan. Coop's in a tight spot, and we gotta get him out of it."

"Yeah . . . yeah . . . ," from Britain. "I'm feelin' it." He starts to sway like we're in our final time-out during a close game. So of course, Golly starts really feeling it and swaying, and next thing I know, I'm swaying and getting hyped, too.

Go time, baby.

"So this is what I'm thinkin'," Golly says. "Coop, you need to study Jupiter's moves. Figure out what she does, what she says, how she says and does it. All the stuff about her that's got you twisted up in the game and shit. She's doing something for you that these other girls aren't, and we know it's not about the boom-boom since you ain't gettin' any there. You really got some thinkin' to do."

"Yeah, yeah." I'm nodding with my sway. "I can do that."

"Write all the shit down so you know what you really *need* in a woman. What'll keep you coming back, you feel me?"

"Golly, I hate to break it to you, but this is some real girly shit you talkin' about right now," from Britain.

Golly doesn't stop his sway. "I have *five* sisters, hello? Three of them are in good relationships. I seen them do this shit, so it obviously works. If you can't get with the Game Plan, take your little ass to the bench."

"Okay, brah, damn." *Sway, sway, sway.* "You don't gotta be so harsh."

Golly continues: "Coop, once you got your Team Jupe playbook together, you can consult it when you encounter a *legitimate* prospect. You can't just pick whatever cute girl is available and try to force the feelings, dawg."

How does this giant-ass dude know SO MUCH about my life?!

"All right, all right," I pant. Like straight-up *panting.* The adrenaline is flowing. "Find a real prospect. Consult the playbook."

"In the meantime, keep your bachelor card, but stay *away* from Jupiter."

I stop the sway and stand up.

"Huh?"

"You heard me, dawg," Golly says. "No more *Jupe-and-Coop* or whatever the hell you call it. Don't be hanging around at her house all the time, snuggling and watching movies and sleeping with her and shit."

Yeah, they know about that. I slipped up and told them of

me and Jupe's fairly frequent sleeping arrangements when I had a stiff shoulder from her lying on my arm all night and kept missing jump shots in a scrimmage last season.

"Wait, though. Why do I have to stay away from Jupe?" And why do I feel like he just told me I have to saw through my nuts with a plastic butter knife?

"Did you really just ask him that, Coop?" Britain says.

"Coop, do you know the basic definition of stupidity?" Golly asks.

"Umm—"

"It's doing the same thing but expecting a different result—"

"Pretty sure that's *insanity*, brah."

"Stupidity, insanity . . . ," Golly says. "Point is: How you expect to get clean if you keep shootin' up, man?"

"Damn, Golly. That was deep," Britain says.

Deep. Like the breath I need to take right now.

"What the hell you plan to do if she gets a girlfriend, Coop?" From Golly.

Ping! The *joy* all over her face when she was texting the other night pops into my head. Still don't know who this Rae is—been trying not to think about it—and I haven't seen Jupe with her phone in her hand since, but still. What *will* I do if she gets a girlfriend?

When she gets a girlfriend. Because it's bound to happen eventually, right?

"We'll cross that bridge when we get to it," I say.

"Brah, if you still burnin' for her the way you are now, any bridge you step onto will go up in flames," Britain says.

"Open your eyes, Coop." Golly. "Jupiter is *never* gonna feel the way you feel, dawg. *Never.* You get that, right?"

Yes . . .

No.

Maybe?

Damn.

"Yeah." Damn! "I get it."

"Repeat after me: Jupiter Charity-Sanchez will never be my woman."

"Jupiter Charity-Sanchez will ne—" I stop. Take a deep breath and try again. "Jupiter Charity-Sanchez will ne— Oh, fuck me, I can't say it!" Now my hands are on my knees, and I swear I just ran a suicide.

"*COME ON, DAWG!*" Golly's using the get-fired-up voice. It makes me *really* feel like we're on the court.

"All right, all right." I bounce on my toes and shake my wrists out as I roll my neck from side to side. "Say it again, Golly. . . ."

"You ready?"

Go time. Go time.

GO TIME, COOPER!

"I'm ready."

Golly: "Jupiter Charity-Sanchez will never be my woman!"

Me: "Jupiter Charity-Sanchez will *never* be my woman!"

"Louder!"

"Jupiter Charity-Sanchez will NEVER *be my woman!"*

"WE CAN'T HEAR YOU, COOP!"

"JUPITER CHARITY-SANCHEZ WILL *NEVER* BE MY WOMAAAAN!"

"HAYLE yeah!" Britain and Golly chest-bump and then smack me on the ass.

No clue what I've gotten myself into.

3

It's Said That on the Fourth Day, God Created the Sun, Moon, and Stars, But I Feel Like All Three Have Fallen from the Sky

For one thing, I really haven't slept since implementing the Game Plan.

There's this nightmare I have sometimes. Starts with me on a merry-go-round. At first everything is normal, but then this old TV character, Carousel Carl, pops up at the control panel. Carl was the star of this kids' science show I used to be into because I always felt smarter by the end of the show. He was hella fun to watch and listen to, and I loved that he was the same color as me, but in the nightmare, he looks scary as hell—all red-eyed and gray-skinned and rotten-toothed. He grins at me with this sinister smile, and the unicorn I'm on moves up and down faster and faster, then the merry-go-round spins faster and faster, so I shut my eyes. . . . But when I open them, I'm in a car, and the car is spinning, and the sky is spinning, and there's a tornado spinning, spinning, spinning, and rain, thunder, lightning, screeching tires, my dad's face, then *CRASH*—

That's always when I wake up. Usually sweaty, panting, dizzy as hell, and with no clue where I am. I do know what the nightmare references—it's something I've stuffed deeeeeeep down and never talk about—and when I'm sleeping next door, Jupe's always there to like . . . *ground* me, I guess is the word, and I'm able to go back to sleep.

When I'm at home, though? By myself?

It's bad, man.

To add insult to injury, she's just going on about her life like me not being around has no effect on her whatsoever. Case in point: on Thursday, Golly drops me off after cheer practice—guy's been driving me everywhere, since Jupe and I technically share the car Papi and Dad Charity gave us—and as he's pulling away, a bubblegum-pink Jeep whips into Jupe's driveway.

Breanna Banks. The college sophomore Dad Charity introduced Jupe to last year after she sat in on his History of the African American Experience course—Dad's a professor at Emory, by the way—because he thought they'd "really vibe."

He was right, unfortunately.

What I know about her from Jupe: she does a lot of social justice stuff—organizes protest marches and goes around to high schools, ours included, to get students "active in their communities." She's also an apprentice grant writer for "a handful" of nonprofits, and she's the VP of her university's Pride organization.

And yes, I committed all this to memory. One cannot

best an adversary without full awareness of said adversary's strengths.

Speaking of strengths, she's also . . . really good-looking. Brown-skinned with curly hair she keeps cut in a frohawk, as I've heard Jupe call it—looking at her now reminds me I need a damn lineup. Dark brown eyes. Pretty face. And yeah, she dresses "like a guy," but she's certainly not shaped like one. Also always has her nails painted, which I only notice *because* of the way she dresses.

And she has more swag than me.

Am I feeling threatened as she hops down from the Jeep in her Jordan 5s and her pink chino shorts and her short-sleeved denim button-down with plaid bow tie and her dope-ass forearm tats—something I'm not even old enough to get—all on display?

Yep.

Jupe *swears* there's nothing between them but friend-ship. "She's too old for me, Coop. And not my type. A little *too* swaggy." But knowing that this gorgeous human Jupe *could* be into is about to hang out with her when I haven't all week?

Before I know what I'm doing, I'm three-quarters of the way across the wide strip of green that separates my drive-way from Jupe's. "Hey, Breanna! Hold up!"

Now I'm jogging. Yeah, shaking my head, too. Trust me.

"Mr. Cooper!" she says once I reach her. We do that hand-shake/hug-with-the-opposite-arm thing that I usually only do with my boys but feels totally natural with her. "What up, my dude?"

"Chillin', chillin'. You and the Jupe-ster got plans this

lovely evening?" WOW, that came out way wacker than I intended.

Breanna smirks. *Knowingly*, I'd say. Gives me a once-over that makes me feel like a little-ass kid.

I don't like it.

"Yeah, you could say that," she replies. "Some of the kids I work with are doing a poetry slam to raise money for juvenile justice care packages. You . . . uhh . . ." She looks over her shoulder up at Jupe's bedroom window, then back at me. Smiling openly now. "You wanna come?"

"Oh. Nah, I'm good. I, umm . . . have homework?"

Her eyebrows lift. "You sure about that?"

I can't get my lips to move.

"You don't sound very sure, Cooper." Smirks again. She's enjoying every second of this.

I clear my throat. Jam my hands into my pockets. "I'm, uhh . . . gonna get going. You two have fun with . . . whatever it is you're doing."

"Yeah, aiight. Enjoy that 'homework.'" And she winks at me and *swags* up to Jupe's door with the confidence of Kevin Durant playing Horse with a toddler.

This is not a good feeling.

Once I'm inside my house, I basically lose it. Takes everything in me to not say screw this Game Plan bullshit and just bust up next door to take my girl back. Tell Save-the-World Breanna to take a damn hike.

For what it's worth, up until now, I *have* been doing my part. I grab the Jupe playbook from my bedside table and open to the list I put together that first night I couldn't sleep:

What I Love About Jupiter Charity-Sanchez
By Courtney Aloysius Cooper IV

1. She's always there when I need her.
2. She completely accepts me. Well . . . at least everything she knows.
3. She's hella confident. Doesn't need anybody to validate her existence. Most of the girls I've dated spent more time asking me insecure questions than actually enjoying our time together—Do you think I'm pretty? Does this make my ass look small? Am I a good girlfriend? You really like me, right? It got ridiculous.
4. She genuinely cares about people and is really focused on fixing what she sees wrong with the world.
5. She's so damn beautiful, but she's not wack about it. Like some of the pretty girls I've dated who spent more time checking mirrors than actually interacting with me.
6. She's got this way of lighting up a room and making it feel warmer just by being in it.
7. She's secretly a hopeless romantic. In sixth grade, we had a babysitter from Mama's church who wore this charm bracelet. When Jupe asked her about it, she explained that each of the five gemstone charms represented a different intimate act—there was even one for dropping the L-word—and she was supposed to give each charm to whoever she did the corresponding activity with for the first time. I thought it was corny as hell, but Jupe got this look on her face like she was seeing a sunrise for the first time. Color me surprised when she asked for a similar bracelet for her Quince. Said she loved

28

*"the symbolism" and the idea of giving all her "firsts" to
the first person she would "truly love."*
  8. She still has all the gemstones.

In other words, she's a damn unicorn and this is hopeless.

When I showed Brit and Golly the list two days ago, Golly shook his head and said I was *idealizing* her too much: "acting like she has no flaws so you can hold on to the idea that she's perfect for you." Might have to start calling this guy *Guru*, by the way.

So I went back in and tried to add some stuff I *don't* like.

For instance, (a) she's a little *too* tough sometimes. For example: when she found out her surrogate—a black woman named Sunnie—had died, Jupe shrugged it off. "Whatever, it's not like I knew her," she said. But then she didn't eat for a week and a half.

This would also be a good time to mention that Jupe was a twin. Her brother, Mars—Dad and Papi let Sunnie choose the names, and I kid you not, she named the babies *Mars* and *Jupiter*—died when they were seventeen days old. The most interesting part of all this, and brace yourself if you're squeamish about biology stuff: for the IVF, Sunnie was implanted with a mix of eggs—some of the ones they harvested were fertilized with Papi's sperm, and some with Dad's. Meaning Mars and Jupiter could've had totally different fathers. Wild, right? Anyway, they've never checked—Jupe said she didn't want to know—so it can't be said for sure, but she definitely looks more like Papi than Dad.

Also, I would never let her hear me say this, but (b) it

bugs me that she never seems to *need* me—not the way I want her to, at least. Like she'll ask me to go get her tampons and salted-caramel gelato when "Aunt Flo" makes her monthly visit, but she's never called me crying or asked me to come climb a ladder or kill a bug for her or anything. This is the kind of stuff I remember Daddy doing for Mama, and she'd always call him her *hero* afterward. I'd give my left thumb to hear Jupe say that, but it just doesn't happen. Probably never will.

And this last thing is dumb, but (c) I wish she were more demanding of my time, if that makes any sense. She's obviously not jealous of my girlfriends, but I sometimes wish she were less okay with me ditching her for weeks without thinking twice.

Like the fact that I can hear the crank and rumble of Breanna's Jeep outside my window is killing me right now. I haven't seen Jupe in four days, and though she's texted a few times asking me to hang out, when I tell her I can't, she just says, **K.**

K??? What *is* that?

There hasn't been a single *"What are you doing that's so important?"* or *"Coopie, this bed is so empty without you!"* (Not that she'd ever actually say that second one.) And as a result, I've been spending *way* too much time wondering how much she's been talking to this *Rae* person since I'm not around to stop her.

It's torture.

Has she made sure I'm alive? Definitely. She checks in at least twice a day. But she doesn't seem to miss me. Which in some ass-backward way just makes me miss her even more.

My phone *pings!*

Bre said she invited u 2 to the Slam. You should have come w us, loser 😊. With a selfie. Of her and Breanna. Leaned all close together in the Jeep.

I swear there's a mocking glint in Breanna's eye.

I toss the phone onto my carpeted floor and look around my lifeless, everything-Jupe's-isn't bedroom—my plaques and trophies are actually on display, my clothes are either in the hamper (dirty) or folded and put away (clean), and my walls are pale blue instead of white and are hung with posters of Great Men with Girly Names: Connie Hawkins, Dominique Wilkins, Courtney Lee, Shannon Sharpe, Tracy McGrady, Sasha Vujačić, Dana Barros, and Marion Barber III.

I lie back on my perfectly made, perfectly Jupe-less bed that I can't actually get any sleep in, and I stare up at the ceiling. Rivers are running into my ears, but I don't even care right now.

What the hell am I *doing?*

"Courtney?" a voice calls from downstairs.

Shit, what is Mama doing here?

I wipe my tears on my shoulders and throw an arm over my eyes so it looks like I'm sleeping. Of course because Mama is Mama and the sun hasn't gone down, she strolls right in and "wakes me up."

"Sweetheart?"

"Hmmm?"

"I just came from next door." I feel her sit down. "What are you doing here?"

Is she serious? "I live here, Ma."

"Coulda fooled me . . ."

Yeah, not responding to that.

"Sit up." She pats me on the thigh.

With a nice fake groan, I oblige.

"Honey, are you all right?" she says. "You've been looking a bit run-down this week. Are you sleeping okay?"

Whoa, she actually noticed? "I'm fine, I'm fine."

For a few seconds, she stares at me with her eyes narrowed. *Examining* me like I'm one of her patients. I hate when she does this.

"Courtney, your eyeballs look like they're smothered in hot sauce."

"Five cool points for the simile, Ma."

"Don't change the subject." She pulls the penlight out of the collar of her shirt and shines it into my eyes. "Have you been using drugs, sweetie?"

"What? *No*, Mama."

"You know you can tell me the truth, right? We can get you the help you need—"

"*Neetaaaaaa—*"

"Do not call me that, Courtney Cooper. I am your *mother.*"

I close my eyes and shake my head. "I promise I'm not using drugs, Ma."

"Have you ever used them before?"

"Can we not talk about this right now?" I fall back onto the bed.

"It's a yes-or-no question, baby."

I take a deep breath. Push up onto my elbows and look her dead in the eye. "Yes, Mama. I've used drugs before. I had a hash brownie at a party once, and it was the worst six hours of my life, so I don't plan to ever do it again," I say. "Okay?"

Now she wants to look all *taken aback*.

"You asked." I lie down again and return my arm to my face.

"You're not having that nightmare again, are you?"

Oh boy. It *might* be said that I told her I stopped having it three years ago because she was talking about sending me to therapy. And no shade on therapy . . . Just didn't want to talk to some stranger about my subconscious fear of former kid-show stars and merry-go-rounds. "Huh?"

"You heard me, boy."

"I mean, every now and then, I'll have a bad dream. . . ." Not a lie. "But it's nothing to worry about, Mama. Pretty sure everyone has bad dreams occasionally. I know Jupe does."

That is a lie. I know no such thing.

She doesn't respond. And I refuse to look at her because then she'll *know* I'm lying.

"I'm gonna take a quick nap and then hit my homework," I say, rolling over onto my stomach. "Cheer practice was a doozy today."

She still doesn't say anything.

I crack an eyelid. She's standing with her arms crossed. Giving me the Mom Look.

"I promise I'm fine, Mama."

"Yeah, all right," she says. "I'll take your word this time, but don't take that for granted."

"I appreciate that."

"And watch the sarcasm." She finally moves toward the door. "You might be bigger than me now, but I'll still lay you out."

This makes me smile. Which feels nice considering how rarely I've done it over the past four days. "Yes, ma'am."

"Oh, by the way, we're entertaining some guests on Saturday," she says as she opens my door. "There's a new doctor on the pediatric ward who just transferred here from Alabama, and he and his daughter will be coming over for dinner. Pretty sure she's around your age."

"Cool."

"Troy, Emilio, and Jupiter will be joining us as well. Six-thirty sharp, okay?" With that she leaves the room.

Hmm . . .

Logic says that since I'll be forced to see my best friend against my will at this dinner, it's a good idea to go to her house now and wait for her to come home so it won't be an awkward reunion in front of strangers, right? I'm sure me hug-attacking her and refusing to let go would make our guests uncomfortable, and I have no doubt that if I wait until then to be in the same room with her, that's exactly what'll happen.

I stand up, change my shirt, spray on some cologne, and head to the bathroom to wash my face. Pull myself together and all.

I grab my backpack (homework!) and change of clothes for school tomorrow. There's no way I'm coming back to this wack-ass room.

4

Britain and Golly Won't Even Look at Me the Next Day

They knew exactly what was up when I texted Brit this morning to let him know I didn't need a ride. But I feel too good, too *refreshed*—no nightmare for the first time all week—for their insults to get me down.

It isn't until we're changing out of our cheer uniforms after the football game that tomorrow night's dinner comes up. "My brahs," Britain says, bare-chested after removing his cheer top. And yeah, at the sound of the word *brah*, my eyes drop to his pasty adolescent man-chest. "So my new lady invited me to a party tomorrow night—"

"New lady, huh?" Golly pulls a giant polo over his head and jams his arms into the sleeves.

A dreamy look overtakes Britain's face. "Yeah, man."

"Things are official, then?" I ask, zipping my jeans.

Britain's eyes drop. "Well, not *yet*. We're just talkin' right now, but I think this one will stick."

"Yeah, all right, dawg." Golly and I peer at each other, and I know we're thinking the same thing: this girl's gonna play Brit like a Texas Hold 'Em hand.

"Like I was saying before the yeti interrupted"—Brit glares at Golly—"y'all should join me. Hella new girls to peruse." He rubs his hands together like a creeper.

"Can't," I say. "My mom planned a dinner at our house for these people who just moved here from Alabama." I toss my empty water bottle at the trash can across the locker room—*bang bang!* "Some doctor and his daughter."

Britain stops in the middle of putting on his shirt. "Daughter?"

"Yep."

He and Golly exchange a look. "How old is this daughter, man?" Golly says.

I shrug. "Around our age, I guess."

"You guess?"

"That's what my mom said."

Both fully clothed now, they look at each other again. "You thinkin' what I'm thinkin', Golly?" Brit says.

"Yep." Golly knocks on a locker. "You hear that, Coop?"

"Hear what?"

He knocks again. "Sounds like *opportunity.*"

"Sure does," says Brit.

And I'm confused. "What the hell are you fools talking about?"

"He's hopeless!" Brit tosses his hands up in defeat.

Golly: "Coop, this could be a brand-new prospect, un-tainted by Decatur High politics."

"Okay . . ."

"Could she be a troll with more bass in her voice than little Brit over there? Yes."

"Quit with that 'little' shit, brah."

Golly goes on, unfazed: "But she could also be exactly what you need, man."

And now they're both staring at me.

Truth is, in the state I was in yesterday, all I heard when Mama mentioned the dinner was *"Jupiter will be joining us."*

And yeah, I slept last night because I was with her, and I'm not worried about Breanna—Jupe told me how Bre "even had a bunch of *straight* girls trying to get at her at the Slam, and it's way too much, Coop, and I just *cannot*"—but I basically went into attack-dog mode every time Jupe got a text message because while I hadn't heard any more about *Rae*, every *ping!* made me think of her.

"You'll let us know how it goes?" Brit says.

After thinking about it for a sec, I nod. "Yeah. I'll let y'all know."

Because maybe they're right.

Maybe all I really need is something new.

Except within sixty seconds of our dinner guests' arrival, I know all is lost.

The moment we open the door, Jupe squeals—something I've *never* heard her do before. Then she throws her arms around the girl on the other side of it.

The girl's dad looks about as startled as I feel.

After the longest rocking hug I've ever witnessed, they let each other go. "You got your hair trimmed!" Jupe says, reaching out to touch it.

"Mmhmm. You like?"

"I *love* it. Though it makes you even prettier. Which is annoying."

The girl snorts. "Peeked in a mirror lately?"

Jupe blushes. Like full-on rosy cheeks.

What the hell is even happening right now?

"Hi, I'm Jupiter," Jupe says, extending her hand to the girl's father.

"Kenneth Chin," he says with a smile. "It's great to meet you, Jupiter. I swear you're all Rae talks about these days."

Jupe looks like she just stumbled into an underground cave filled with enough gold to end world hunger. I take a quick glance around to make sure I'm still in my Earth house and not some whacked-out alternate-universe version of—

Wait.

"You're *Rae?*" I say. "As in *the* Rae?" *Rae* of the giggle-inducing text messages Rae?

Fuck you, universe.

"Umm . . . yes?" Her eyes bounce back and forth between me and Jupe. "Is that bad?"

"Oh, ignore him," Jupe says, waving me off.

Is she serious right now? "Actually, don't." I extend a hand to the dad first. "It's nice to meet you, Dr. Chin. I'm Courtney."

"Oh, call me Kenny," he says. Like Mama would let *that* fly.

"And, Rae, it's nice to meet you," I say. "Jupe's told me almost *nothing* about you, but I know y'all text a lot—"

"Coop!" Jupe elbows me in the ribs.

38

Rae laughs. She really *is* pretty. "Nice to meet you, too. Well, *formally* at least."

As my big-ass hand basically eats her little dainty one, I take her in. Just like Jupe, she's hard to pin down. Dr. Chin is East Asian, and you can see that a little bit in the shape of Rae's eyes, but said eyes are green and she's got a *lot* of freckles. Nice lips, too. The hair Jupe *loves* (rolling *my* eyes) is cut super-short, and there's a spot over her left ear where it's a reddish color, but the rest is dark brown. She's probably got Jupe by an inch or so height-wise, but completely opposite body type: slim, kind of willowy.

And I recognize her now.

"I've seen you at school," I say. On one of the days I was avoiding Jupe, I saw her talking to a short-haired girl in the hallway and didn't think anything of it because Jupe is *always* talking to someone.

Now I feel like a dumbass.

"Oh, wonderful, our guests have arrived!" Mama says as she approaches from behind us. "Come in, come in!"

Rae and her dad step into the house.

"Right this way," Mama says. "The guys are in the living room."

Dr. Chin and Rae follow Mama, but I catch Jupe's wrist to hold her back. She turns to me, still beaming.

"You knew she was coming?" I say.

She nods. Eyes *sparkling* like the Fourth of damn July. "We figured it out yesterday," she says. "She was saying she and her dad got invited to dinner at a coworker's house, and when I asked where her dad worked, and she named your mom's hospital, we put two and two together."

"And you didn't tell me?" That this *girl* who obviously makes you *so happy* was coming to MY house for dinner?

"What was there to tell?" And she pulls out of my grip and bounds after Rae with more spring in her step than I've ever seen.

I get to the living room just as Mama finishes the introductions. It's dead obvious from the shock trapped in Dr. Chin's raised eyebrows after meeting Troy and Emilio that he got no forewarning about the nontraditional family next door. Which is fine, of course. I can just tell he doesn't know what to do with the information.

We live in a pretty "progressive" area, as Mama likes to put it, and barring one incident in ninth grade involving some bigots picketing at one of my basketball games in deeeeeeeeeeep South Georgia, the two-dad life has never really been a big deal. I'm *so* used to it not being a big deal, in fact, that Dr. Chin's shock catches me off guard.

And now I'm really curious about Rae.

It's crystal clear to me that Jupe was flirting with her, so Rae either didn't realize or didn't mind. Definitely seemed like there was something mutual going on, but it's not like Rae has I LIKE GIRLS tattooed on her forehead, so it's difficult to know for sure.

What if Rae is batting for the same team as Jupe, and Dr. Chin doesn't know it? If his daughter was gay, and he knew, he probably wouldn't have been so shocked by the Dad/Papi revelation, right?

But then again, he looked so *happy* about whatever was happening between the two girls.

As a matter of fact, all five of us can see them sitting at the dining room table, giggling and touching each other's hair and examining each other's nails and complimenting each other's best features. I just heard Jupe say, "Dude, your eyes are *amazing*. They're like the inside of a just-ripe avocado."

Rae's reply? "Oh my gosh, *yours* are like tree sap backlit by sunlight."

Again, Dr. Chin looks thrilled. Is this a normal thing for girls to do?

Jupe says Breanna isn't her "type." . . . Is Rae?

Which leads to other questions: How much *have* they been talking? Do they see each other outside of school? Did they hang out at all during my Game Plan hiatus?

During dinner, I keep my mouth shut and my eyes on my plate to keep from staring at them—*"What the hell you plan to do if she gets a girlfriend, Coop?"*—but then Mama has one mojito too many—Papi made a freaking *pitcher*—and starts blabbing. "So, Rae, you should know you're a lucky girl. Courtney and Jupiter are Decatur High royalty."

"Mama, put the glass down, please."

"What? I'm just making sure she knows she doesn't have to worry about making friends!"

Jupe snorts. "You can say that again."

"Oh, you shhh," Rae replies with a blush.

I'm missing something here. *What am I missing? This is driving me bonkers!*

"Courtney, I hear you're quite the basketball player," Dr. Chin says.

My cheeks burn, not that anybody can tell. "Ah, I'm not too bad."

"Don't let Mr. Humble Bumble fool you, Doctor," Papi says with a wave of his fork. I smile in spite of myself: I used to watch *I Love Lucy* with my dad, and when I met Papi at age seven, I thought, *Wow, a blue-eyed Ricky Ricardo!* Learning Papi was born in Santiago de Cuba just like Desi Arnaz? Definitely one of the highlights of my childhood. "Cuatro has been the leading scorer on the team every year since the fourth grade, isn't that right?" And he winks at me. Papi's called me Cuatro for as long as I can remember. Said it was because he'd never met a *fourth* before.

Mama jumps back in: "And Jupiter is class president *and* the head of a number of civic groups, right, honey?"

Jupe smiles at her but looks at me and crosses her eyes really quick. It's this little thing we do when one of the parents is getting too parent-ish.

So she *hasn't* forgotten me in the face of a pretty girl. Good to know.

"Mmhmm," Jupe says, before shifting her attention to Dr. Chin. "I'm in charge of a couple of volunteer organizations, and I run Iridis, our school's GSA."

"GSA?" he asks.

"Gay-Straight Alliance," Jupe says.

"Oh—so you're also . . ."

"Gay? Yes, sir, I am."

Dr. Chin's face goes crimson, and he smiles and looks down at his plate.

I can't decipher Rae's reaction because she literally

42

doesn't have one. No pause of her fork or rapid blinking or twitch of a finger or small smile.

It's maddening.

"So what about you, Rae?" Mama is practically singing now. *Dear Lord, don't let her be asking Rae if she's gay. . . .* "Did you participate in any extracurriculars at your old school?"

Thank God.

"Rae was in the Eight Hundred Club," Dr. Chin says, grinning. "She was the only freshman to get a perfect score on the PSAT verbal—"

"Oh my gosh, Daddy, that's not an extracurricular."

"Sorry. Proud dad moment," he says. "She also constructs incredible crossword puzzles."

Now Rae groans.

"I think that's amazing." From Jupe, batting her eyelashes, the asshole. "I knew your vocabulary was pretty impressive just from talking to you, but seriously?"

Rae blushes even deeper, and Dr. Chin laughs. "At three years old, the only item on Rae's Christmas list was a dictionary."

"Daddy!"

Mama, Papi, and Dad all chuckle. Rae puts her face in her hands.

"Hey now, nothing wrong with beauty *and* brains," Jupe says. She nudges Rae, who just *beams* at her.

This is torture.

"So were you involved in anything else at your old school?" Mama asks.

Rae nods. "I was a cheerleader."

OPPORTUNITY! "Oh yeah?" I say. "Which position?"

"Flyer." She looks at me and grins. *Finally!*

"Do you not *see* her, Coop?" Jupe interjects. "You really had to ask?" She nudges Rae again, and they explode into a fit of giggles.

"I didn't want to make any assumptions." *And how 'bout you stay the hell out of it, Jupiter?* I say in my head. Full disclosure: I'm not used to girls not paying me any attention, and it's bothering me a *lot* that Rae's into Jupe instead of me. Courtney Cooper, thou hast been brought *low*, brah.

"You know, Coop's a cheerleader, too," Jupe says.

"Mmhmm. I saw him on the sidelines at the game yesterday," from Rae.

Am I not sitting right here?!

Jupe's face lights up like it's Christmas. "Coop, you should see if you can get Rae on the squad!" she says. "It would be perfect!"

Oh, *now* she's okay with cheerleading? I take a sip of water to help me swallow down *Well, we wouldn't want to subject her to the male gaze, now, would we?* Especially since Rae is staring at Jupe like her idea could bring world peace.

Am I being petty?

Yeah, don't care.

I force a smile. "I'll see what I can do."

I don't say a word for the rest of dinner, not that anyone notices, and once we're done, everyone pairs off: Dad Charity and Dr. Chin go to the den to continue their conversation about Dr. Chin's humanitarian medical work in Tanzania, Mama and Papi head to the back porch with the rest of the mojito pitcher, and Jupe and Rae disappear altogether.

As in, I collect the dishes from the table and take them to the kitchen to load the dishwasher, and when I return, Jupe and Rae are nowhere to be found.

I go out back. "It's been eleven fucking years, Emilio," Mama says. It stops me in my tracks because I *never* hear her use profanity. She must be drunker than I thought. "Eleven years, and I still miss Al like he died yesterday."

God, what did I step into?

"Nobody on this earth could ever love me like that man loved me. And poor Courtney . . ." She shakes her head.

Well, this is uncomfortable.

As I'm going back into the house, the deck creaks. They both turn, and Mama's eyes go wide.

"Cuatro!" Papi says, trying to break the ice.

"Shit, he looks just like Al." Mama whips away from me and lifts her cup.

I grab it before she can get it to her lips. "No more mojitos for you, Neeta Cooper. Out here cussin'."

She waves me off and shifts her focus across the yard.

"You're such a good boy, Cuatro," Papi says. "Jupiter is lucky to have you, you know? Your dad would be so proud."

I gotta get outta here. "Hey, speaking of Jupiter, any idea where her and Rae went?"

"*She* and Rae," Mama says. "And they're up in my room going through old photo albums."

Aw, *hell* no.

I drop off Mama's glass at the sink and rush up the stairs. Mama's door is barely cracked. I'm about to push it open, but then I have a thought: What if the girls are kissing or something? What if they're . . . doing more?

No way, though, right? It's my *mama's* room. Jupe wouldn't do that.

Would she?

I can't help but imagine, though. I wonder if Rae has freckles everywhere else. It'd be like a salted-caramel-and-vanilla swirl with sprinkl—

"Check out those *ears*!" Rae squeals.

"Coop, we know you're at the door," Jupe says. "Stop being a creeper and come in."

My palms go damp, and I can feel the heat in my face and sweat at my hairline. "It's cool . . . I know you're having girl time." There's no way I can look either of them in the eye right now. Especially Jupe. She'd see inside my head to what I was thinking and never speak to me again.

"The parents wanted me to make sure you two were all right up here," I lie.

"Okay! We're fine," Jupe says.

I jet downstairs and put my headphones on, crank my music up loud, and try to keep myself busy: I straighten the dining room, clean the entire kitchen, rearrange the pantry, which doesn't take long seeing as there's never any food in this house—dinner was ordered in—and when the dishwasher shuts off, I unload it.

I've just finished putting the glasses away when someone smacks me on the butt. I whip around and pull the headphones down to find Jupe grinning at me. And now my heart is pounding. "Thanks for doing the dirty work, Mr. Clean," she says. "Come on, the Chins are leaving."

She takes my hand and pulls me just outside the front door, where we all say our goodbyes. I stand there, taking up air and space I don't feel entitled to, while the parents smile and hug, and Jupe and Rae stand locked in what appears to be a lovers' embrace for e-frickin'-ternity. When they finally break apart, Jupe tells Rae she'll be over tomorrow, and Rae tosses an indifferent half-wave in my general direction before heading to her dad's car.

Seriously feel like I just shot a game-losing air ball at the buzzer.

But then . . .

Jupe looks up at me and smiles the way she does. "Wanna go watch a movie?"

I wonder if she can see my shock. "Uhh. Sure . . ."

"Awesome," she says. "I'm gonna change and make popcorn. See you in five?"

"Five it is."

She reaches up to tug on my ear, and I exhale.

For the first time in my life, I'm thankful for that bracelet she wears. I know she and Rae didn't do anything: all five of the charms are still there.

5

If You Start Walking Around Decatur High, Talking and Laughing with Jupiter Sanchez Like You're Her New Bestie, Everyone Notices

Everywhere I go in these hallways, I hear people talking about Rae Chin. . . . How nice she is; how interesting; how pretty; how cool; how *chic*.

I've heard she spent time in Tanzania (true); I've heard she surfed in the Maldives (maybe true); I've heard she's biracial, but descended from rulers of the Ming dynasty (possible, I guess); I've heard she created maps for some uncharted portion of the Amazon rain forest (doubtful, but who knows?)

You'd think Rae Chin was some infectious disease, based on the epidemic curiosity about her.

Is this weird for me? Yes. Especially considering people come to *me* with their questions, assuming that if Rae's tight with Jupe, I'm the third Musketeer.

But the thing is, Rae hasn't really spoken more than a few words to me since the dinner. She's not deliberately rude or anything. She gives a generic "Morning!" as she hops into the backseat when we pick her up for school, and she'll throw a closed-lip smile and half-wave in my direction if I pass her in the halls, but beyond that, the longest sentence she's said to me is "Hey, can you tell me how to get to B wing?"

It'd be one thing if she were weird/standoffish with everyone *but* Jupe. Then I could chalk it up to Jupe's awkwardness-repelling sorcery. Or, fine: to something romantic going on between them, but I refuse to think about *that* because (1) I get pissed at the thought of some admittedly cute girl swooping in and stealing the affections of the woman I've wanted since I was seven and (2) it devolves into depraved imaginings involving Jupe's brown skin and Rae's freckles *pretty* quickly. So it would obviously, definitely have to be the sorcery, case closed.

Bottom line, if she were *Jupe-only*, I could still feel okay about myself.

But that's not the case at all. I am literally the only person Rae's not smiley-happy-friendly with.

Since we've already established that I like winning, I've gotten into this idiotic thing where I try to get Rae's attention and make her smile just for the sake of knowing I can.

True to my word, I get her a tryout for the cheer squad.

After our warm-up laps, we all gather on the blue mats and find Rae standing next to Coach Q in standard cheer-practice garb—sports bra, tank top, and cotton shorts that reveal *just* how long and toned her legs are. When everyone sees her, the thrill of collective excitement is so electric, I almost expect each person's hair to stand on end. As I mentioned before, she's all anybody's been talking about.

"Guys, this is Rae Chin, though I assume you already knew that based on the way you're all looking at her," Coach says.

A few people laugh.

Rae turns that pinkish color beneath the freckles and giggles. "Hi, guys," she says with a little wave. And I can't help but smile. She really is crazy cute, even if she confuses the hell out of me. Or maybe *because* she confuses the hell out of me?

Who knows how these things work?

"CC"—Coach nods in my direction; I hate when she calls me that—"asked me to let her try out, but since we're already two games into the season and stunt partners are more or less set, I figured it'd only be fair if I ran it by the whole team since it'll involve some flyer rotations. Anyone object?"

Like anyone would.

"All right," Coach says. "Everyone clear the mats. Rae, if you wouldn't mind throwing the toughest tumbling pass you can land without a spot, please. And no need for multiple handsprings."

Rae nods and goes to one end of one of the forty-two-foot strips of carpet-bonded foam. Apparently no one's actually breathing, because it's so quiet in the gym, you could hear a cockroach fart. After a couple of seconds with her face scrunched in determination, she takes a deep breath, rises up on her toes, and then launches herself forward into the pass: *two steps, roundoff, back handspring, double full twist.*

As in she rotates her body 720 degrees while doing a straight-bodied backflip.

Eyes bulge out of head.

"Holy shit!" says Shanna Wilmington, team captain, before clapping her hands over her mouth and throwing Coach a terrified look. Coach is too busy trying to pick her jaw up off the ground to make Shanna sprint a lap and do a hundred squat-jumps—standard fare for cussing.

"That was . . . umm . . ." Coach Q, like the rest of us, is at a loss for words. "Wow. All right, then. You've flown single-base before?"

Rae, who hasn't finished blushing from all the wonder in our eyes, nods. "My old squad was coed."

"How tall are you?"

"Five seven."

Coach's brow creases for a sec before a smile tugs at one corner of her very thin lips. They're nothing like Rae's full ones. Not that I'm looking at Rae's full lips when she talks or anything.

"C'mere, Jess," Coach says. Just as she won't call me Coop, she refuses to call Jesse Golly. I dunno what it is with Coach Q and the girly-ass nicknames, but regardless of what she called him, I've never seen my dear friend Jesse "Goliath" Cox move so quickly.

"You afraid of heights, Miss Chin?" Coach asks, wrapping an arm around Golly's waist.

"Not in the least, ma'am."

"Jess here—"

"Call me Golly," Golly says, extending a hand to Rae, who blushes again and smiles up at him as his mitt swallows her hand.

"*Golly,*" Coach continues, "is what, six foot seven?"

"And a half." Golly grins.

"That means at full extension, your head will be . . . somebody do the math for me—"

Britain: "About fifteen feet above the ground." If only he were as good with women as he is with numbers.

"You okay with that, Miss Chin?"

Rae's green eyes sparkle. "Totally."

"We'll start with a toss to half-press." Coach steps away from Golly and gestures for Rae to take her place in front of him. "Whenever you're ready," Coach says.

Golly whispers something to Rae that none of us can hear, but it makes her smile. Then he counts off, squats low, tosses her straight up into the air, and catches her in a full extension instead of a half-press like Coach said. They're solid as stone.

"Damn," Britain says.

"Drop and give me a hundred mountain climbers, Brit," from Coach.

Britain sucks his teeth and glares at Shanna, who sticks her tongue out at him.

Golly pops Rae off his hands, catching her waist as she comes down.

"What else you got?" This from Shanna, who I think is feeling threatened—she's Golly's regular flyer, after all.

Rae looks at Coach Q for the approval to do another stunt, and when Coach nods, Rae turns to Golly and beckons him down to her level. His eyes get big, but he recovers quickly, which is good: I'm sure Coach would try to stop whatever's coming if she'd seen it.

When Rae finishes telling him what she wants to do, he

swings his arms around, shakes his hands and legs out, and rolls his neck.

Highly doubt I need to mention that the rest of us are riveted.

They get in pretoss position, and this time Rae grins. Golly counts off, tosses, and—BAM—one-arm liberty. Golly's holding Rae up above his head with one arm, and she's standing on one foot—this is technically illegal at the high school level in our state.

We've all got our chins on the floor, and then she stretches into a scorpion. She's . . . flexible.

Golly pops her off, and before her feet touch the ground Coach Q is asking her when she can come by the office and pick up a uniform.

By the time practice comes to a close, she's totally become a part of the team. Everybody's congratulating her and giving her high fives and telling her how awesome she is. So I'm thinking: *I've done it! She'll get to me and thank me, and smile real big like she does for everybody else.*

That's logical, right?

She doesn't even glance my way. Just a curt "Thanks, Courtney" in passing.

Forgive me for sounding arrogant, but this is so far outside my realm of experience, I can't even figure out how to feel.

Like it's one thing to piss a girlfriend off, get dumped, and *then* be avoided, but to have a girl who doesn't know me refuse to even look at me? And *only* me? It's like everyone else is basking in this Rae of light that moves every time I try to step into it.

I'm too baffled to even be offended.

She and Jupe have been spending a good bit of time together, so I'm sure I could ask Jupe if she knows what Rae's
deal is. Something interesting: I came home after hanging
with the guys one night to find Jupe and Rae in their pj's
at *my* house with *my* mom. "We're having a slumber party,
Courtney!" Mama giggled as she looked up from polish-
ing Jupe's toenails. Rae didn't even glance in my direction.
But the handful of times Jupe and I have been alone, I've
resisted the temptation to bring Rae up at all.

Three reasons:

1. Our whole life, Papi has stressed the importance
of *minding your own business:* "If people want you to
know, they will tell you, Cuatro."
2. It seems a little pathetic to ask, doesn't it? *Jupey, why
doesn't Rae like me?* Wah, wah, wah. *So* wack.
3. I know if I ask her that, I'll wind up asking her that
other question: "So . . . you and Rae?"

She's still got all the gemstones on her bracelet. Yes, I
check regularly at this point—can't help it.

But I'm not ready to go there because I have no idea how
I'll react if she says they're more than friends.

Like right now, I'm sitting in the La-Z-Boy with an *I Love
Lucy* episode playing on the TV, but my eyes keep drifting
to the glory that is Jupiter Sanchez lying belly-down on her
bed in leggings and one of my old jerseys. As I mentioned,
the niceness down bottom is in amazing proportion to the

niceness up top, and right now that bottom is just sitting there like a majestic mountain I'd like very much to climb.

I have the blanket over my lap.

The idea of some girl getting to touch what I can't?

Yeah, not feeling that at all.

"Hey, Coop?" She turns onto her side to look at me.

Dear Lord, please don't let her have caught me staring at her ass. **Shifts blanket and thinks about butt-naked grandmas posing suggestively on top of glaciers.** "Mmhmm?"

She sits up. "Will you come over here? I want to talk to you about something."

I feel like she just dropped a seed of doom down my throat and now it's growing and spreading poisonous vines that are wrapping around my internal organs.

But of course I go.

"What's up?" I say, sitting beside her. Then for good measure: "Everything okay?"

For a second she just stares into my eyes, and I really feel like we're having a *moment*. Definitely a struggle not to look at her lips. I do clear my throat, though, because it's getting a little hard to breathe with her gazing at me like that.

She shifts her focus across the room and takes a deep breath. "There's something I want to tell you, but you have to promise you won't get weird."

Damn.

"Okay. I won't get weird."

"Promise?"

Damn damn *damn*. "Yeah. I promise."

"Okay." *Here it comes . . .* "Well, you've been an amazing

friend to me, and I just wanted to tell you that I . . . umm . . ."
Her gaze drops to her hands in her lap.

Just say it already, woman!

Another deep breath, and then her eyes are on mine
again. "I really appreciate you, Coopie."

Huh? "Huh?"

"Ugh." She puts her head in her hands. "You know vulner-
ability is not my strong suit!" And yet another deep breath.

"Okay, this is the thing," she says. "You're the best friend
I've ever had, and I really appreciate you for that, Coop. I
try not to like, impose when you have a girlfriend or whatever, but I want you to know that when you're gone, I miss
you, and being with you is the safest, happiest place in the
world for me."

I, Courtney Aloysius Cooper IV, am at a total, utter, *complete* loss for words.

"Oh God, I made it weird, didn't I? Did I make it weird?
Shit." She covers her face.

I gulp and pull her hands down. "Thank you for telling
me that, Jupes. It means a lot to me."

She smiles.

Fireworks in the heart.

"Cuddle?" she says.

I lie back and put my legs up on the bed, and she nestles
into her spot beneath my arm.

"So what brought on the mushy gushies?" I ask.

"Well, I've been hanging out with Rae a lot—"

"Ya think?"

Sorry, couldn't help it.

She kicks my ankle. "Shut up," she says. "I like being

around her. She's got this way of charging into relationships with eyes and arms wide, where I've usually got mine
crossed and am wearing sunglasses. She just makes me want
to *feel* more. Not be so guarded, I guess."

"Ah."

"She's also biracial like me. Her mom is Irish. But her
parents divorced when she was little, and her mom moved
back to New Hampshire where she's from, so it was just
Rae and her dad and her older sister."

"Older sister, huh?"

"Yeah, but then she left, too. Went to live with their
mom."

Damn. "For real?"

"Yep. So Rae's all about not taking people for granted.
Which is amazing to me. If I'd been through that kind of
stuff, there's no way I'd be like her," Jupe goes on. "You
know how many friends that girl's made already? She's just
so *open* to everyone. Lets people in without thinking twice,
you know?"

I *don't* know because apparently I'm the exception.
Though I can't complain about the effect she's having on
Jupe. I haven't felt this *connected* to her in a long time. "In-
teresting."

"Yeah. I just feel like I need to acknowledge—out loud—
that you mean everything to me, Coop. I'm really thankful
for you, and I totally hate admitting this, but I wouldn't be
half the person I am without you. You're my rock."

Note: this is not helping the Game Plan. I know she's saying all these things as a friend, but *Jupiter Charity-Sanchez
just said I'm her* ROCK, *yo!*

In lieu of a response—because I'm a little choked up—I kiss her forehead, and she squeezes me tighter.

Time to change the subject.

"Speaking of Rae," I say, "any idea why she's so weird around me?"

"I did notice that," Jupe says. "But no. No clue. You know I don't get how the minds of straight girls work."

OH HO!

"So she's straight?"

"Seems to be. Had a boyfriend named Corey for a year. It's possible she's equal-opportunity, but I haven't asked so I'm not sure."

The relief is so immediate, and the sigh I breathe so deep, I forget Jupe has her head on my chest and can feel it. "Ah, so you're relieved," she says. "Does Courtney Cooper have a crush?" She looks up at me with her eyebrows dancing.

I laugh. "No, Jupiter." And then, spurred on by her honesty, I decide to tell the truth. "Just glad I won't be losing my best friend to some *girl* anytime soon."

"Oh, hush."

I kiss her nose and she giggles and snuggles in deeper.

"Will you stay here tonight?"

I look up at the ceiling. Shake my head and smile.

"Course I will, Jupes," I say. "There's nowhere I'd rather be."

6

Except for the First Time Ever, the Jupe High Doesn't Last

Because as much as I want to just accept that Rae Chin is wide open to everyone in the world but me, I can't. Especially after hearing she's *probably* straight.

No idea why I care so much. I'm sure Jupe would say something about a "fragile male ego" like she did the first time I expressed astonishment over getting dumped. And I know I can't *force* Rae to talk to me if she doesn't want to. But I figure if I spend as much time around her as possible without crossing into creep territory, I'll eventually win her over.

This is the thinking behind my decision to forgo my usual post-football-game ritual of knocking out homework while waiting in my room for Jupe to get home from do-gooding so we can watch movies for most of the night, and instead accompany my squad mates to a carnival that popped up in the empty parking lot of an abandoned Kmart.

Still in uniform, a bunch of us pile into Shanna's Toyota Sequoia. By the way, it should definitely be illegal for a person as dramatic as her to drive a car this big. Rae sits shotgun, and I wind up in the third row, so there's zero chance of charming her into talking to me on the way over.

Then as soon as we're all out of the car, Rae grabs Golly and this other guy and *jets*. Doesn't even look back. Shanna heads off in a different direction with the girl who usually flies for Britain, and the three people who came in another car are already in line for the Tilt-a-Whirl.

Which leaves me alone with Brit—clearly a sign that the whole night is a bust. All *he* wants to do is snarf corn dogs and gawk at all the "fine-ass honeys" we pass as we stroll around.

He *did* get played by that "new lady" of his, by the way. Said he showed up at that party and found her "all up under this lumberjack-looking asshole she introduced as her boyfriend."

Within half an hour, I have a raging headache from all the lights, and the funnel cake I force down . . . well, let's just say it doesn't do me any digestive favors.

Missing Jupe like there's no tomorrow right now, and *way* ready to go home, but of course, I didn't drive. ALL of us are at the mercy of a girl currently leaning forward to give the slimeball running the Shoot-the-Duck game a peek down her top in an attempt to swindle a stuffed hippo out of him without actually playing.

"Come on," Brit says, glancing at his phone. "We're supposed to meet everyone by the merry-go-round."

"Cool." Hopefully that means we're merry-go-*rounding up* to leave.

When we get there, Rae is literally sitting on Golly's shoulders, laughing her head off. Even the guy with them seems to be having the time of his life.

"Coop, you gonna ride the unicorn?" Golly says once he sees us.

And then . . .

Well, I'm not really sure what happens.

All I know is the moment I *look* at the merry-go-round—like actually focus my eyes on it—it feels like the Hulk has wrapped one of his big green hands around my midsection and is squeeeeeeezing. My heart is beating too fast, and I'm trying to inhale, but I can't get my lungs to expand. And just when I'm *sure* I'm about to die, all the neon lights start spinning like some nightmare carnival tornado.

So I shut my eyes . . .

7

. . . And by the Time I Open Them, I've Traveled to Another Dimension

Or so it seems.

First, there's this piercing two-toned shriek that makes me feel like I'm being stabbed in the eyeballs from the inside.

Then I notice a bunch of giant men all around me. Some are in variously colored tank tops and short sets, and others are wearing helmets, strange big-shouldered shirts, and unnecessarily tight pants that stop at the knee. All are frozen in motion.

The two-toned shriek sounds again.

I roll over onto my stomach and groan. See a lamp, a clock—11:42 a.m.—and a framed photo of me and Jupe standing at the edge of the ocean.

I take another glance around. Giant men = my posters.

How the hell did I wind up in my bed?

Another shriek.

It's the doorbell.

I pull a pillow over my head and try to go back to sleep.

More ringing. Once. Twice. Three times. Doorbell ringer ain't giving up.

By the time I stumble down the stairs, I'm pissed.

Ringing, ringing, ring—

"WHAT THE FU—" I yank the front door open.

And stop.

It's Rae.

"I'm sorry!" She covers her face but peeks between her fingers. "Your mom told me to keep ringing until you answered."

"Oh. Uhh . . ."

There's a very awkward silence.

She drops her hands and her eyes latch on to my forehead. "Wow," she says, and she bites her lip.

My head whips left so I can look into my entryway mirror. There's a purple knot the size of a golf ball above my right eyebrow. "Holy shit!" I reach up to touch it and . . . *"DAMN,* that hurts!"

"It was a little worse last night, believe it or not," Rae says.

Last night? "Huh?"

She takes a deep breath. "Can we talk? There's some stuff I need to tell you."

"Mmmm . . ." I'm so confused right now. "Yeah. Come on in."

She does, and I shut the door behind her. "We'll talk in the living room, I guess?" I say. "I'm gonna grab some water. You want anything?"

"No thanks. I'll just wait on the couch if that's okay."

"Sure."

I'm not actually thirsty, by the way. Just need a minute to regroup or prepare or breathe or make sure this isn't a dream or *something.* Instead of drinking cold water, I go to the sink and splash some on my face.

Rae's sitting so stiffly when I come back into the room, I almost laugh. She's obviously just as nervous as I am.

"So," I say, slouching down in the chair adjacent to the couch and clasping my hands over my midsection like I've got ALL the chill in the world. "You wanted to talk?"

"Yeah, I do, but I promised your mom and Jupiter I would make sure you're okay first and send them each a text."

No clue what to say to that.

"Do you remember anything at all from last night?" she asks.

My eyes drop. "Nah, not really."

"I figured as much. You hit your head pretty hard when you fell. I was shocked when your mom said you didn't have a concussion."

Wait . . . "Sorry." And I shake my head. Which hurts. "Would you mind starting from the beginning?"

"What's the last thing you remember?"

"Coming to the merry-go-round." Just saying the word makes my stomach flip.

"Ah. Well, you passed out."

"I *what?*"

"You and Brit stepped up to the carousel, and this funny look came over your face like you were flabbergasted. Then

64

you just fell over forward. Your head hit the edge of the platform."

She can't be serious.

"I called your mom, and she left the hospital to come get you. Checked your eyes and said you didn't have a concussion. Golly carried you to her car and your mom took him home on the way back to the hospital this morning."

"Wait, Golly *slept* here?" And I had no idea about it?

Rae grins. "Guy wouldn't leave your side," she says.

Wow.

"So you're really okay?"

I shrug. "Seem to be." Though I am embarrassed now, and this headache is a motherfu—

"Good." She pulls out her phone and starts tapping.

"You're texting my mom for real?"

"Yep. And Jupiter. Who left about twenty minutes ago for a volunteer thing she couldn't cancel."

"Okay, then . . ." Definitely in another dimension. Gotta be.

Her phone pings, and she nods and smiles. "Jupiter says she's glad you didn't die or she would've had to kill you."

I grin—and wince 'cause it hurts. Typical Jupe.

Pings again.

She smiles even bigger. "And your mom said to tell you there's Cream of Wheat on the stove, and you better study for the physics test she knows you have on Monday. And she loves you."

Not even responding to that. "So was there something else?"

"Oh." Her whole face changes. Smile vanishes, cheeks go pink, eyes drop.

Damn. "Sorry. Wasn't trying to be rude. It's just that . . . uhh . . . well, you've never really *talked* to me before, but now you're, like, texting my mama." Comes out a little saltier than I intended, but whatever. It's true, and my head hurts.

"Ah. Right. Umm, about that . . ." She takes a deep breath, then pulls something out of her back pocket and passes it to me. "I saw that in one of your mom's photo albums a couple of weeks ago and slipped it into my bag when Jupiter went to the bathroom," she says. "I went to a Carl's Carnival just before my family began to crumble, so seeing that photo stirred up a lot of stuff I thought I'd dealt with a long time ago. I haven't been able to look you in the eye since I took it." Her gaze falls to her hands. "And I honestly wasn't planning to give it back, but then . . . Well, with what happened last night, I realized it might be a bigger deal than I initially assumed. Figured it was time to return it and tell you I'm sorry for absconding with it."

Absconding?

I'm so busy trying to process the facts that (1) Rae Chin is sitting on my sofa, inside my house, *talking* to me, (2) she's a dirty little thief—!!!—and (3) her being weird had to do with the dirty thievery, not some problem with *me*, it takes a minute to process what she said, pick up on *Carl's Carnival*, and look at the picture.

When I do, my eyes open so wide, I'm surprised they don't *pop!* out of my face and roll across the floor.

It's a picture of Mama and me. And Carousel Carl—the guy from that science show I used to love.

At Carl's Carnival.

My literal worst nightmare immortalized.

I haven't looked at this picture in almost twelve years: it's a throwback to the worst day of my life. That terrible dream I mentioned having whenever Jupe's not around? There's a reason it starts with me on a merry-go-round and ends with a spinning car crash.

The day my dad died, Mama and I were in Alabama. *The Carousel Carl Show* did a live-action five-city tour, complete with a science-fair-like carnival, and I begged Mama to take me to the Birmingham one even though I knew Daddy wouldn't be able to go with us.

And everything was cool at first. Pictures with Carl were taken just inside the entrance, then we were cut loose to enjoy the carnival part: rides, games, delectable delicacies like Koolickles and deep-fried Ho Hos, the whole deal.

But when the time came for the actual show, things got . . . weird.

First we were all herded into this big-top tent, where we took our seats. In the center of the floor was a massive grand carousel, brightly lit with a top that looked like a gilded crown or something. The theme song from the show filled the air, and the merry-go-round started flashing and spinning and the horses began to rise and drop. And it was kinda eerie-looking with no one on the thing, but overall: fine.

But then all the lights shut off, plunging us into a darkness that, to my six-year-old mind, was worse than death *and* Brussels sprouts. A loudspeaker crackled just before we heard what sounded like a man sobbing. Then there was a mind-numbing screech of feedback, and everything went quiet.

I, for real, thought the world was about to end.

After what felt like a geologic era, the lights came back on and a lady's voice came over the loudspeaker apologizing to everyone: *"Ladies and gentlemen, I regret to inform you that Carousel Carl has fallen ill. The remainder of the show has been canceled."* There was something about "a full refund" and "proceeding to the exits in an orderly fashion," and next thing I knew, we were caught in the tide of folks shoving their way out to the parking lot.

We drove the two hours to get home, and I went to bed with my head still spinning. Once in bed, I tossed and turned, worried out of my skull about Carl. Had that been him on the loudspeaker? What did *fallen ill* mean? Was he gonna be on TV come Monday?

I evidently dozed off at some point, because Mama came and woke me up in the middle of the night. At first I thought it was *so dope* because I'd never been up that late before, but when I came into the living room and saw the policemen, I knew something was wrong. That's when I noticed how strange she looked. Like she'd seen a ghost or something.

I kept my eyes on her the whole time the policemen were talking. Caught the important words: *tornado* and *wet roads* and something they called a *spinout*.

By the time they left, I understood: my daddy was never coming home. It's like the carnival incident was some kind of premonition or bad omen or something.

And I've never told anyone about it. Not even Jupe. Hell, I've spent the past eleven years pretending none of it ever happened, and outside of the nightmare, I've been success- ful at keeping it shoved waaaaay to the back of my mind.

But now, thanks to *Rae*, cold-shouldering queen of thieves, I'm staring at a painful reminder of everything I wanted to forget.

Shit sucks.

"Courtney?" She's kneeling in front of me. When the heck did that happen?

"Huh?"

"You're crying."

I touch my cheek. My fingertips come away wet.

"Are you okay?" She puts a hand on my knee. Just like Jupe did when I first met *her*. It was the day we moved in, and I was sitting in this same living room in Dad's La-Z- Boy, crying my damn eyes out, when a snaggletooth beige girl with frizzy hair strolled in carrying a fancy covered cake plate. The moment she saw me, Jupe sat the cake down on the ACTION FIGURES box and rushed over to kneel in front of me.

And she put a hand on my knee.

So this is weird.

"Sorry about that." I wipe my face on my sleeve. "If you, uhh . . . wouldn't mind keeping this between us—" I point to my wet face.

"Yeah, of course."

Cue loaded pause where this very confusing girl stares up at me from the floor like all my facial features have been rearranged.

Then: "Courtney, can I ask you something?"

"Didn't give me much of a choice there, Rae."

Her eyebrows shoot up.

"It was a joke."

She cocks her head to the side and squints at me.

"Because that *was* a question—"

"Yeah, I got the joke. Just didn't take you for the type to use humor as a defense mechanism."

Whoa. Maybe liked it better when she *wouldn't* look at me. Now I feel like she's mind reading all my secrets, Professor X style.

I clear my throat. "Ask away."

"How old were you in that picture?"

"Six. Why?"

"This wasn't taken at the Atlanta carnival, was it?"

"No." I'd had a karate tournament and couldn't make the Atlanta one.

"Which city?"

I gulp. Not sure I like where this line of questioning is headed. "Birmingham."

Rae nods. "That's what I figured."

She's from Alabama, and *she* said she went to one of the carnivals. "You were there, too?"

She nods again. "Were you in the big top when the lights went out and Carl started weeping over the loudspeaker?"

My turn to nod.

She sighs. "That was his last public appearance, you know? They canceled his show right after."

Is this really happening, or did I hit my head harder than I realized?

70

"I was devastated," she says. "My love of Carl was akin to hero worship. And it wasn't just about the show. The day I turned four, I got a call 'from' him wishing me a happy birthday and saying his famous line: *'Always remember: you could be anything—'*"

"*'—It's* SCIENCE!*'* " I complete the quote. Which shoves me the rest of the way into the damn twilight zone— another show Daddy used to love, by the way.

On the first-ever *Carousel Carl* episode, Carl went over the life cycle of stars and explained that all things on earth, people included, are made of atoms that came from exploding stars. Aka we kids "could be anything." It became his farewell tagline. Looking back, it's pretty corny, but it still makes me smile.

Rae's smiling, too. "Exactly!" she says. "So I told my parents I wanted to write Carl a letter to thank him for calling—of course now I know it was some automated thing they signed up for, but back then, it was like the highlight of my young life. So I write this letter in my four-year-old chicken scratch, and my parents were all about sending it, but only after they were *sure* I understood he probably wouldn't respond."

"Gotta love those parents with their dream crushing," I say.

"Except he *did* respond."

"Wait, for real?"

"Yes! I couldn't decipher his loopy cursive, so my dad had to read it aloud to me, but he basically thanked me for thanking him and told me I had great parents and a bright future ahead. I *begged* my parents to take me to the carnival after that."

"Wow." Is it weird that I'm a little jealous right now?

"And I was *so excited*, Courtney. Took the letter with me and everything. They kept the photo line moving too fast for me to introduce myself, but just *seeing* him in person was a bigger miracle to me than the Immaculate Conception."

I chuckle at that one. She's cute as hell, this *Rae*.

"But then those lights shut off and that moaning started?"

I swear the temperature in my living room just took a nosedive.

"I'd never felt terror that raw before."

I nod. "Agreed."

"Then right after Carl vanished, my parents split, and my mom took off."

"Dang."

"Yeah. I think I had an inkling stuff was *off* between them, but I guess I was too young to realize what that meant. All I knew was something bad happened at the carnival, and Carl was gone, then my parents' fighting got worse, and my *mom* was gone." She shakes her head. "Probably sounds dumb, but the end of Carl felt like the end of *normal* for me. Eventually my sister left, too. It was like . . . the catalyst for this foundation-shifting chain reaction."

She's staring at me again, though I got nothing in terms of a response. Those freaky green eyes, I swear.

"Anyway, seeing your photo churned all that back up. And then when you passed out last night and it happened to be by the carousel . . . well, I kinda wondered if maybe you'd been at that Birmingham show and were negatively impacted, too. You know?"

I gulp but don't speak. A pause heavier than Golly's bench-press load stretches into next week.

Then she shakes her head real fast. "What am I even saying? Of course you don't know." She sighs. "*And* I just feely-vommed all over you. Told myself I wasn't gonna do that and now here I am—"

"Rae?"

"Hmm?"

Am I really about to open the vault? To a girl I don't even know outside of cheerleading practices and football games? Hell, a girl who, up until fifteen minutes ago, wouldn't even look at me, let alone *talk* to me?

Because she stole my Carl's Carnival picture.

She loved Carousel Carl and was even at that carnival.

And bad things happened in her life afterward, too.

"You're wrong," I say.

Her brows tug down. "Huh?"

"I *do* know."

And I tell her everything.

8

And Then I, Courtney Aloysius Cooper IV, Commence Living a Triple Life

Maybe even quadruple.

Life number one is Coop-and-Rae, or Crae Crae, pun very much intended.

After discovering our shared Carl's Carnival experience and subsequent traumas, Rae and I have the following discussion:

Rae: "You know, I actually feel a lot better now.
    Having talked to someone also deeply affected by
    Carl's demise?"
Me: "So do I."
And it's true. I feel the way I do when I step out from
    under a squat bar with 300 pounds on it.
Me and Rae: **Awkward silence.**
Me: **Clears throat.**
Rae: . . .

Me: "Remember how yesterday you wouldn't even talk to me? Kind of a one-eighty, huh?"

Rae: "We should launch an investigation."

Me: *What?* "What?"

Rae: "Into Carl. We should like . . . try and find out what happened to him. Where he disappeared to."

Me: *Why in the holy hell . . . ?* "Why would we do that?"

Rae: "I dunno. Maybe it's a sign, us meeting each other. You know the show was filmed here in Atlanta, right? He had to have lived here at some point. Maybe we're *supposed* to solve this mystery together."

Me: *Mmmmm . . .* "To what end, though?"

Rae: ***Shrugs.*** "Maybe that's a bridge we won't be able to cross until we get to it. I just feel like we need to figure out what happened."

Me and Rae: ***Awkward silence.***

Rae: "Maybe he *needs* us to find him."

Me: *Now she's* really *gone off the deep end. . . .* "Huh?"

Rae: "Maybe he needs to know there are kids he impacted who still care about him."

Me: *I really don't want to be a downer, but . . .* "What if he's dead?"

Rae: "He's not."

Me: "How do you know?"

Rae: "Google."

Me: *Wellllll . . .* "Wouldn't Google also know where he is and what he's doing if he were still alive?"

Rae: "Not if he doesn't want it to."

75

Me: *Are we really discussing Google like it's a sentient being?* "Okay . . ."

Rae: "Trust me, if he'd died, we would've heard about it. Carousel Carl was a major childhood icon for a lot of people: no matter where he's been or what he's been up to, his death would've made national news. Like there was some guy named Mister Rogers or something like that? He died when you and I were toddlers, and my dad *still* bemoans 'the loss.' "

Me: *Bemoans?* "Fair enough." *I guess . . .*

Rae: "Anyway, I think it's worth a shot. For *his* sake. It's not like we've got anything to lose, right?"

Me: *Besides our standing as rational human beings?*
I mean, who goes searching *for the person who's a reminder of life's shittiest events?*

But the way she looks at me—with the green eyes all bright and the nice lips all parted and the cute face all expectant—if she told me we needed to chase Big Bird across the country and cliff-dive into the Pacific Ocean in the dead of winter to find out what's *really* in Oscar the Grouch's trash can, there's a good chance I'd go along with it just to see what would happen.

Needless to say, after this first real encounter, I totally get what Jupe was saying about how Rae Chin makes her want to "not be so guarded." And fine: now that I've been *forced* to think about Carl, I am curious about where dude ended up.

Anyway, three weeks after launching Operation Crae

Crae, or the Carl Conundrum, as Rae calls it, this is what we've learned: he checked into a psychiatric facility just outside Augusta, Georgia, right after that Birmingham show, and then someone reported seeing him panhandling off I-20 in downtown Atlanta five years ago.

That was creepy as shit. To think the guy whose downfall basically took our respective childhoods with it was begging for change fifteen minutes from my house six years later?

And yeah, I still feel weird about the fact that we're actively *"trying to solve this mystery,"* as Rae puts it—and partially because thinking of Carl makes me think of my dad, which is a whole different can of worms—but I can't lie: the time I get one-on-one with her because of our sleuthing is . . . nice. A couple of times a week after cheer practice, she and I spend a little over an hour poking around online for Carousel Carl clues in my basketball coach's computer science classroom, and it's during these sessions that I discover just how much *fun* she is to be around. Like she makes *everything* seem like the best/funniest/cutest/most-exciting thing ever: "Oh my gosh, Courtney, you have to see this dancing puppy compilation video I found on YouTube. It's the *BEST*!"

And I can't even count the number of times she's said "I need to think" and then busted out her graph-ruled composition notebook to make a crossword puzzle.

By hand.

Like we're in the computer lab now and hit a snag fifteen minutes ago, and Rae's been hunched over that notebook ever since. I peek at her handiwork. Three down reads:

Force that acts on a body moving in a circular path and is directed toward the center around which the body is moving. She blocks off eleven boxes.

"Nerding out again, huh?" I poke her in the side.

She squeaks and jumps—"Courtney!"—then she shuts the book and turns bright pink the way I knew she would.

Shit's adorable. And it really has been a nice deviation from the norm.

But speaking of *the norm,* the uncomfortable part—for me at least—is that Jupiter doesn't know about any of it.

Which leads me to life number two: Jupe-and-Coop 2.0.

Now, I'll confess: I don't feel too terrible about more or less chucking the Game Plan because I'm hanging out with Rae a bunch now. But I have to also confess that things with Jupe have gotten a bit out of hand, albeit in a different way.

Remember how she said being with me is "the safest, happiest place in the world" for her? Well, she's gotten a lot more up-front with her *enjoyment of our friendship*, I guess would be the way to put it.

Like her text messages have gone from **Busy?** to **Jupe-n-Coop + La-Z-Boy + movie = T−7 mins, k?**

And she's way more open with stuff she's never really talked to me about before. Like how nervous she gets before a big community service event or how frustrating it is when straight girls flirt with her. She even told me she thinks Breanna-Queen-of-Swag-and-Social-Justice might be into her, and Jupe feels weird hanging out with Breanna sometimes because Jupe doesn't "wanna give Breanna the wrong idea, though she is *wicked* hot, and I'd be a goner if she ever tried anything."

Like I needed to hear that last part.

The hardest thing about all this is trying to make sure *I* don't get the wrong idea. Because this new Jupe? If I didn't *know* she wasn't into guys, I would definitely, definitely get the wrong idea.

Observe: We're a week out from November, and it's starting to get chilly, so Jupe organizes this community outreach thing she calls Burgers and Blankets. She rallies over a hundred volunteers, Rae and me included, to go around the city hand-delivering, you guessed it, hamburgers and donated blankets to the local homeless.

The event is a huge success, and Jupe is glowing so much on the ride home, she looks almost radioactive. As soon as Rae leaves the car, Jupe turns to me with her eyes all glossy and says, "That was so amazing I can hardly stand it, Coopie!" She squeezes my thigh one good time.

And then she just . . . leaves her hand there.

On my thigh.

Keeps it there the whole way home.

(Holy shit.)

We get into her driveway, and I rush out of the car thinking I'll head to my house for a subzero shower and thoughts of the glacier grandmas, but when I take a step toward my door, she gives me this *look*. Like she's appalled or something.

"You're not coming up?" she says.

"Oh . . ." I shift my feet, hopefully inconspicuously. "I kinda need a shower."

She pouts. Like actually *pouts*.

And then before I know what I'm doing, I say: "I'll make it quick and come over right after, okay?"

Ridiculous.

When I get over there precisely seventeen minutes later, she's also showered and changed and has *I Love Lucy* season four cued up on the TV. Once I'm seated in the La-Z-Boy, she sits cross-legged in my lap and pulls my arms around her waist.

See what I'm talking about with the whole *getting the wrong idea* thing?

No matter how hopeless I know it is, I like it too much to "extract" myself from "the toxic circumstances." That's what Golly said when I slipped up and told him about a similar encounter a couple of weeks ago.

Jupe is just so warm and soft and sexy and she smells and feels so damn *good*. It's quite the predicament.

After four episodes, we climb into her bed and turn the light off.

"Coop?"

I love how her voice sounds in the dark. "Yeah?"

"Have you ever been in love?"

Well, that was unexpected. . . . "Not in a way that could ever amount to anything."

"What does that mean?"

"Eh, dude stuff." That usually shuts her up.

"Oh."

Bingo. *And* I told the truth. **Five points for the Coop-ster.**

"So . . . ," because of course I have to ask now even though I really don't wanna know. And yeah, that's probably a little selfish of me—or maybe a lot, whatever—but considering

80

my feelings, I thought it'd just be better if I stayed in the dark about this part of her life.

Guess that's over . . .

"Have *you* ever been in love?" I say.

"Nope."

Dammit, why did my heart leap just now? "Really?"

"Really. Never even been close, I don't think. Well, besides Delaney. It's too bad she moved."

Delaney Patterson kissed Jupe on the lips in the fourth grade, thereby stealing Jupe's heart and simultaneously smushing my soul to dust between her puckered little lips, the wily seductress. It's actually *not* too bad she moved.

"I've had some crushes here and there," Jupe continues. "Between you and me, I think I might be developing a pretty dangerous one as we speak. But I still have all my gems"—I hear her bracelet jangle in the dark—"because I haven't found the right girl to give my everything to yet."

I will not ask about this crush even though I feel like I just caught a knee to the nuts.

I kiss her temple. "You're a very special woman, Jupiter Sanchez. Whoever winds up with that charm bracelet will be one lucky chick."

"You did *not* just say the C-word . . ."

"What? *Charm?*"

"You better be glad I love you, Coop." With a backhand smack to the ribs.

"Hey hey, so which one of these is mine now?" I find her wrist and tap the bracelet. "There's an 'I love you' one, right?"

"Not like *that*, ya ding-a-ling."

Yeah, yeah. I know. It was worth a shot.

But now I can't resist asking. "Jupe?"

"Mmhmm?"

"Who are you developing a dangerous crush on?"

Her diaphragm expands and I hear her yawn.

Then she nuzzles into my neck. "Like I'd tell you."

9

In Third Grade, Jupe Asked to See My "Wiener"

(Subtitle: Welcome to My Third Life)

1. Jupe, Rae, and I are going to a movie tonight.
2. Football cheer season is almost over—two games left and then the playoffs if we make it—which means basketball preseason is in full effect: I had four hours of conditioning this morning.

What does one get when one puts one and two together? Courtney Cooper needs a shower.

What does Courtney Cooper do when he needs a shower? I take one. At *my* house.

So when I step into *my* bedroom butt-ass nekkid after drying off and leaving the towel in *my* bathroom where it belongs, the last person I expect to see—stretched out on *my* bed and reading my Miles Morales novel like she owns the place, the hypocrite—is Jupiter Charity-Sanchez.

But there she is.

"Oh." And that's all she says.

I am frozen just inside the door. As in I am so shocked by her being there and my being naked at the same time, I can't actually move. Or unhinge my jaw to speak. Or blink.

"Uhh . . ." And then she looks me over from head to toe before zeroing in on it.

Yes. That *it*.

"Wow," she says.

Wow???

I try to respond, but all that comes out of my mouth is this strangled sound like a frog dying.

"It's a lot bigger than I remember—"

"You *remember*?"

"I mean . . ." She looks up at my face and blushes. "Yes?"

No words.

"Ugh!" She covers her face but looks at *it* again through the spaces between her fingers, and then up into my eyes. Sighs and drops her hands. "It's the only one I've ever seen. . . ."

And I *swear* she starts full-blown checking me out. Her brow crinkles, her head tilts, she bites her lower lip, and her eyes roam: up, down; left, right; shoulder to shoulder; head to toe.

It's a look I've seen before. A dude *knows* when he's being checked out.

And the fact that Jupiter Charity-Sanchez is doing the checking? Well . . . it's certainly getting my blood flowing.

First come the goose bumps.

And then . . .

84

"Oh!" And the flush in her cheeks rises simultaneously with my—yeah, you get it.

And now I can move. "Holy shit!" **Turns and runs into the closet; no pun intended.**

The doorbell rings.

"ThatshouldbeRaewe'llbedownstairsbye!" Jupe's voice trails off like she's rushing out of the room, and then there's a slam.

My head falls against the inside of the closet door with a *thunk*.

After I pull it together, I force myself downstairs and find Jupe and Rae talking and giggling on the couch. Jupe's head is in Rae's lap, and Rae's running her fingers through Jupe's curls, something *I* would get murdered for if I tried to do—and I have.

Welcome to Croopiter—also known as life number three.

Three. As in *third wheel*.

Now look, when I'm with each girl separately, I have an existence that the other doesn't know about; see lives one and two. As such, I'm under no illusions about the fact that they have a separate life that doesn't involve *me*.

Thing is, when the three of us are together, *their* life-together-sans-Courtney is what comes to the forefront. There are moments when I can feel *my* separate-life tension with one or the other of them—like Jupe will get extra touchy-feely when Rae isn't looking. And if I had a dollar for every time I've looked up and caught Rae staring at me—and instead of turning away, smirking flirtatiously—I'd have enough to pay for all three of us to go to this movie tonight.

But in general, when the three of us are together, Jupiter

and Rae are giggling, talking, laughing, whispering, touching each other's hair, linking arms, etc., and I'm more or less driving, chaperoning, mascotting, tagging along like some unshakable older sibling.

Frankly, I really shouldn't hang out with them at all, since I tend to end up evacuating small soldiers while indulging depraved thoughts after watching them flirt with each other for hours.

I don't know how much longer I can live like this.

As a matter of fact, before we even get out the door—with the two of them arm in arm, of course—I've decided I'm going to ditch them when we get to the movie theater. I text Golly and Brit to meet us there because there's no way I can handle this shit tonight. Especially not after Jupe gobbled my naked body up with her eyes the way a starved sex goddess would.

My inability to handle it intensifies when on the way there, Rae, *out of nowhere*, says, "Jupiter, you have the nicest boobs," from the backseat.

"Oh God, they're totally out of control," Jupe says, rotating in her seat to look at her complimenter. "Did I tell you I was a freaking C cup at thirteen?"

"What are you now?"

"Thirty-six D."

Yes, I do take my eyes off the road to glance at Jupiter's incredible breasts. They fill the mustard-colored V-neck sweater she's wearing quite superbly. Thankfully she and Rae are too immersed in this conversation I don't/do want to hear to notice me looking.

"Ugh, you're so lucky. I'm a thirty-two *A*," Rae says.

"Yeah, but it fits your frame," from Jupe.

"My mom is shaped like you," Rae says. "All voluptuous and everything? My sister is, too, actually."

Jupe doesn't respond.

Then Rae says: "You also have a really great butt."

I promise you, it's like I can *feel* Jupe blush as she turns forward again. "Oh, stop it," she says.

I wonder what this conversation is doing to her.

"I'm only telling the truth," from Rae. "Your body is downright exquisite."

And Jupe is silent.

I cannot tell you how happy I am that we're turning into the parking lot now, and that Golly's old Ford that's propped up on massive wheels and rumbles like a tyrannosaurus when he pushes down on the accelerator is already there.

"Is that Britain and Golly?" Rae says. "What an awesome coincidence!" Both guys climb down from the truck cab— Well, Britain climbs down. Golly just steps out.

"Oh, this isn't a coincidence." Jupe glares at me. "You're totally ditching us!"

Sometimes I miss the days when she didn't seem to care what I did with my time even if it did involve ditching her.

"Sorry, ladies. Need some time with my boys, if you don't mind."

"Of course we don't, Courtney!" Rae says all Rae-of-sunshiny before squeezing my bicep, tossing me a wink, and hopping out.

Jupe isn't so quick to let me off the hook. She won't even look at me. Taken with the whole peen-peering thing earlier, I'm confused *as all get-out*, as Mama would say.

"Jupe?" *Are you secretly in love with me?* "Is everything okay?"

"Yeah, it's fine."

You've been super-clingy lately. For real, are you secretly in love with me? "Don't be mad at me, all right?"

"Not possible, unfortunately."

Can we talk about how I was totally naked and you were looking at me like you wanted to eat me? "What's not possible?"

"Being mad at you, Coop. I definitely want to be because you're ditching us, but I can't because you're *you*. You suck."

Jupiter, I wish you wouldn't say things like that because it's very confusing for me. Don't you realize I'm passionately in love with you, jackass? "Hey . . ." I take her chin and turn her face so she's looking at me. Yes, this is ridiculous. "I'll be home later, okay?" *And by* home, *I mean your* home, *but of course I don't have to say that because you know what I mean, and now your eyes and face are lighting up like the Fourth of damn July and I HAVE NO IDEA WHAT TO DO WITH THAT.*

In this moment, I can't help but wonder if that *dangerous crush* she mentioned is on ME.

I gotta ask: "Hey, before you go, what's the latest with your 'crush'?"

Jupe rolls her eyes. "The girl is clueless," she says.

And my hopes are smashed again.

No idea why I keep doing this to myself.

This was supposed to be the part where I talk about my fourth and final life: Coop-and-Everyone-Else. But it's currently rolling into the third: when we get back to my house, all Britain and Golly want to talk about is Jupe and Rae.

We're eating pizza in the living room with an NBA game playing on the TV, but I'm the only one paying attention to it. "So, Coop . . . ," Britain says, picking up the remote and hitting Mute.

"Dawg," I say. "Party fucking foul."

"Hmph. Somebody's testy," Golly says with his mouth full.

"And anyway, this game is a repeat and you already know who won," from Britain. "So tell us: What's the deal with Rae and Jupiter, man? We saw them go into the theater arm in arm. . . . *Everybody* at school is wonderi—"

"Everybody at school needs to mind their own damn business."

"Pump the brakes with all that attitude, brah. I was just asking 'cause *I* wanna know," Britain says. "I'm thinking about asking Rae to tutor me for the SATs. She's in my AP Lang class, and her vocabulary is thicker than Nicki Minaj." With stars in his eyes.

I think Britain might have a crush on Rae, though he would never admit it. "What the hell does SAT tutoring have to do with Jupe and Rae?"

"Well—"

"It really don't even matter," Golly says, downing another half-slice of pizza in one bite, then taking a swig of Dr Pepper straight from the two-liter. "*All* girls do that shit," he says. "My sisters—even the ones with boyfriends—are *all* like that with their girl friends. They constantly touch each other and snuggle and play in each other's hair and shit, too. It's a girl thing."

"Yeah, but as you just verified, your sisters are straight. Jupiter is not."

Like I needed the reminder.

Okay, fine, I did need the reminder.

I hate all almost-four of my lives right now.

"So, Coop," Golly says, "Little B's dumbass question aside, what's going on with *you* and Rae? Y'all seem to be gettin' real close."

"Yeah, don't look too far into it." How to put this without sounding like I'm completely bonkers? These guys would look at me more-than-sideways if they knew about my nightmare and the whole *Find Carousel Carl* thing. "We get each other, is all," I say. "Both live with single parents who work in the medical field, that kind of stuff."

"Yeah, but wasn't she hella cold-shoulderin' you?" Britain says. "What changed?"

"She was just a little nervous around me at first because she knew I'd lost my dad, you know?"

Okay, shocked at how easily that lie came.

"Can't say I know personally, but I get you," Golly says. He doesn't like talking about sad things so this is an easy out, thank God. "I guess there's nothing really there to talk about, then, huh?"

See?

"Nope . . ." *Except (1) I think Rae might have a thing for me, (2) I think Jupe might have a thing for Rae, and (3) I am so wrapped around Jupe's pinkie, the tip is surely turning blue, and I can't wait until she gets back so I can kick you asswipes out of my house and go curl up with her to watch* To Have and Have Not *before we crawl into her bed together and I can sleep without having the nightmare related to the manhunt Rae and I have embarked on to find our fallen favorite childhood TV star.*

"Nothing that would interest y'all, anyway."

10

But Then Every 248 Years, Neptune and Pluto Switch Places, and the Solar System Changes

This little factoid, which I learned from some Discovery Channel documentary I watched with Jupe earlier tonight—an activity that involved having her in my lap for ninety-three minutes, yes, there was some strategic positioning—is what I'm thinking about as I drive to Rae's house at 3:17 a.m. a week before Thanksgiving.

Something I left Jupe alone in bed to do, mind you.

She sleeps like a corpse, so unless she's woken up in the past nine minutes, Jupe has no idea I'm gone. And despite feeling like I made the right choice in leaving, I'm admittedly a little scared to find out what she'll say/think/feel when she realizes I not only left her, but left her to go to Rae's.

We fell asleep at around eleven—me on my back, her tucked under my arm with half of her bodacious physique draped across me—and my nightmare had just started the way it always does, but instead of merry-go-round music, I heard the intro to this old rap song I like (and Jupiter hates). Carousel Carl appeared, looking like he'd stepped right out of the nineties, and then the rapper's voice filled the air: "I like . . . big . . . BUTTS and I cannot *liiiie.* . . ."

Turns out, my cell phone was ringing.

Which, once I was awake enough to connect the dots, almost made me pass out again: my brain immediately jumped to the time I was awakened in the dead of night post-carnival eleven years ago and told that my dad wasn't ever coming home.

Jupe had shifted off me by that point and I was able to move, but I was too busy bracing for the worst to actually *look* at who was calling. So when I croaked hello and heard "Courtney?" in Rae's voice, it was like somebody Tased my brain or something.

"Rae?" I sat up straight. "Everything all right?"

"I'm sorry for waking you—"

"Don't apologize. Are you okay?"

"I, umm—"

And she sniffled.

Now look, I don't know if it was a manly instinct, a friendship instinct, or both, but the second I realized she was crying, I stood up to put my shoes on. What I gathered before I grabbed the keys and slipped out: she was alone and she was afraid.

So now here I am, pulling into the driveway of her two-story brick colonial at one of those ungodly hours during which, according to Britain, "the only thing open is legs."

Like he would know.

I don't have to ring the doorbell because she's sitting on the porch steps, all bundled up in one of those puffy coats with her breath fogging the air in front of her face. As a matter of fact, by the time I put the car in park, unbuckle my seat belt, and reach to shut off the ignition, she's opening the passenger door and climbing in.

"Leave it on," she says, holding her hands up to the heater vents.

"As you wish." I drop my arm.

"You know, you really didn't have to come."

"Says the girl sitting outside in subglacial temps while the vampires are out looking for a snack with sprinkles." I tap a freckle on the back of her hand.

She laughs and looks down at the floor, and I have zero doubt her cheeks are all pink.

I can't begin to tell you how good that makes me feel right now.

She looks over at me—shyly—and I grin.

"So, you okay?" I ask.

Her eyes drop. "Well—"

And then she starts to cry again. "I'm so sorry," she says.

Side note: I for real hate when people apologize for crying. Like what the hell is there to be sorry about?

"Come on, let's get in the backseat." Under *no* other circumstances would I ever say those words to a girl. I can just see the look of horror on Jupe's face if she heard me. Man, I sure hope she hasn't woken up yet. . . .

Once we're in back, I lift my arm. "C'mere, you."

Rae slides underneath it. "You smell nice," she says as she rests her cheek against my shirt. At first it makes me smile, but then she says, "You know what it reminds me of? That stuff Jupiter uses in her hair."

Uhh . . .

"I actually almost called her," Rae continues.

Whew, off the hook. "Why didn't you?"

She looks up at me. "You cannot *ever* tell her this."

"Okay . . ."

"I needed a guy," she says.

"You needed a guy?"

"Right. It might be said that I have fairly extensive abandonment issues when it comes to women since my mom left and my sister eventually joined her?"

"Ah. I see."

"I'm working on it, but when I get to where I am right now, I need a big, strong *dude*. You know what I mean?"

I laugh. "Can't say I do, but okay. Big, strong dude at your service. Thanks for the compliment, by the way."

"Oh, shut up." She smacks my stomach.

Yeah, we've been getting more and more flirty when no one else is around these days. And by *no one else* I mean Jupe. Is this wrong? I'm not sure. Though I feel guilty about it sometimes because it does feel deliberate.

Like Rae and I deliberately don't touch each other or banter or flirt if Jupe is around. It feels like I'm going behind Jupe's back or something. Like I'm cheating on her. Which is bullshit, right? It's not like she's my girlfriend.

And really, why should I feel guilty for flirting with a cute girl who actually likes dudes? The fact that Rae feels like she has to keep it from Jupe that she "needs a guy" sometimes is laughable because whether Jupe's willing to admit it or not, she obviously needs a guy sometimes, too. I don't see her calling any of her *girl* friends to come cuddle with her to watch movies and then hold her all night long.

Now that I'm thinking about it, it kind of makes me mad, you know? That I'm sitting here feeling *guilty* about flirting with a girl who's okay with flirting back? That I feel *guilty* about leaving Jupe alone in a bed very few people even know we share? It's like I'm this dirty little male secret of hers. She never "came out of the closet," so most people assume there *is* no closet for her. . . .

But there is. *I'm* inside it. She comes in there when she needs a "cuddle-buddy" or a bedmate or whatever, and then goes back out all gay-guns blazing when she's done.

Wow, I am really pissed off right now.

"Do you ever miss him?" Rae says, tugging me back.

"Huh?"

"Your dad."

"Oh. Uhh . . ." Well, that was unexpected. "I mean, I was pretty young when he passed, so I don't remember a whole lot about him."

Except that's a lie. Matter of fact, I have a *ton* of memories. Was just looking at pictures of him the other day. And I do miss him.

Why's it so hard for me to say it?

"So where's *your* dad?" I ask Rae, slamming a lid back on *my* dad box and trying to refocus things. It's getting close to four, and we do have school in the morning.

And, all right, despite being pissed, I'm still not sure I want Jupe waking up to an empty bed if she hasn't already.

I really hate myself right now.

Rae sighs. "He had to go to some AAP conference in Nebraska."

"AAP?"

"American Academy of Pediatrics."

"Ah. And he just left you here?"

"Ugh." She puts her forehead in her hands. "It was *my* idea?"

When she looks at me this time, I swear to you the air in the car changes. It's like the way I felt that night Jupe let her guard down and said all those things that sucked me deeper into the inescapable abyss that is being in love with Jupiter Sanchez while in biological possession of a penis.

"If I tell you something, do you promise not to judge me?" Rae says.

"Of course."

She takes a deep breath. "So you know how I'm all exuberant-shiny-happy-nicey-nice-vivacious all the time?"

I laugh. "That's one way to put it."

"Well, it's all a lie."

"Huh?"

"None of it's real." She pulls away, and I can tell she's about to cry again. "Honestly, the only time I'm *legitimately* happy is when I'm with you or Jupiter. The rest of the time, I'm just"—she looks down—"unshakably disconsolate."

Not real sure what to say to that. Partially because I have no idea what the hell *disconsolate* means. But she doesn't go on, so I guess I have to come up with something.

"What do you mean by that, Rae?"

Shut up. It was the best I could do.

"Well, in a word, I'm sad. Last time I remember being really and truly happy was before Carl disappeared and everything fell apart. That's the real reason I want to find out what happened to him."

"Wow." Now I'm super-uncomfortable because I tend to want to *fix* things, but I can't even come up with a decent response.

She goes on: "I really do want *other* people to be happy, though. My dad's wanted to go to this conference for four years now, but this was his first time being invited as a speaker. He was *so* excited until he saw the dates. Normally he'd take me with him, but this time it's five days instead of just the weekend, and he didn't want to pull me out of school. I saw how badly he wanted to go, so I convinced him to accept. Told him I'd stay at Jupiter's."

"Okay . . ."

"He tends to go with whatever I tell him because of some . . . points of contention with my sister. She barely speaks to him now because he went all helicopter parent on her after my mom left."

"Dang."

"And then when *she* left me I—" She shakes her head. "Never mind. Anyway, he asked if I was sure, I said yes. So he left."

Hmm. Not sure where the sister thing was going, but probably shouldn't pry, right? And I'd comment on Dr. Chin's parenting, but my mom would've done the same thing, so who am I to judge? "Gotcha."

"Thing is, I have sleep terrors," she continues. "Sometimes

I even sleepwalk. It was *way* worse when I was a kid, but when I get stressed—like I was tonight because I was alone in this new house—I tend to have episodes. I, uhh . . ." She gulps. "Woke up in the attic."

"Whoa."

"Yeah. Also took me a minute to figure out where I was. I had my phone in my hand, so I called you as soon as I did. Needed to hear the voice of a friend. Haven't felt *that* alone in a long time."

"Wow, Rae." She wipes her tear-streaked face, and I pull her back in and rub the top of her arm.

"Sorry for unloading on you."

"Don't apologize. As you said, I'm your friend. It's what I'm here for. Though I'll admit I had no idea you were going through all this."

"Well, that's the point, isn't it? I pretend so no one *will* have any idea. My dad made me see a therapist for a while, and she used to say I had an issue with 'people-pleasing.' Hence the *everything is jolly, yee-haw!* act."

Didn't judge Dr. Chin's parenting, but definitely judging Rae's use of *yee-haw*. "So why didn't you come to Jupe's?" I ask. "I have nightmares sometimes, and she's usually the person who's there to bring *me* back—"

Holy hell, why did I just say that?

She hesitates for a second before pulling away and looking down at her hands. "I didn't want to impose," she says. "I'm not sure if she meant to, because she seemed embarrassed about it afterward, but a few weeks ago, Jupiter let it slip that you guys hang out most nights."

Is she serious? "Are you serious?"

She turns to the window and clears her throat, and I swear to you, a wall drops down between us. "Mmhmm."

So that's weird, right? Open book to brick barrier in less than a second? She's dead silent now and won't look at me. Which means she's totally not telling me something.

Right?

Or maybe I'm overthinking things?

See what I mean about not-Jupe girls being hard as hell to read? Though even *she's* like a foreign language at this point. Like she's *embarrassed* about Rae knowing we hang out? The hell's up with that?

"Well, I'm taking you to my house now," I say. "You can sleep in our guest room tonight and then go to Jupe's tomorrow. Or maybe the two of you can have another sleepover with my mom if she's home."

Before I have a chance to consider the weight of what I just said, Rae turns back to me and smiles like I just offered her the galaxy or something.

And just like that I've set the following two facts in stone:

1. Jupiter Charity-Sanchez will definitely wake up alone.
2. She and I will not be sleeping together for at least the next three nights.

Thing is, looking at Rae right now—at the light in her face that wasn't there when she got into the car, at the relief in her shoulders—I don't even care that I didn't get

Jupe's permission. Matter of fact, I *know* in this moment that I'm going to do everything in my power to help her solve the Carl Conundrum.

It clicks for me then: there's something really delicate and vulnerable and not-Jupe about Rae. It makes me wanna like . . . protect her. Rescue her, even. And despite the fact that Jupe would shit glitter if she heard me imply that *any* girl needs to be rescued, it feels *good* to want to do that for Rae.

Not sure if I'm brainwashed by the *friggin' patriarchy,* or if it's just part of being a dude, but knowing she "needed a guy" and *I'm* the one who came through makes me feel really damn good.

Don't get me wrong: I love Jupe's strength and independence and all that. It's great—and sexy as hell, I won't lie.

But this gorgeous, whip-smart girl sitting here gazing at me the way she is right now?

I'm feelin' this.

"Come on," I tell her before opening the door, grabbing her hand, and pulling her out of the car. "I'll walk you in to get your stuff."

Once she's out, I push the car door closed and turn to lead her up to the house, but she stops me. "Hey, wait . . ."

So I turn around.

I'm still holding her hand, which is soft but cold and kind of bony. Compared to Jupe's meatier, always-warm hands, it's a strange sensation . . . but not an unpleasant one.

She's staring up at me, and things are a little tense. Not like we're-going-to-kiss tense, but something's definitely different between us.

"Thank you," she says.

"For what?"

Yeah, fishing for the ego stroke. Deal with it.

Her eyes drop.

Just the *thought* of her freckly cheeks being all pink is making me smile really hard and feel this strange warmth in my chest.

She clears her throat, squares her shoulders, and raises her chin to look me in the eye—cutest show of bravery I've ever seen.

"For being the guy I needed," she says.

And just like that, the planets realign.

Game Plan?

Game on.

Book Two

A Sesquipedalian Search for a Simplified-Science Savant*

Across

2 A state or quality marked by seriousness, gravity, or solemnity.

4 More than is required; unnecessary or needless.

6 Of or pertaining to sisters.

7 Division or separation; discord, disharmony.

8 A confused or chaotic state; "Situation Normal: All Fucked Up."

Down

1 Overwhelmed with amazement; astounded; astonished.

3 Ready to or in the process of falling.

4 Progressing by leaps.

5 The simultaneous occurrence of causally unrelated events and the belief that the simultaneity has meaning beyond mere coincidence.

6 An alignment of three celestial bodies, as the sun, the earth, and either the moon or a planet.

---

* Crossword created by Rae E. Chin.

11

STUPEFIED

*(adj.) overwhelmed with
amazement; astounded; astonished*

Exhibit A: Rae Chin, veritable home invader, wide awake
in a paisley-wallpapered guest suite across the hall from
Courtney Cooper's bedroom.

How on earth did I even get here?

Better yet: *Who* is this guy who would get out of bed at
3:30 a.m. on a school night to come get me and bring me
to his house so I wouldn't be alone? It's one thing for him
to humor my Carousel Carl shenanigans, but this? This is a
push past plausibility.

There's a knock. "Rae?"

"Come in," I say.

Courtney sticks his head in the door. "Sorry to wake you."

"No worries. I wasn't sleeping."

"Oh. Did you get any sleep at all?" His eyebrows pull
together and I have to look away because . . . well, I'm a

little embarrassed. About being here. In his house. Because he basically rescued me.

Jupiter would have a conniption.

"I got enough," I lie.

"Okay, good." His shoulders relax. "We need to leave for school in forty-five minutes. Just wanted to make sure you had time to get ready. You brought your cheer uniform, right? Game tonight. Should've asked before we left your house . . ."

I smile. "I brought it."

"Okay, good. Towels are in the bathroom closet."

"Got it. Thank you!"

"Oh! My mama told me to tell you—Uhh . . . Hold on." He pulls his phone from his back pocket, taps the screen, and holds it up to his face. "*'Hi, sweetheart. Hope you slept well. Guest room is yours whenever you need it, and let me know if either of my knucklehead children gives you any trouble.'*"

Utterly speechless.

"Sorry if that was weird." Phone returns to the pocket. "She . . . made me write it down. Said she was gonna ask you if I delivered. So . . . there ya go." Now he won't meet my eyes.

I clear my throat. Try to keep my grin from overtaking my *entire* face. "I'll let her know you did."

"'Preciate that."

He doesn't move. Just stares at me. It's giving me heart palpitations.

"I'm, uhh . . . I'm glad you're here, Rae."

"Really?"

He laughs. "Why wouldn't I be?"

"Is that rhetorical?"

He laughs again! Am I *funny*?

"Oh, Coooooopiiiiiiie!" a voice trills from downstairs before I hear the front door slam.

"Jupiter?" I ask.

Coop rolls his eyes, which makes *me* laugh.

"Girl thinks she owns the place," he says. "I'll let you get ready."

"Does she know I'm here?"

It's out of my mouth before I can stop it, and part of me feels asinine for asking, because it really shouldn't matter: we're in *his* house. It's just that looking around this room and at this beautiful boy standing in the doorway, I feel like I'm encroaching on something sacred. Something definitively *hers*. And while I can't say I know her *that* well, Jupiter Charity-Sanchez doesn't seem the type to take kindly to encroachments upon her territory.

Not that Courtney Cooper is mere *territory* . . .

What the heck did I get myself into by calling him in the middle of the night?

"She doesn't," he says. "But she's about to find out." He winks before closing the door.

I guess Courtney's revelation of my presence goes over well, because when I get downstairs, Jupiter greets me with such exuberance—and *quite* the embrace—one would assume we hadn't seen each other in months. It makes me wonder just how much Courtney told her. Hope he didn't mention my faux-joviality . . .

Though pretending to be ecstatic to see her when I'm

107

this self-conscious about the circumstances is . . . challenging. "Hi, Jupiter," I say, once she releases me. She's wearing an apron: KISS THE COOK, BUT DON'T TOUCH THE BUNS. I smile, but now I'm thinking about *her* "buns," and I can't get my eyes to lift past her lips.

They are very lovely lips. Covered in a shimmery gloss that I bet is sweet to the taste.

I swallow.

"Come," she says, grabbing my hand and pulling me into the kitchen. She deposits me in front of a meticulously arranged place setting. I take a seat, and within seconds, her 36Ds are in my face as she puts a plate down in front of me. "Eat fast, we gotta leave in eleven minutes. Iridis meeting this morning." And she sashays away.

Courtney grins at me from the opposite end of the table, where he's got his chair kicked back on two legs and is nursing a glass of orange juice.

I drop my eyes to my plate, *sure* my face just spontaneously combusted. Did I seriously call him at past three in the morning?

Clearly I did, because here I am at his kitchen table with the fragrance of an omelet smothered in some kind of tomatoey-oniony-garlicky sauce tickling my olfactory epithelium.

I take a bite.

Holy ambrosia, what is *in* this stuff?

"It's called sofrito," Courtney says with another smirk. Is he really watching me eat? "It's nuts, right?"

"Mmhmm!" I stuff another mouthful.

108

"Milk? Water? OJ?" Jupiter removes the apron and hangs it on a hook.

Coffee is what I really want, but is that weird? Also, she didn't offer that, so "Water is fine, thank you."

She brings a pitcher and fills the empty glass in front of me. Smiles. "Food okay?"

More than okay is what I want to say, but "Oh yes!" is what comes out. I take a gulp of water before I can make a bigger idiot of myself.

She's still beaming at me. "I'm happy you're here, Rae-Rae."

And now I choke.

"Oh my God, are you okay?" Jupiter rushes over and smacks me on the back.

"Yeah, yeah. I'm fine," I say. "Minor epiglottal failure."

Now she and Courtney are *both* beaming. "I can't even handle her!" Jupiter says.

"Oh, me neither," he replies. His eyes fix on me. "Best morning I've had in weeks."

"Oh my gosh, *stop*," I say, my face aflame again.

Now they're laughing. For the second time this morning, two people I deeply admire have told me they're glad to have me around.

I wonder how many more times it would take for me to actually believe it.

School is surreal.

Actually, no: *everything* is surreal.

There's nothing outwardly different. . . . Jupiter is driving this morning, so despite it being November and fifty degrees, we ride the entire twelve minutes with all the windows rolled down and a blend of Queen and Halsey ("This woman might be Freddie Mercury reincarnate," Jupiter once said. "They're both bisexual, both incomparable songwriters, both have voices like angels . . .") blasting from the speakers as Jupiter sings into the wind.

I typically stretch my legs across the backseat and work on a crossword, but this morning, I can feel the beat thrumming at the base of my spine, almost like it's inside me. There's a string quartet on this track that makes my hair stand on end, and some of the melodies and harmonies are so rich, my eyes literally prickle with tears.

This hyperawareness continues all day. People smiling at me and saying hello in the halls both overwhelms me with joy and makes me want to flee to the bathroom and hide. In AP Language, Britain touches my arm to ask me a question, and I startle so intensely, my pencil goes flying and I almost fall out of my desk.

Eventually I *do* flee to the bathroom just so I can regroup.

I've never felt this out there before. All exposed like some sort of stripped wire that'll *zap* anyone who gets too close.

It's times like these I miss our massive backyard in Alabama and how easy it was to just go out and tumble until I'd flipped so many times, it felt like my brain had realigned.

Knowing Courtney Cooper's aware of the truth about me and my duplicity is one thing.

Knowing he's *fine* with it? That it didn't make him turn tail and run?

That's another thing entirely.

12

SYZYGY

(n.) an alignment of three celestial bodies, as the sun, the earth, and either the moon or a planet

I stay at Jupiter's house all weekend, and then the following Thursday, on the morning of our inaugural Thanksgiving in Georgia, she invites me over to help prep a few items for the dinner her dads are hosting. We're working on a cake that involves three varieties of milk when she turns to me and smiles.

It makes me blush. "What?"

"Just glad you're here."

There it is again. "You are?" Why does this keep surprising me?

"I am," she says. "It's totally selfish, but you coming here has been the best thing to happen to me since Coop moved in next door."

"Oh." I don't know if my face has ever been this hot.

She goes on: "How ironic that the person who taught me the importance of letting people know I appreciate them is embarrassed by my appreciation." She bumps me with her hip.

"Could you stop?" I look away. This flattery to the point of fluster happens more often than I care to admit when she's around, and it was unnerving at first because I'd never reacted to a girl that way before. But the more time I spend with her at school, the more I realize that pretty much everyone gets inarticulate around her—guys, girls, teachers, administrators, janitors, librarians, classroom pets. Even Courtney does at times, and they've been friends for an eon and a day.

Anyway: To have the most enchanting human being I've ever encountered tell me *my* move to her town is the best thing to happen to *her* in ten years?

"Did you inhale too much flour dust or something?" I say.

She laughs. It's nothing short of pure resplendence.

"You totally don't get it, do you?" she says.

"Can't say I do. Sorry."

"Okay, I'll explain, but you have to promise you won't pass out from all the compliments I'm about to give you."

"Oh, shut up." I blush again, and there's more laughter from her. It's a marvel we ever make it through a conversation.

"So my whole life, I've never really *fit* anywhere," she begins. "And I'm not even talking about being gay. Not that it was super-*easy*, but having gay dads and super-accepting people like Coop and Neeta made it possible for me to not really struggle with that part of myself."

"Okay."

"But when it comes to other stuff like being biracial and growing up without a mom? While it was never a 'big deal' because those things just *are*, and I've never known different, you being here makes me feel less singular because I know you *get* those things," she says.

She's looking at me with her golden eyes all squinchy like she's waiting for a response. But I don't have one, because I've only ever felt like an oddball. How ridiculous is the notion that I've made another human being feel like *less* of one?

I guess I look just as baffled as I feel, because now her smile is fading and her eyes are opening so wide, the gold of her irises looks molten and is threatening to spill over onto her cheeks.

"Shit, was that totally insensitive?" she says. "I promise you I wasn't implying that our mom situations are *remotely* the same—I'm so sorry, Rae!" She closes her eyes and her chin drops to her chest.

"Wait, no! That's not it at all . . . I just—"

And now she looks hopeful.

How did I wind up in this position with the most popular—and beautiful and funny and kind and compassionate and socially conscious and, and, and, and, and—girl at my new school? "No one's ever said anything like that to me before." I look at my feet. "Just sounds a little strange because *I've* never 'fit' anywhere."

"Really?" She globs a can of sweetened condensed milk into a mixing bowl and follows it with a can of evaporated milk (because apparently they aren't the same thing?) and a cup of heavy cream.

"Jupe, I grew up in Flintley, Alabama," I say. "My dad was the only Asian in like a hundred-mile radius. The next town over was like ninety-six percent African American, so I saw nonwhite people all the time, but I was definitely an anomaly."

She turns to me with her eyebrows furrowed like this is the most interesting thing she's ever heard. "Tell me more."

"My sister and I both got bullied when we were younger because we didn't look like everybody else. It was your standard anti-Asian dreck: pulling out the corners of the eyes, yelling stuff like 'ching chong' and 'hiiii-yah!,' asking if our dad was Bruce Lee." I shudder at the memory. "It was actually a lot worse for her than for me—she's got black hair, dark brown eyes, and porcelain skin without freckles, so kids used to say she was a witch and a devil worshipper."

"Those fuckers!" Jupiter says.

I giggle. There's something refreshing about a beautiful girl's use of "profanity" after living in the land of Southern Etiquette and debutantes for so long. "It tapered off for me in middle school because I started to look less Asian, but even after I got into cheering and it was clear people liked me, I still didn't *fit*."

"Here, stir." She passes me the bowl of milks and a whisk, then goes to grab the cooled cake from the wire rack next to the stove. Once she's beside me again, she starts poking holes in the cake with a fork. "So where's your extended family?"

"My mom and her parents are in New Hampshire—my sister moved there when she was thirteen and goes to Dartmouth now—and most of my dad's family is in Jamaica."

Her eyebrows lift. "Jamaica?"

114

"Mmhmm. That's where he's from. My grandparents were born there, too. That's pretty much all I know about them, though. I've never met them. When we were younger, my sister told me they cut ties with him when he married our mom, and while I've never had the guts to ask him, I sort of believe her. The one time we met my dad's brother's family, our cousins made fun of us for not being Chinese enough."

"Dad's family cut ties with him when he came out," Jupiter says. "He's actually got an ex-wife and two kids."

"Really?"

"I mean, his 'kids' are grown now, but yeah," she says. "It's sad, you know?"

I nod. "It really is."

"Well, whatever slightly depressing path led you here, I'm really glad you came, Rae. You really do fit with Coop and me. I seriously feel like the three of us belong together. Here, taste . . ." Jupiter dips her finger into the bowl and holds it up to my mouth.

I hesitate—my dad is a doctor, after all, and holy unhygienic, Batman!—but then she starts wiggling it and making her eyebrows dance. "Come onnnn. You know you wanna."

Capitulation is inevitable.

She laughs as I stick the tip of my tongue out and lick off the three-milk mixture that gives the *tres leches* its name.

So *that's* what belonging tastes like.

Thanksgiving dinner at La Casa de Charity-Sanchez is unremarkable.

Okay, that's not entirely true. . . .

Because it was a "special occasion," the parentals said we

could each have *una copa de vino* (that's how Papi said it). So we each did, but *I* might have also potentially snuck into the kitchen to imbibe a glass of that mojito stuff Papi makes. And since I only weigh 117 pounds and have only had alcohol one time before, I *might* have been a little woozy by the time I got back to the table.

It might also be said that everything at dinner after that is fuliginous at best. So let's just fast-forward to the nonce and be done with it.

Scene: *After an uneventful Thanksgiving dinner, the three friends retire to Jupiter's bedroom to while away an indeterminate number of hours while the parentals embark on whatever it is parentals embark on. Within said bedroom, Jupiter is at her desk on her laptop, likely putting the finishing touches on tomorrow's community service outreach, Courtney is reclined in his special chair watching a black-and-white film featuring a middle-aged white man who talks funny and appears to have a penchant for younger women, and Rae is lying prone on Jupiter's bed, reading the cover story in a magazine entitled* Feminist Monthly *about a group of European women who stage "topless protests" to combat religion and patriarchy by writing activist-ish messages across their breasts. Rae doesn't understand the purpose of such brazen self-exposure, but it does bring another question to the tip of her tongue. . . .*

"Jupiter, what's it like to have sex with a girl?"
Frickin' frack, did Rae really say that aloud?

116

Guessing I did by the way Jupiter rotates in her chair with her eyebrows raised, and Courtney continues to stare at the TV but blinks rapidly for a few seconds before clearing his throat.

No point in turning back now. "I mean, there's no boy part," I say. "So what do you like . . . do?" I sit up.

Whooooa, too fast, room spinning.

"Wow, um . . ." Jupiter rubs her nose ring. Seems to be her *apprehensive* tell. "That was kind of out of nowhere, Rae."

Courtney "coughs," but I can tell he's really laughing into his hand. My suspicion is confirmed when Jupiter glares at him.

"Well, Jupiter?" He clasps his hands in his lap. "What *is* it like?"

Jupiter picks up the unicorn Beanie Baby from her desk and lobs it at him. Now he's laughing openly.

"I've never actually done it, Rae," Jupiter says.

"Really?" Le plot thickens! "But what about Breanna?"

"What about her?"

"You haven't hooked up with her? I know you two hang out a lot. Seems like a missed opportunity."

Courtney looks back at the TV and pulls his lips between his teeth.

"I—" Jupiter shakes her head. "Breanna and I are just friends, Rae."

"Oh. Okay. Well, what about kissing a girl, then? What's that like?"

"Well, I assume it'd be like kissing anyone with a mouth." (Is it me, or does she sound a little perturbed?) "But I wouldn't know because I haven't done that, either."

117

"Wait, so how do you know you're gay, then?"

Courtney's eyes go wide, and he and Jupiter look at each other. This is when I know I'm drunker than I realized: from the looks on their faces, if I'm reading their expressions correctly, I just said something offensive.

But I genuinely want to know.

Like, sometimes I totally find myself looking at Jupiter's mouth and wondering what it would be like to kiss her. Does that make me gay? Well . . . I guess *bi* would be more accurate because I've thought about kissing Courtney, too.

Then again, my boy-sex experiences weren't satisfying in the least. Would I like it better with a girl? And what if I *did* kiss Jupiter and liked it? I would totally have to be gay or bi then, right? How does she even *know*?

"I know that's a little forthright, but seriously, how do you know you're gay?"

"Well, Rae," Jupiter says, and she definitely looks aggravated now, "did you have to kiss or have sex with a guy to know you're straight?"

"No . . . ," I say. "But I don't really *know* if I'm one hundred percent straight. These boobs in your magazine, for instance . . ." I hold the page up for them to see. "Well, they're kind of nice to look at, and it's a little confounding because the more I look at them, the more tingly I get down in my—"

"Whooooa there, Sprinkles." Courtney rises from the chair to take the magazine from my hand. "Might be a good idea to lie down now. You've obviously had a *bit* too much to drink."

"Oh."

"How much *did* you drink, Rae? I've heard of 'lowered inhibitions,' but this is a lot, baby girl," Jupiter says.

"Aww, you called me baby girl!"

Okay, maybe they're right.

"Sorry if I crossed a line," I say. "I just really wanted to know. I've had sex with a boy, and it honestly didn't feel all that great, so I wondered if maybe—"

"Wait, you're not a virgin?" Courtney says.

"No."

"For real?"

"Why is that so shocking?" Jupiter asks. "Besides, 'virginity' is a misogynistic patriarchal concept historically used to control female sexuality—"

"Huh?" I say.

"We'll talk about it when you're sober, sweet pea. Just know you have no reason to be ashamed." She glares at Courtney.

"Dawg, I didn't say *anything* about being 'ashamed.' It just surprises me that she's had sex—"

"Well, it shouldn't!"

"Whatever, Jupiter. You can't tell me you're not surprised, too."

"I'm not as surprised as *you* are."

"Well, she doesn't seem like the type, does she?"

"What the hell is *that* supposed to mean?"

Wow, they're really going at it over my vagina. I cock my head to look at Jupiter—well, more like my head plops to one side, since I no longer have much control over my neck. Anyway, I don't think I've ever seen her this mad before.

Courtney just waves her off and looks at me. "I'm *surprised* because you're only fifteen, Rae."

"I'd just turned fifteen when I did it the first time," I say. "It was basically terrible."

Jupiter's eyes expand. "Did he *force* you?"

"*That's* quite the conclusion to jump to, Jupit—"

"CAN IT, COOP! Did he, Rae?"

"Not exactly . . ."

"Was it consensual?"

I shrug. "More or less."

She gets up and comes to sit next to me. "Rae, this is serious. Did you give *full permission* when it happened?"

"I mean, I definitely said 'yes' out loud," I say. "He wouldn't do it until I said the actual word, so I said it. Just wish I hadn't. It's not like I loved him."

"Oh, Rae." Jupiter puts her arm around me, and I lay my head on her shoulder. She's so cozy.

Courtney leaves the room and comes back with a box of tissues. He sits on my other side, and Jupiter pulls a tissue from the box and wipes my face with it. Not sure when I started crying.

"So what happened?" Jupiter asks.

"Wait, maybe I should leave." Courtney moves to stand, but I stop him.

"No, stay," I say. "It's not much of a story, anyway. My ex, Corey, wanted to do it, so I said yes. I just wanted him to be happy."

"Ah," Courtney says. "The people-pleasing thing?"

Jupiter: "She's a people-pleaser?"
Courtney: "Yep."
Jupiter: "That explains a lot."

Me: "What's *that* supposed to mean?"

Jupe: "Sweetie, nobody's *that* damn happy."

Me: "So you knew I was faking?"

Jupe: "Rae, do I look like I was born yesterday?"

Courtney: "Can we get back to *Corey* or whatever his name is?"

Me (internally): *Wait, does Courtney Cooper sound a little jealous?*

Me (aloud): "Well, we only did it a few times before he broke up with me. Said he could tell I wasn't into it, and that his 'inability to satisfy' me was destroying him."

Jupe: "Of course the dickhead made it about *him*. . . . Friggin' patriarchy—"

Coop: "Not the time, Jupe . . ."

Jupe: "Whatever, Coop. You know I'm right. Anyway, we're so sorry that happened to you, Rae."

Jupiter kisses my forehead.

I look up at her again. Her lips look so *soft*. Like little flesh-covered pillows. Her boobs feel really nice against my arm, too. Also quite pillowy. It's doing a lot for my hampered proprioception. "Hey, Jupiter?"

"Yeah, babe?"

"Can I kiss you?"

Courtney snorts. "Welp, definitely time for *me* to go." He stands.

Jupiter gulps. "You should lie down now, okay?"

I nod and let her guide me to the pillow.

13

SUPERFLUOUS

*(adj.) more than is required;
unnecessary or needless*

Our beloved football team loses the state semifinals, which concludes my inaugural varsity cheerleading season at Decatur High.

But of course there's still a *grande fête* at the quarterback's lake house.

Not that it's any fun for me. For one, I'm sad the season's over. Practices and games were downright life-giving because they were my one reminder of my former life. Now I feel untethered.

For two, I'm *trying* to pretend I'm having the experience of my very existence, but every time I look up and see Courtney and Jupiter dancing/laughing/bantering/being Best Friends Forever, I want to vamoose into thin air and never return—yet simultaneously squeeze in between them so they make a sandwich out of me.

I've been feeling this way since waking up in Jupiter's

bed a week ago on the day after Thanksgiving, and it's very confusing.

"Rae-Rae!" Britain crows as he approaches with red cup in hand. I'm nauseated just *thinking* about what might be inside it (again: Thanksgiving).

"Hi, Britain." I force a smile.

"Don't think I don't know you're over here faking the funk, girl," he says, pointing at me for emphasis. "What's really going on? You bomb that AP Language essay like I did?"

"No, nothing like that." I try not to look past him at Courtney and Jupiter, who are currently slow-dancing . . . despite the upbeat Drake song currently throbbing through the speakers.

I obviously fail.

"Earth to Rae-Rae . . ." Britain's waving his hand in front of my face, and I send a silent prayer of thanks to the universe for his inebriation. Were he sober, all he'd have to do to find the answer to his question would be to follow my eyes.

"What are you talking about, silly goose?" I say with a gentle shove. "I'm having a great time!"

"You know how I know you're lying?"

I draw back. Can he really see through me that easily?

"You didn't use an SAT word!" He lifts his cup and flashes the most self-congratulatory grin I've ever seen.

It makes me laugh. And thaws my frozen heart just the slightest bit. Seeing as Courtney and Jupiter are too lost within their little microcosm to check on measly ol' me, I thank God for Britain in this moment. I might be overthinking, but despite Jupiter saying I "fit" with her and Courtney, lately, when I'm around them, I feel a bit redundant.

"Come dance with me," Britain says.

I agree—there is really no *dis*agreeing. But I come to regret it, because of course he pulls us into orbit around the star formation that is Jupe-and-Coop. If I didn't know better, I'd swear they were madly in love with each other.

"So what's new, Rae-Rae?" Britain says, beginning a restrained two-step-type move from side to side. He dances like a white guy who can't dance. Which I find surprising despite the fact that he *is* a white guy.

"Nothing at all!"

Courtney whispers something in Jupiter's ear, and she tosses her head back in riotous laughter.

My heart falls into the five-inch wedge boots I shouldn't have worn because who am I trying to impress? No one who's actually acknowledging my presence right now, that's for sure. Though that might not be a bad thing, because in this moment, I can't tear my gaze away from Jupiter's beautiful neck.

What I'm not telling Britain: Thanksgiving night, I woke up in Jupiter's bed at 3:47 a.m. because my bladder was on the verge of paroxysm, but when I came out of the bathroom, I accidentally went to the guest room, where I normally sleep when I stay over.

Since I'd fallen asleep in Jupiter's bed, *she* was in the guest room. Which made perfect sense.

What was odd was that Courtney was in there with her.

I got all the way to the bed before I noticed—thank God they didn't wake up—that they were all curled up together on their left sides. He had his arms around her waist from behind, and she was tucked into the curve of his body. Like two human spoons nestled together in a silverware bed.

In the grand scheme of things, I guess it wasn't *that* bizarre. Dane Greaves, this gay guy back home, and his female best friend, Maisie Phillips, used to literally sleep together all the time.

It's perfectly permissible for Jupiter and Courtney to do the same. They've been friends for an eon, and technically, *I'm* the interloper, so no big deal.

Except I'm jealous.

"Spin move!" Brit exclaims, twirling me so haphazardly, *he* almost falls.

"You good over there, Lil Brit?" Golly's to our right with Shanna Wilmington basically grinding on his knees. It's a sight.

"Hush, fool," Brit says.

"We're going to find some water," Jupiter says, taking Courtney's hand but turning to me. "You good, baby girl?"

Courtney beams down at me, too.

So they *are* cognizant of my existence. I smile in spite of myself. "I'm good."

"Take care of our girl, Brit," Courtney says.

"Aye-AYE, *Cap'm*!" Britain replies. Then Jupiter kisses my cheek, and she and Courtney are off.

I watch them go. I'm sure Jupiter would terminate our friendship if she heard me say this—she's pretty vocal about how much it annoys her that people assume she wants to "bang every girl" she lays eyes on—but there've been times when I've wondered if she's into me that way. Like she'll give me a certain look, or she'll say things that seem a bit coquettish. Though I usually brush it off, because she's the same way with Courtney.

Either way, I often wonder if I'm feeling stuff for *her*. Like right now, my face is still tingling where her lips touched it, and I haven't taken my eyes off her even though she's across the room.

It's possible my attraction is rooted in the fact that she's such a force and everyone adores her, so it's fairly exhilarating when her attention is on me. But I do sometimes get the same light-headed, fluttery sensation from her that I get from Courtney. And there is *certainly* some more-than-friendship attraction with him.

I'm trying my best to suppress *all* attractions because I don't want to upset the preexisting equipoise, but HE makes me feel accepted and secure, while SHE makes me feel beautiful and powerful, like there's nothing I can't conquer. If I could combine them, they'd make the perfect boy/girlfriend. Birlfriend?

Not that I really believe in love or those kinds of relationships anymore . . .

They come back. "So I think we're gonna go," Jupiter says. "Can't find anything to drink around here but Kool-Aid and liquor. Rae, you coming?"

I look at her, and she's smiling with that signature Jupiterian twinkle in her eye.

"Yeah, I'm coming."

As if I could say no.

14

SYNCHRONISM

*(n.) the simultaneous occurrence
of causally unrelated events and
the belief that the simultaneity has
meaning beyond mere coincidence*

Courtney takes his eyes off the road to glance at me in the passenger seat. "You're pretty mum over there, Sprinkles. Everything cool?"

We're headed to investigate what I think is a pretty promising lead in the Carl Conundrum. I found it the day after the football team's literal pity party, but we're just now getting around to checking it out—*nine* days later—because basketball season is in full swing, so Courtney isn't around very much.

I turn to meet his eyes, then sigh and shift my attention back to the miserable late-autumn landscape on the other side of the windshield—all cold and dreary and bereft of life. "Just have a lot on my mind," I say.

Few seconds of silence and then: "Yeah. I feel that."

"You do?"

"Yeah."

Another long pause, then he takes a deep breath. "You remember asking me if I miss my dad?"

I nod. "Mmhmm."

"Well . . . I do."

"Oh."

"I'm, uhh—I'm glad we're doing this. This search for Carl thing."

"You are?"

"I am. So thank you."

"Oh. Okay," I say. "You're welcome?"

And he laughs. Which makes *my* stomach flip over with delight. And throws me back into my tangle of unaskable questions and conflicted emotions.

Which of course he notices. "So what's up with you? Wanna talk about it?"

"Indubitably" is how I'd like to respond, but I can't seem to get the word past my lips. What would I say afterward? That, while I do feel more integral to the trio as of late, I still can't stop thinking about finding him and Jupiter in bed together? That I've come *this* close to asking Jupiter about it on a number of occasions—especially when I think about some of the mortifying stuff she told me *I* said while under the influence? But I always lose my nerve because, really, is it any of my business? That even thinking about it right now, I can't figure out if I'm jealous of *him* for getting to be that close to *her*, or *her* for getting to be that close to *him*? That these questions have been my constant cognitive companions over the past two and a half weeks?

That this Carl Conundrum jaunt is actually meant to be a distraction from all that, but it isn't working?

"Courtney, can I ask you something?" is what I say, and I know the next question will shock him, but if I can't talk about what's on my mind, I have to talk about something else.

"If I make the joke about you not giving me a choice, will you say I'm being defensive?" He winks at me.

The Courtney butterfly in my stomach flutters in a haphazard circle; there's a Jupiter butterfly in there as well, which is confusing, and that's why I have to ask the question. "It's kind of personal," I tell him.

"Shoot."

"Have you ever questioned your sexual proclivities?"

He doesn't respond.

"I just mean like, being as surrounded by gayness as you are—Oh God, am I allowed to say 'gayness'?" I put my hands over my face. "Was that totally offensive?"

He laughs. "It's all good, Sprinkles. Not sure I understand what you mean, though."

I sigh. "Well, you grew up surrounded by people who are gay. Have you ever thought you might be like them? Just seems like something someone would wonder, being around it so much." I hope I don't sound as ignorant as I feel.

We lapse into this profoundly awkward silence where he's squinting and chewing half of his lower lip—a lip that is just as nice as Jupiter's, I might add, but now I feel bad because I obviously made him uncomfortable. I look down at my chipped nail polish as we pull to a stop at a traffic light.

He turns to me. "What I'm about to say to you stays *in this car,* got it?"

My mouth goes dry.

"Well?"

I nod and drag my index finger and thumb across my lips. *Zip!*

When the light turns green, he takes a deep breath and eases the car back into motion. "The only other person on the *planet* who knows about this is Jupe, so if it gets out I'm gonna know it was you." He cuts me a look that I assume is meant to intimidate but is really just a reminder of his plentiful sex appeal. It makes me blush and giggle.

"I can't believe I'm telling you this," he continues, shaking his head, "but yes. Before I realized 'gayness' isn't transferable, there was a point when I wondered if maybe I'd be gay because I spent so much time with Jupe, Dad, and Papi. Let's just say I did an experiment with some pictures to 'check.'"

"Ah. How old were you?"

"Fifth grade, so eleven. Bottom line, the pictures of guys did nothin' for me, but the pictures of women? Well, I vividly remember the first one. It was this lady wrestler in this white bikini, and . . . yeah. You get it."

"So that was it?"

"Yep."

I see his Adam's apple move like he's gulping, and his hand muscles are flexed from where he's gripping the steering wheel so hard.

I shift in the worn leather seat. "Are you wondering why I asked?"

"Nope."

"You aren't?"

"Not at all." Now he looks at me. "It was pretty clear a couple weeks ago that you're questioning, Rae."

"What do you mean?"

"You asked Jupe if you could kiss her. Yes, you were drunk, but you know what they say about alcohol being the first FDA-approved truth serum."

I can't even respond. It's like my jaw's been wired shut.

We stop at another traffic light. "You good?" He pinches my cheek. "You're all pink beneath your sprinkles."

I swallow. Hard. Clear my throat. "I asked her *what*?"

"Well, you had a number of interesting queries, but you flat-out said, 'Can I kiss you?' You don't remember?"

Criminy and sugar biscuits. "No!"

Courtney laughs.

"It's not funny, Courtney!" I swat him on the arm. "Ugh, this is so embarrassing! She told me I asked some relatively inappropriate questions, but she didn't mention *that*."

He's laughing so hard, there are tears in his eyes. "I can't believe she didn't tell you."

"Me either!"

"Actually, no." He shakes his head. "I take that back. It makes perfect sense."

"*How?*"

He goes silent. Which is bizarre considering how hard he was just laughing. He's got the furrowed-brow/lip-chewy-ponder-face thing going again, but this time he looks at me. "Okay, I'll say two things, and then let's switch subjects, because I don't like talking about Jupe when she's not around."

"Duly noted."

He takes a deep breath. "Number one: I personally don't see anything wrong with questioning, Sprinkles. Not that you asked me, but I think it's your life, and ultimately, *you* have to choose how to live it, yeah?"

"Yeah." I'm smiling so hard, it feels like my face might split. I *really* love it when he calls me Sprinkles. Though I've noticed he doesn't do it around Jupiter. Which is intriguing.

"Number two, and I'll only say this once because it's none of my business, but as your friend, I feel like I should warn you: if you do get some kind of experimentation urge, Jupiter is *not* the girl to try and satisfy it with."

"Oh." Why did that give me vertigo?

"She's just not that girl, Rae."

"Okay . . ."

"Between the two of us, yeah, Jupe's all *I-am-feminist-gay-woman-hear-me-roar*, but she's also a hopeless romantic. She wants all of her firsts to be with the same person."

"Firsts?"

"Kiss, 'I love you,' anything sexual . . ."

"So she's never been in love before, either?"

"Apparently not. You know that charm bracelet she wears?"

It appears in my mind's eye. "Yeah."

"She got it for her fifteenth birthday. Each of those charms represents a different . . . uh . . . *intimacy* act, and she's supposed to give the charm to the first person she does each act with." He looks at me. "She still has all of them."

"Wow," I say. "I don't even know what to say to that."

He laughs. "You're surprised about all this?"

132

"A little." And also ashamed, because why would I presume any differently?

"Don't feel bad, Rae," he says. "Most people assume Jupe is more experienced than she is. You know Shanna from the squad?"

"Mmhmm."

"Well, she's been trying to get with Jupe since we were freshmen."

"Wait, Shanna's a lesbian?" Actually, she'd have to be bi, because she's dating a guy right now. Unless she's not out? I can't bring myself to say any of this aloud.

"She's 'romantically straight,' as she puts it—"

"Ah, heteroromantic."

His brows lift.

"I've been doing my research," I say.

"I can see that." He grins, and my cheeks heat. "As I was saying, Shanna—among others—is allllll about 'going gay' for Jupiter Charity-Sanchez. They're convinced Jupe is some lesbian sex goddess."

This doesn't alleviate my guilt over my own assumption, but okay.

"Anyway, if you're looking to do a kissing version of my naked picture test, just know Jupe's not the person to go to."

I nod again, admittedly a smidge defeated. "Got it."

Courtney signals to turn left onto a gravel road. I recognize the street name from the address I plugged into his map app. We pass a crumbling brick mailbox and turn down a drive lined on both sides by massive trees without leaves.

"Thanks for telling me that, Courtney," I say, just to be saying something. "You're a good friend."

He looks at me and laughs as a brick mansion comes into view ahead of us. "Don't thank me, Rae."

"Why not?"

"My motives weren't the least bit pure."

We pull into the driveway, which circles a filthy, non-functioning fountain with a stone merry-go-round at its center. Which makes me nervous. Hope there's no repeat of the recent carnival fainting incident—Courtney's certainly too heavy for me to lift, and I only have a learner's permit, so I couldn't drive us back. Not legally, at least.

Thankfully he doesn't seem to notice it.

"What do you mean, your motives weren't pure?" I say.

He parks, pulls the emergency brake, and then turns to me. Compared with the desolate scene outside the car, his eyes look like the dancing flame of a lit match.

"If you want the truth, Sprinkles, I'd be a little jealous."

He winks at me again and gets out of the car.

I do the same—exit the car, I mean—but my grip on reality is feeble at best. *Did Courtney Cooper just say he'd be jealous if I experimented with Jupiter? And he obviously meant he'd be jealous of her, right? Which would mean he's interested in doing something beyond what friends-bound-by-love-for-a-mutual-childhood-hero do with me. Because he couldn't possibly mean he'd be jealous of me getting to do that stuff with Jupiter, since he's known she likes girls for as long as she—*

"So *this* place is creepy as hell." He snatches me back from the edge of a thought spiral.

We stare up at what looks like a mansion plucked out of a Civil War film. It's perfectly symmetrical and has four massive white pillars holding up the rounded roof of the porch. We can see the neon NO TRESPASSING sign on the oversized front door, and literally all the windows on the first floor of the front façade are either boarded up or broken.

"Probably should've asked you to be more specific about where we were going *before* driving an hour and a half to get here," he says. "But what exactly is this place?"

"Well, I was poking around online and stumbled onto this blog that lists all these conspiracy theories about individuals who starred in children's television shows? There was a whole section dedicated to a guy referred to as 'The One Who Spun,' and they mention this place by address." I point at the house.

"Okay . . ."

"I was able to find a public record listing Carlswald Fingleblatt as the last owner."

"Car swallow finagled *what*?"

"Carlswald Fingleblatt. It's Carousel Carl's full name."

One of Courtney's eyebrows lifts. "A black guy named *Carlswald*? Come on now."

I shrug.

He takes a look around, and I see his eyes widen. He found the carousel fountain. "Whoa."

Please don't faint please don't faint please don't faint . . . "Yeah."

He clears his throat. "Guess that's a little hard to explain away." Clearly uncomfortable now. "You were saying?"

I gulp. "Umm ... right, so the house went into fore-closure in 2009. That's a year before he was spotted pan-handling in the city."

"Ah ha."

"It adds up, right?"

He looks over his shoulder at the fountain again, then back at the house. "I guess."

The air around us is so heavy, it wouldn't surprise me if birds began to fall from the sky. But now I'm too focused on the golden doorknob—the only thing on the house with any luster left—to be bothered by it.

"Sooooo, here we are at Carousel Carl's old house," Courtney says. "What do we do now?"

I'd like to say, *We go in and search for clues like the Argo-nauts we are*, but even the *thought* of those words is ludi-crous. So, instead of speaking, I take a step toward the wide concrete stairs that will carry us to the door.

"Whoa now." Courtney catches my wrist. "Big, creepy house plus unsupervised teenagers never adds up to any-thing good, Rae."

"Oh, come *on*, Courtney," I say. "We *have* to go in! What if there's a clue or something?" I know I've gone off the deep end now, but the longer I stand here looking at the house, the more desperate I am to go inside. How many times in life will I get an opportunity to explore the for-mer home of the man whose disappearance played a major part in two-hand-shoving me out of childhood? While I'm old enough to *know* Carl's disappearance had nothing to do with my mom leaving, there's no disconnecting the two in my mind. Such is the nature of childhood trauma, I guess.

I need to find out what happened to him.

"But what if there's like . . . a torture chamber inside?" Courtney gulps. "Or a cellar full of dead bodies? You know what folks say about meeting your heroes . . ."

"Highly unlikely."

"But how do you *know*?"

"I mean, I don't *know* know," I say. "I just think the same rationale behind why I doubt he's dead applies here, too: if Carousel Carl had committed some heinous crime, we'd have heard about it—"

A chilly breeze whips past, and I get a serious case of the collywobbles.

We're so *close*, though.

"I have to go in there, Courtney. I *need* to know what happened to him. I still remember my mom waking me up before dawn to tell me she had to 'go see Daddo and Nanna for a little while,' and then turning on the TV a few hours later to find some show with talking trains instead of Carousel Carl. It upended my whole damn universe!"

His eyes go really wide, but they seem to be filled with—wonder? "Did Rae Chin *cuss* just now?"

Oh. "It slipped."

"Well, shit, then, Rae." There's a pause as Courtney looks back at the house. "If this means enough to have you using that kinda language, I guess we have to do it."

I look up into Courtney Cooper's insane hazel eyes. "For real?"

137

"I mean, you *do* need a guy right now, right?"

I can't reply because the butterfly's doing loop-de-loops, and it feels like my tongue has glued itself to the roof of my mouth.

He takes my hand and turns back to the house. "Come on," he says. "Let's go set some skeletons free from some closets."

The wood of the doorframe is all rotted, so it only takes a few blows from Courtney's boulder-shoulder to get the door open. The first things we see once we're inside are the merry-go-round unicorns standing guard at the foot of each side of the double staircase. The whole setup is faintly backlit by light filtering through grimy windows at the opposite end of the house.

Courtney pulls out his phone, turns on the little flashlight, and points it upward to illuminate the second-floor balcony overlooking the foyer. In place of a chandelier is a hanging lamp shaped like the sun with nine different-colored balls of blown glass dangling around it (clearly made before Pluto got planet-demoted).

Looking up at this bizarre light fixture while standing between two cracked and peeling, yet somehow still majestic, horned carousel stallions, all I can think about is watching the solar system episode in Mom's lap. Carl explained just how tiny we are: how while the earth seems enormous to us, over a million earths could fit inside the sun, and how the sun is diminutive compared to other stars not only in our galaxy, but in the observable universe.

I was so bewildered, I burst into tears.

Mom comforted me and tried to explain how much of a privilege it is to be alive and loved, and for a while, it all made sense.

But then she left.

"Heliosphere," I mumble.

"Huh?"

"It's the eleven-letter word for the bubble in space that contains our solar system."

He doesn't respond.

"She's a cruciverbalist," I say.

"Huh?"

"My mom. Her name is Siobhan, and she's a cruciverbalist."

"What's that?"

"A person who creates crossword puzzles. She loved language and rare words and puzzles and things that reminded her of how awesome the human mind is relative to how minuscule humans are in comparison to the universe." As I blink and the first tears roll down my cheeks, I look over at him. He's holding his light up toward the second floor but is staring at the nearest unicorn.

Uh-oh.

"Come on," I say, grabbing his arm. "Let's look around a little and then go. It'll be dark soon, and we need to use the available light."

We walk beneath the solar system and into what must've once been the living room. The floor-to-ceiling windows curve outward and are covered in dust and grime, and there's a giant stone fireplace in the wall to the right, but no furniture.

As a matter of fact, the whole house is empty. The kitchen has holes where appliances should be, the dining room has an empty china cabinet built into the wall and a perfectly round chandelier that looks like it's made from conjoined metal toilet paper rolls dangling at eye level in the center of the room, and there's a high-ceilinged space full of dust-laden shelves that must've been a library.

Upstairs is more of the same, except it's easier to see: none of the dirty windows are boarded. Just room after room of bare walls and dusty wood floors.

Until we reach a room at the back of the house that we have to go up a small flight of stairs to enter.

I'm so in awe of the floating dust particles in the air, I don't notice that Courtney has stopped dead just inside the doorway until I smack right into him; he doesn't budge.

When I look past him, I see why.

While a large window giving a view of the backyard and woods beyond takes up a decent portion of the rounded wall opposite the door, every other inch of space is covered in pictures. And every picture features a family standing with Carousel Carl at various Carl's Carnivals.

"Whoa." I come around to stand beside Courtney. My stomach churns, but I can't move another inch.

When I look at him, his eyes are focused on a spot to the left of the mammoth window. His lips are slightly parted, and he looks as though he's sighted a poltergeist.

Which makes me nervous. Were he to drop here and happen to fall backward, down these few stairs he'd go.

"Courtney, are you okay?"

"Do you see them?"

Okay, really scared now. "Do I see what?"

"The pictures."

"Yeah. They're everywhe—"

"No, the *pictures*."

I follow his gaze, and then my feet are leading me closer to the wall, because it looks like—

But there's no freaking way.

I pull out my own cell phone and turn on my little flashlight. Maybe three feet to the left of the window, right at my eye level, is the picture of Courtney and Ms. Neeta with Carousel Carl.

And right next to *that* picture is a picture of another family I know: Carousel Carl is standing beside a thin Chinese man who has his arm around a curvy woman with rosy cheeks, flaming red hair, and a smile as bright as the North Star. In front of the man is a lanky girl with pale skin and jet-black hair, and in front of the woman . . .

Is four-year-old me.

15

SOBRIETY

(n.) a state or quality marked by
seriousness, gravity, or solemnity

If Courtney and Jupiter take notice of my drearier de-
meanor post-field-trip-and-photo-discovery, neither lets
on. I would guess he told her the whole story—he looked
a bit shell-shocked when he dropped me off, and he said
he'd be at her house if I "needed anything"—but he hasn't
mentioned the trip since, and neither has she.

On the one hand, I'm thankful: I have no idea what I'd
say were either of them to bring it up. However, halting
our investigation without discussion and keeping everything bottled up is taking its toll: my always-happy face has
begun to falter at inopportune times.

Like in class.

This morning in chemistry, for instance, as the teacher
droned on about the importance of synthetic elements, my
mind drifted off to what I've been calling (inside my head

at least) the Rounded Reliquary: that convex room in Carl's house where we discovered the carnival photos.

No idea how long I was out of it, but the guy sitting next to me, who I believe is class president, put a hand over mine and said, "Hey, are you all right? You look like you're about to cry."

I got excused to the bathroom.

And then there's now, evidently.

Britain and I are at our regular table in the school library having our final lunch-hour SAT study session before holiday break when I hear him say: "Rae-Rae, you good? Lookin' a little *lachrymose* over there, girl," and see him grin in a very self-satisfied way.

"Ten vocab bonus points, Britain."

"Don't try to change the subject," he says. "You were zoned out for a good five minutes. Why you look so sad?"

"Hey, Rae!" someone shouts from across the room. The timing is perfect, because I'm forced to stick a smile on my face. I keep it there as I turn back to Britain.

"Uh-huh," he says. "Go ahead and *disavow* whatever notion is telling you that fake-ass smile is gonna work on me."

My jaw doesn't hit the table, but it falls far enough.

"Bet ya didn't know I knew *that* one," he says. "Now spit it out."

Initially, I don't respond. Just sit there, locked in a stare-down stalemate. Except I'm predestined to lose because my resolve is weak, and now I'm starting to feel like I have to make this wasted study time worth his while. Plus, I don't want to be a bad friend.

I sigh and glance around the room. "Do you have any siblings, Britain?"

"Diana and Jack-Jack. Age five."

"They're twins?"

"Mmhmm. And holy terrors."

I grin. "I have an older sister," I say, still not looking him in the eye. "Bess."

"You don't seem too thrilled about it. . . ."

And just like that, I'm on the verge of tears.

"I haven't seen her in a long time," I say. "Not in person, anyway. Our parents divorced when I was four and she was eight, and then when she turned fourteen, she moved to New Hampshire to live with my mom."

"Oh. Sorry to hear that."

"Which part?" I finally lift my chin.

"Uhh . . . all of it, I guess?"

I nod. "Thank you."

"So did y'all like fall out or something?"

"Huh?"

"You and your sis. Is there a reason y'all don't talk?"

"I mean, we're mutuals online so there are intermittent likes and comments on posts—" More from her than me, now that I'm thinking about it. "But as far as why we don't communicate in real life, I'm not really sure."

Except I am. As soon as the words are out of my mouth, I know *exactly* why we don't talk. And why seeing that picture in Carl's old house—more specifically, *her* in it— has made it so hard for me to "fake the funk," as Britain would say.

She left me.

It was one thing for Mom to leave. Not that the divorce wasn't devastating, but I was young, and Daddy made Bess and me both see a counselor. As flippant as it might sound, I feel like I've dealt with that part enough for it to no longer be debilitating.

But Bess? Bess is the one who put *me* back together after Mom left. She's the one who would crawl into my bed and hold me when I cried out for Mom in the middle of the night. She's the one who made my lunches just like I liked them and helped me with my homework. She's the one who promised she'd always be there for me.

And then she left, too.

I didn't realize it before now, but *Bess* leaving is what killed my belief in romantic love. Clearly it didn't work for my parents, and what's more, if love between two *sisters* couldn't keep one of them around, there's no way any type of love between two people who don't share DNA could ever last.

Eventually, one person will get sick of the other one. And they'll leave.

Just like Mom—and then Bess—left me.

"Aww, man, Rae-Rae, don't cry!"

"Oh my gosh, I'm so sorry." I quickly wipe my face with the heels of my hands.

"You don't need to be *sorry*," he says. "Just—well, why don't you call her? Bess, you said, right?"

I nod. "Yeah."

"I'm sure whatever the issue is, it's squashable, right? Blood is thicker than water."

I sniffle. "That doesn't mean what you think it does, but

duly noted." At this point I just want the conversation to end. "Calling her would definitely be the way to go," I say. "Thank you."

"Of course, Rae-Rae. You know you're my favorite." He reaches over to squeeze my hand. It makes me smile and is unexpectedly settling.

"Ready for the next word?" I say, holding up an index card with the word *aberration* written on it.

"Aberration," he says. "A state or condition markedly different from the norm."

Go figure.

Later, I'm stretched out on Jupiter's bed, studying for finals—she and Courtney are doing the same, her at the desk and him in the La-Z-Boy—and all I can think about is how much it's going to take for them to get tired of me and decide they were better off as a duo.

Jupiter chooses that exact moment to look over her shoulder at me and smile. I've been staring at the back of her luscious curly hair, so we wind up locking eyes. "You okay?" she says, brows tugging together in concern.

Of course Courtney looks up.

As melodramatic as it likely sounds, they're both so beautiful it makes me want to cry. Well, that combined with their kindness/goodness/purity of heart and garnished with my certitude that this glorious triad I somehow finagled my way into is definitely, definitely temporary. I *want* to force myself to smile, but I think my heart might be breaking. Don't think I realized it's still capable of such a thing.

"You're not thinking about that *Corey* asshole, are you?" Courtney says.

I literally choke on my gum.

The look Jupiter gives Courtney is so disdainful, *I* feel cut to the quick.

"The hell you looking at me like that for?" he says to her. "Perhaps *you* don't remember because you're obviously not as good a friend as I am"—he winks at me (and for all intents and purposes, I die on the spot)—"but the last time Rae looked this sad, she was telling us about *Corey*."

I shake my head. "I'm not thinking about Corey." Well, I wasn't. But now that I am, I wish I weren't. He's another one who left—

My phone rings.

"Hi, Daddy," I say, beginning to gather my stuff. "Are you outside?"

"I am," he says in my ear. "I can come in and say hello to Troy and Emilio if you need a few min—"

"No, no, I'm ready," I say. "Besides, they're not even here."

I cover the mouthpiece as I stand. "I'll see you guys tomorrow," I say to Jupiter and Courtney. It's ridiculous and I know it, but right now, the compulsion is to get away from them before I wear out whatever welcome I still have.

They look at each other.

Ugh, they're totally going to talk about me when I'm gone.

Also, Daddy hung up. I'm just keeping the phone to my ear so I won't have to really say anything on my way out. They ask too many questions, and I can't not answer them, so . . .

"Call us?" Jupiter says.

I nod, and then I'm out the bedroom door.

But when I get to the bottom of the stairs, I hear, "Hey, Rae?" and I turn around to find Courtney coming down behind me. He stops with literally six inches between us and looks down at me.

I'm sure my blood pressure is through the roof in this moment.

"You sure you're okay, Sprinkles?" he says, eyes narrowed.

"Mmhmm!" I nod. Way overzealously. His proximity is making my brain melt.

"I know we haven't gotten to hang much or work on the Carousel Carl thing," he says. Very strange hearing him acknowledge it, and it's a bit of a morale boost to see he still cares. "But know I'm here for you, all right?"

And now my heart is on the verge of detonation. "Thank you."

"I mean it. If you need anything, don't hesitate to call me. You've got the number."

"Okay."

He pulls me into a deeply soul-soothing hug, and my nostrils are flooded with what I'm sure is the olfactory embodiment of nirvana. "Catch you later?" he says.

I nod because I can't speak.

He pinches my nose, then heads back up the stairs, and even after I hear Jupiter's door open and close, I stare after him.

My phone rings.

"Sorry, Daddy," I say. "I'm coming."

16

SORORAL

(adj.) of or pertaining to sisters

Over the next week, Jupiter, Courtney, and I slip back into a semiartificial normal. I do my best to get a leash on my catastrophizing, and we commingle, converse, and serve the community.

Once winter break hits, the three of us are together pretty much perpetually, and it feels good not to have to think about tests or homework or other school things. Just like with Thanksgiving, Daddy and I get invited to participate in the inviolable Charity-Sanchez-Cooper Christmas countdown: "C minus five days" is the twenty-four-hour cookie bake—we all get together and bake literally hundreds of cookies that on "C minus four" will be delivered to three different children's shelters across the city; "C minus three" sees us in elf costumes (Jupiter had one made for me) reading stories aloud at the children's hospital, and "C minus two" involves a soup kitchen.

On Christmas Eve, there's abundant basting, boiling, browning, braising, and more baking, then the evening is spent at the Coopers' drinking spiked eggnog and having a massive Uno tournament. We all sleep over at Jupiter's house, and since I'm expecting Courtney and Jupiter to sleep together (which I'm now convinced they do more often than not), I'm more than a little surprised when he heads downstairs to sleep on the pullout sofa, and Jupiter pulls me into her room.

Once the door is closed and she turns to face me, my guess is she can see my shock, because she blanches.

"Oh," she says. "Sorry, I just assumed . . . um . . . I know you usually sleep across the hall, but since your dad's in there . . ."

I can't get my mouth to work.

"I mean, you can totally go in there with him if you want," she rushes on. "I just figured . . . uhh . . ."

Of *all* the times for me to go mute!

She sighs and looks at the floor. "Look, if it's too weird for you to be in here with me—"

"What? No!"

She picks her head up. Waiting for me to go on, apparently.

"It's not *that*," I say. "I'm just a bit taken aback by the invitation to sleep in here."

Her brows come together. "Why's that?"

"Well . . ." I certainly can't mention Courtney, so: "You've never invited me to sleep in here before."

"Oh. I mean, I always figured you'd want your own space when you're sleeping over, but since the guest room is occupied, I figured we'd do the slumber party thing. If . . . that's okay with you?"

I smile. "Let's do it!"

We wind up raiding Jupiter's dad's collection of Disney VHS tapes and watching *The Lion King* on Courtney's dinosaur . . . I mean VCR. We laugh together when the picture fritzes out and the sound warps (guessing the tape is degraded), and cry together when Mufasa dies, and by the end, my right arm is entwined with her left, our legs are tangled, and I've got my head on her shoulder.

Then we crawl into bed.

"Sweet dreams, Rae," Jupiter says, turning off the lamp beside her.

"Good night," I reply.

But as the darkness settles over the room, my senses kick into hyperdrive. The pillow I'm on smells like her hair, and the sheets have a tinge of her sweat (maybe Courtney's, too?). She's lying on her side facing away from me, and I can see the dip of the blanket at her waistline preceding the rise that marks the curve of her hip. It's a queen-sized bed, and there's a fairly sizable gap between us, but it doesn't prevent me from feeling the warmth of her body. And wanting to move closer.

I could totally reach out and touch her sumptuous derriere right now. And I have to admit: being in the dark with her like this does make me wonder what it feels like.

What *she* feels like.

"Hey, Rae?"

She even *sounds* different in the dark. More . . . breathy. I know I was under the influence when I asked to kiss her, but

151

hearing her now makes me *really* want to know what it'd be like. I have to resist the urge to clear my throat. "Yeah?"

"Thanks for not being weird about this," she says. "A lesser straight girl totally would."

Why does *straight* feel so loaded? Is this a test? The air feels super-electrified. Charged with secret possibility . . .

But there's no way, right? I'm totally overthinking it.

I need to go to sleep.

"You're welcome," I say.

She sighs. "'Night."

I'd almost say it sounds like disappointment.

Of course Christmas Day in the Charity-Sanchez home with the Coopers is nothing short of spellbinding: love and laughter and light, cuisine and cookies and comfort, bliss and booze and bounty. It's the most wonderful time of the year indeed.

I'm still floating the day after, so you can imagine just how far and fast I fall when I return home after a movie with Courtney and Jupiter to find a pale-skinned girl with long black hair and dark eyes sitting on our couch eating a pint of (my!) cookie-dough ice cream. She's wearing Wonder Woman leggings and an oversized Dartmouth sweatshirt, and she's completely immersed in that "reality" TV show where all the women's names begin with *K*.

Bess.

As in my big sister.

My big sister, whom I've spent the past fifteen days constantly shoving out of my consciousness like a game of cognitive Whack-A-Mole.

I get the irresistible urge to flee, but as I take a step backward, Daddy comes out of the kitchen. "Oh great, you're back!" he says.

Bess's head whips in my direction, and her jaw drops. "Oh my GOD, look at *you*!"

My *sister* is looking at me all bright-eyed.

And Daddy is smiling like he's feeling the sun on his skin after a lifetime in a crepuscular cave.

What the heck is going on?

"Look who's here, honey!" Daddy says as though Bess and I aren't already gawping at each other. After she left us, I started traveling with Daddy instead of going to stay with her and Mom, and she never once took him up on his invitations to join us.

It's been *five years* since we last saw her in the flesh.

Now I've got this sickening blend of shock/bewilderment/fear/fury/frustration whipping around in my gut because all I can see is that accursed Carl's Carnival picture of our unbroken family.

Then Daddy says, "Your big sis came to surprise you, Rae!"

Bess tosses her bangs out of her eyes to smile at me, and the light ripples over her ebony mane. I do have some first-rate memories of her: she used to let me style her hair all wacky, and then she'd polish my fingernails afterward; we both loved Neapolitan ice cream sandwiches and would sneak them after Daddy went to bed on Saturday nights; from kindergarten on, she'd share her headphones during the hour-long car ride to the one authentic Chinese restaurant in a hundred-mile radius of our house for Sunday dim sum; and she's the one who taught me how to read. . . . Mom did her part, but Bess made it all make sense.

She was the sun in my sky after Mom left. My true north. Then after one particularly rough day of fifth grade for me, the doorbell rang.

When Daddy opened the door, my mom's mom and dad were on the other side of it. I remember being confused because I knew our mom lived near them and their house was far away—not that I'd been to visit since the divorce; Bess went for almost every holiday, but I always stayed home because I didn't like the idea of Daddy being alone—but half an hour and some formalities after arriving, they were leaving with Bess and three giant suitcases in tow.

I couldn't sleep that night because the house was too quiet without her music playing in the next room, so I went looking for Daddy. I'll never forget secretly watching as he poured half a glass of brown liquid, drank it in a couple of gulps, set the glass on the table, and promptly burst into tears.

Now he's standing here smiling at me like this is just the absolute best surprise ever. Like Bess packing her stuff and leaving didn't mangle what was left of his broken heart.

"Why are you here?" shoots out of my mouth with enough potency to punch the joy right out of her smile, but there's no use doubling back to stuff the anger like I normally would. There's just too much of it.

She looks at Daddy, wary. "I came to surprise you. Like Daddy said."

"Oh, so you pop up after half a decade to 'surprise' me like we've been sororal sweethearts from a distance this whole time?"

"Rae, what's gotten into you?" Daddy says. "Bess has been planning this trip for months. I thought you'd be happy to see her."

My heart is a petrous lump. "Why would I be happy to see someone who abandoned us without warning and never looked back?"

"*Excuse* you, young lady—"

"No, Daddy. She's right." Bess looks at me, and I cross my arms and turn away. My eyes moisten and sting, and then I lose all control of my jaw and the chin-quake begins. "Dad, can you give us a minute?" I hear her say.

My guess is that he responds nonverbally, but I don't know for sure because I can't look at him, either. What remains of my composure will blow to smithereens if I do. All these years, he and I have been what's left of that carnival picture, because Bess left us. She left *me*.

My mom walked out, and I needed my sister.

But then she left me, too.

"Will you come sit with me?" she says the moment Daddy's gone.

I comply and take a seat on the couch but still don't look at her. She pulls my arm, and I let her take my hand. Hers is fleshier than mine, and warmer—kind of like Jupiter's.

Except Jupiter's actually been here for me.

I hear her take a deep breath and blow it out. "Rae, I'm—"

"You *LEFT*!" Lid's off. "No warning whatsoever. You just *left*! I had *nobody*, Bess!"

"I know," she says, and now she's crying. "I'm sorry, Rae-Bee." It occurs to me how awful that nickname is: Calling

155

your needy little sister something that's one letter off from a viral infection that causes acute inflammation of the brain?

I'm shaking now, I'm so furious. "I didn't have a mom, and I started my period all by myself, and I *needed* you because I can't talk to Daddy about boys, but you weren't there!"

She reaches over to pull me into her chest, and I instinctively wrap my arms around her waist. And I sob like a traumatized toddler with a boo-boo on her knee. "I was stuck in that hick-ass town with all those stupid fucking white people, and you *weren't there*, Bet-Bet!"

Her chest shakes beneath my cheek, and at first I think she's crying because I just called her what I used to when I couldn't pronounce the *S* sound . . .

But no. She's laughing.

"Don't laugh at me, it's not funny!"

"You do realize we're half white, right?"

"Shut up. You know what I mean."

I sit up, and she presses the heels of her hands into her eyes. "I'm really sorry for leaving you, Rae," she says. "I just . . . Mom *begged* me to come with her when she left."

"She did?"

"Yeah. She wanted you to come, too, but she knew you wouldn't want to leave Daddy. You were so attached to him."

I sniffle.

"And I turned her down because *I* couldn't leave *you*," Bess goes on. "Well, partially. The other reason I stayed is because I was mad at Mom and wanted to punish her. Daddy hadn't actually done anything wrong to her, you know? They met in med school, and she got pregnant with me and dropped out. Spent most of her marriage to Dad regretting the whole thing."

"Wow." I had no idea. Looking back, I could tell Mom wasn't happy, but I didn't know the whole story. Honestly never really wanted to. Phone calls with her were easier if I kept my questions stuffed down and stayed relatively detached.

"Mom needed someone, Rae. The divorce wrecked her—"

"Wrecked *her*? *She's* the one who left! What about *us*? What about Daddy?"

She nods like she knew that last question was coming. "Mom wasn't doing well, Rae. Daddy knew. He's the one who convinced me to go live with her."

Pause. "Huh?"

"He could also see that me trying to *be* Mom for you was taking a toll on me. I was only fourteen, you know? He thought me moving to New Hampshire to live with her would be best for everyone."

There's no way. "Daddy *knew* you were leaving?"

Her black—and perfectly sculpted—eyebrows tug down. "Of course he did, Rae."

I feel like my whole world just flipped over. "And neither of you thought to *tell* me?" Now I'm crying again.

"Aww, Rae!"

Bess opens her arms, and I fall back into them.

After a few seconds of me sniveling into her collarbone, I feel her shake her head above me. "It's my fault," she says. "I asked Daddy not to tell you because I wanted to do it myself, but then I just . . . didn't."

"Why the hell not?"

"I dunno? I guess I was too scared you'd be too sad, and then I'd change my mind about going. But I really *needed* to, Rae. Don't take this the wrong way, but I, like, needed the space to just be a kid. High school started, and my friends were all having fun and exploring new things, but I was too busy trying to fill a role I wasn't equipped for."

The annoying voice in my head goes, *Oh, so what you're saying is I became a burden*, but then I think about the Bess who left five years ago compared to the Bess I see online. To the Bess who's sitting with me now.

Old Bess was always sweet to *me*, but she and Daddy fought a *lot*. And I remember constantly asking her if she was sleepy because she always looked so tired. The skin under her eyes was darker than the rest of her face.

But now? Online, she's always smiling with friends and posting pictures of food and forests ("#myfavoritethings") and it's clear she's thriving.

Which is something that's bothered me since I started following her.

"I still hate you a little," I say, squeezing her tighter. "Even though I missed you. Can't tell you the number of times I've almost unfollowed or blocked you because I see you online living your best life without me or Daddy, and I get all maudlin."

She laughs. "Still a walking, talking dictionary, I see."

"Shut up."

"I missed you, too. I won't ever up and vanish like that again, Rae. You have my word."

"You better not," I say. "If you do, I'll tell Daddy what

really happened to his nine-hundred-dollar Montblanc pen."

She laughs.

As soon as I'm done crying (again), I sit up (again). "You're a terrible sister," I say.

"I know. I'm sorry."

"Ugh, too many *feelings*." I wipe my eyes.

Bess grabs her backpack from the floor. "Don't tuck away the feels just yet." After rifling around for a few seconds, she hands me what looks like a greeting card. *Carl's Carnival* and a picture of a merry-go-round are printed on the front.

As I open it and look at the thing I've spent two weeks trying to forget, I put my head on my sister's shoulder. "Remember this guy?" Bess says, pointing to Carousel Carl.

I snort. "You mean Carlswald Fingleblatt, patron saint of my childhood?"

"Carls *what* le-blot?"

"Ah, never mind."

Bess chuckles. "Man, were we a cute little family or what?" She touches our dad's face, and then our mom's.

I nod because I can't speak.

17

SNAFU

(n.) a confused or chaotic state;
"Situation Normal: All Fucked Up"

The last day of the year finds me struggling to keep my tears inside while staring at the ceiling above Jupiter's bed. I've been covertly crying every night that Bess has been here, though the *why* behind the weepiness remains an enigma.

As Bet-Bet leaves town tomorrow, she and Daddy wanted some one-on-one time, so I've been here at Jupiter's helping prep for Charity-Sanchez New Year's Eve (another party!). Most of our time was spent putting the finishing touches on what Jupiter referred to as the *Año Viejo* doll. It's a scarecrow-like dummy made of paper-stuffed clothes with a papier-mâché head. As I sliced limes for Papi's magical mojitos, he explained that when midnight hits, we'll carry out a series of traditions that include burning the doll to "get rid of any bad juju from this year."

All I know is the face Jupiter painted on that thing is beyond creepy.

"Hello?" Jupiter says from the end of the bed, where she's been sitting for . . . actually I have no idea how long she's been sitting there. "Earth to Rae?"

She sounds like Britain. "Huh?"

She pinches my big toe inside my sock, so I sit up and hang my legs over the edge of the bed. "Pay attention, woman! I just asked if Bess is coming tonight. If she leaves without Coop and me meeting her, we *will* have to disown you." She nudges me with her shoulder.

When I don't say anything—too focused on keeping my chin from quivering—her smile collapses. She puts her hand on my knee and stares into my eyes. There's this depth of concern glowing in her honey-colored irises.

It makes me want to forget everything else going on and just . . . kiss her. Which is confusing.

"Rae?"

"Hmm?"

"Are you okay?"

With her staring at me like that on top of everything else? Pfffffft.

As the dam breaks, I put my face in my hands because I can't look at her anymore. Her hip and thigh press against mine as her arm slips around my waist, so I turn into her and put my head in that godsend of a nook between her jaw and clavicle. Her skin smells like cake.

"Honey, what happened?" she says.

And of course because this saying-what-I-really-feel thing is still new, the moment I part my lips to take a breath, all the feelings come spewing out like water from an uncapped fire hydrant. "It's like my sister swooped in with a little satchel of fairy dust and single-handedly healed the broken things in my dad that *I've* been trying to keep bandaged for years, but *I* got a waist-high pile of new and interesting things about my mother and sister that served to rip my heart open so all the stuff *I* keep suppressed would tumble out, and we halted the Carousel Carl investigation, but I *need* to know what happened to him because it's eati—"

"Whoa, slow down." Jupiter lets me go and reaches across me to her bedside table. When she pulls the little drawer open and removes a small package of tissues, I catch sight of a picture of Courtney taped to the bottom of the drawer. Part of me wonders which one of them put it there, but now I can't ignore the fact that every time she opens that drawer, she sees his face. It's a gut-gripping reminder that there's this whole world the two of them inhabit that I'll never be a part of. Just like Daddy and Bess. And Mom and Bess.

I'm crying again.

"Okay, let's rewind," Jupiter says, pushing the drawer shut and bringing me back.

She hands me a tissue and I say, "Okay," and wipe my eyes (and sniffle).

"You learned some new stuff about your mom and sister? And what the heck does Carousel Carl have to do with anything?"

Wait, did he not tell her? "Courtney's never told you about Carl's Carnival?"

She shrugs. "That's where he and Mama Nee were the day his dad died."

"And he didn't tell you what happened there?"

She cocks her head and squints at me, then shifts her

162

gaze to the La-Z-Boy. Pure speculation, but it seems the idea of *me* knowing something about Courtney that she *doesn't* is . . . well, in my head, I see an image of the planet Jupiter's red spot—which apparently is a massive, angry squall—churning a bit more intensely. Of course the last thing I want is for her to be anything but happy, so now I can feel a wave of *crap-I-have-to-fix-it* word vomit roiling in my gut.

When she looks back at me, it all comes surging out: carnival, excitement, darkness, fear, Courtney, me, death, divorce, bye-bye, Carl, bye-bye, Bess, hello, Bess, new information (but still no Carl). "It's like everything I thought I knew just exploded in my face, and now I feel like I have no purpose. Courtney's been swamped with basketball, as you're aware, so he and I haven't really reconvened since we found that room full of pictures at Carousel Carl's house, but finding out my dad *knew* my sister was leav—"

"You went to Carousel Carl's *house*?"

Oh boy.

I swallow and nod. "Three weeks ago."

"Oh."

The way Jupiter Charity-Sanchez is now staring at the poster on her closet door—flushed cheeks, moist eyes, closed mouth—makes me want to absquatulate into a crevasse somewhere and perish. I open my mouth to launch into another explanation, but she clears her throat and turns to me. "You were saying you feel like you have no purpose?"

The fact that I'm surprised to see genuine concern in her eyes should give an idea of just how far I've fallen into the *oh-my-God-I-ruined-everything-and-now-she-hates-me* pit. I look at the floor because more tears are coming.

"This will probably sound absurd because you're *genuinely* kind and strong and good, but if my life isn't about keeping other people happy—keeping my *dad* happy most of all—what do I have, Jupiter?"

She furrows her brow.

"Ugh. I told you you'd think it's stupid." I wipe my face on my sleeve.

"No, that's not it at all."

"So why are you looking at me like that?" *And why do I sound like a petulant papoose?*

"Rae, when was the last time you did something for *you*?"

"What do you mean?"

"Like when has Rae done something to make *Rae* happy without first considering whether everyone else is taken care of?"

She can't be serious. "The patron saint of community service is asking *me* when I did something for *myself*?"

She shakes her head. "Rae, all my service work is for *me*."

Huh? "That doesn't make sense—"

"It does, babe. Serving the community makes *me* feel good because it's what *I* want to do," she says. "Question is, what do *you* want? And don't say 'to make everybody happy,' because that's not what you want, Rae. You've been succeeding at that for a while now, so if it were *really* what you wanted, you'd be happy, too."

What *do* I want?

What if what I want—what I've wanted this whole time—is currently staring at me with her plumpish lips parted, awaiting my response to her question? (Though this probably isn't what she meant.)

But then I think of my mom. She was on track to become a doctor and then she married my dad instead, and that wound up *not* being what she wanted. The more I consider it, the more I think I do want something *more* with Jupiter, but what if I'm wrong like Mom was? What if this is nothing more than curiosity?

And what if Jupiter doesn't want me back? Should I consider that?

What if she does, though? I can't really know anything unless I put my "wanting" out there, can I? Before I catch it, "Why didn't you tell me I asked if I could kiss you?" is flying from my mouth to hover in the air above us.

She *blinks blinks blinks* before shifting her focus back to the poster on the closet door. "I thought you said you didn't remember—"

"I don't." And then I gulp because I'm about to throw Courtney Cooper under the bus (again). "Courtney told me," I say.

Her eyes narrow.

"In his defense, he had no idea I didn't remember. But either way, I don't get why *you* didn't tell me."

There's a horrifyingly long pause before she gets up and goes to sit in her desk chair. She powers on her laptop. "There was nothing to tell, Rae. People say all kinds of dumb shit when they're drunk."

Dumb shit? "But what if I meant it?"

"What if you meant what?" She eye-stabs me over her shoulder.

"What if I was serious about wanting to kiss you?"

"You weren't." She turns back.

"How do you know?"

"Just do."

"But *how*?"

I see her sigh, and then she spins in her chair to face me. "Rae, let's not do this. You're an amazing girl and we've got a good thing going, so let's not muddy the waters, okay?"

What? "How does me wanting to know how *you* know what I did or didn't want 'muddy the waters'?"

She looks up at the ceiling and takes an exasperated breath (which is annoying). "Whether or not you wanted to kiss me *in the moment* is irrelevant, Rae. Alcohol lowers inhibitions, and most people regret the shit they do while they're drunk."

"What about now?"

"What?" She looks at me, and her eyes narrow in confusion. I should drop it. I really should.

But I can't.

"What if I said I wanted to kiss you now?"

She spins her chair back to face the desk. "You don't."

The instant rift is so acute, it wouldn't surprise me to discover a chasm in the floor between us. "How could you possibly know that, Jupiter? You just sat here asking me what I want and when I tell you, you say I'm wrong? How is that your call to make?"

She shakes her head. "I'm going to the bathroom," she says.

But when she stands up, something comes over me. I grab her arm, and when she turns around I just . . . go for it.

Her lips are even softer than they look, and they taste a bit like vanilla. My hand perfectly fits the curve of her hip, and

I'm hot all over, but I'd be lying if I said I don't like the sensation. It's . . . well, I don't think there's an actual word for it.

Her mouth opens just the slightest bit, and I slide a hand beneath her hair, intending to pull her closer and deepen the kiss—

But then she jerks away.

"What are you *doing?*" she shouts, shoving me a little harder than I'm expecting. I stumble backward.

"I tried to tell you what I wanted, but you wouldn't lis—"

"You don't fucking get to do that! You don't get to *force* yourself on me just because you *think* you want to."

Here we go again. "You're not in my head, Jupiter! You have no *idea* what I do or don't want."

She sighs. Exasperated. Looks me dead in the eye.

It's so intense, I couldn't break the gaze if I wanted to.

"Look: while it's true you might be curious about the more *physical* aspects of female-female relationships, I know you're not *really* into me because I see the way you look at Coop."

All the blood leaves my face.

"I'm not interested in being some straight girl's experimental dip into forbidden waters. If I were, I would've hooked up with half the girls at our goddamn school already."

"That's not what I meant, Ju—"

"It's fine. Let's just put it behind us and go back to being friends," she says. "Pretend none of this happened. I'm going to the bathroom."

I gulp. "Okay."

She makes a swipe at her eyes and then rushes out the door.

18

SCHISM

(n.) division or separation; discord, disharmony

Thus I fracture irreparably my bond with Jupiter Sanchez. Though I do stick around for the New Year's Eve party.

She keeps it small: Courtney is there, of course, as well as Golly and Britain—the latter in a three-piece suit ("Gotta enter the new year with style, Rae-Rae," he says). Daddy comes, and Bess, and Jupiter's dads and Ms. Neeta are there. The only person *I* don't know is Jupiter's college friend Breanna, and she becomes an object of my instant—though unearned—contempt, with her brown skin and neat hair-cut and megawatt, dimpled smile and loose khakis and cable-knit sweater and cool sneakers. Her obvious charm and how easily she makes Jupiter laugh and smile after I made her so upset that I'm pretty sure she cried.

When the clock strikes twelve, we go through what feels like an obstacle course of traditions: first everyone eats twelve grapes and drinks a cup of homemade cider. After that, we each grab a little bucket of water and run to the nearest available door or window to toss it out. Then for the grand finale, we head to the backyard, where the *Año Viejo* doll is waiting in the Charity-Sanchez fire pit.

As soon as we're all gathered around, Jupiter says, "Rae gets to throw the first match." It catches me by surprise, because she's barely acknowledged my existence for most of the night.

Papi passes me a box of long-reach matches, and after striking one, I try to meet her eyes, hoping that the flame in my hand is a symbol of peace blazing between us. But she looks away.

So I toss it.

And when the flame catches, I really do feel an atmospheric permutation. Surely kissing Jupiter Charity-Sanchez without her express permission constitutes bad juju, so as I watch the doll burn, I pray said juju is being devoured. I still don't know what I was thinking. Can one plead temporary insanity in a case like this?

When I work up the courage to look at her again, she's staring across the fire with her eyebrows drawn together. So I follow her gaze.

And I find Courtney Cooper. Staring at *me*.

And grinning.

When our eyes meet, he winks, which makes my face hotter than the blazing inferno in front of us. But then his gaze shifts, and his smile melts off like the bad juju has leapt onto his face. I turn just in time to be withered by Jupe's stare before she rotates on her heel and heads up to the house. Courtney watches her go, his expression mired

169

in confusion. And as soon as the door slams, he looks back at me, and I take an immediate interest in the winter-dead grass beneath our feet.

"I'll be right back," I hear him say, presumably to Britain and Golly. They're standing on either side of him.

Well, they *were*. Now they're side by side because he's headed toward the house.

"Still wrapped, brah," Britain says once Coop is far enough away not to hear him.

"I know," Golly replies. "Shit's ludicrous."

"Can't say we didn't try—"

That's when I decide to tune out.

I'm not sure how long I stand there thinking about the Carl's Carnival picture and letting the fire sear my pupils, but the next thing I know, a voice says, "Going up!" and my feet are leaving the ground. I barely have time to squeal before my skinny thighs settle on a pair of massive shoulders. My arms reflexively wrap around Golly's head, and I'm pretty sure I poke him in the eye.

"Geez, Golly, are you trying to give me cardiac arrest?" I say.

"Rae, tell Brit you like me more than him," he replies from beneath me, rotating so I'm looking down at Britain.

"Man, please," Britain says. "She likes me better, right, Rae-Rae? You and I have *inimitable rapport*." He tugs my foot and bounces his eyebrows at me, and I giggle like a teenybopper.

"No way, dawg," Golly retorts. "I can give her a bird's-eye view, something your little ass will never do. Ain't that right, Rae?" He slowly turns in a circle. "World looks nice from up there, don't it?"

"You gone stop with that 'little' shit, brah."

"Excuse you, wee man. You're in the presence of a classy lady. Watch your mouth."

"Oh dang, my bad, Rae-Rae!" Britain looks up at me, apologetic.

I just laugh, all vestiges of relational conflict shoved aside for the moment.

"For real, though, Rae-Rae, you good?" Britain says. "You were gazing into that fire like you wanted to eat it or something. I have a cousin who for real struggles with pyromania, so I've seen that look before."

I manage to keep my smile from drooping. "I'm great," I practically chirp.

"You sure about that?"

I often forget how observant Britain can be. Thankfully he won't have the opportunity to drag anything out of me tonight: Daddy's coming over.

Golly reaches up to take my waist and then pops me off his shoulders to set me back on the ground. "How's it going, Dr. Chin?" he says to Daddy.

"Great now that my daughter's back on the ground." Daddy grins at me. "I know you're a professional who would *never* drop her. . . ." He looks at Golly and lifts a threatening eyebrow. We all laugh: Golly has a full foot on Daddy in height. "But the whole 'flyer' thing still makes me nervous."

"Oh my gosh, Daddy." I feel my face go red.

He laughs. "Hate to break up the cheer practice, but we gotta go. Your sister has an early flight. And it looks like I'm going to have to *drag* her away from Breanna and Troy." He gestures to where Bess is immersed in conversation with Jupiter's dad and Breanna. It's probably wrong, but I'm kind of glad to see that someone other than Jupiter has Breanna's undivided attention.

Though I'd be lying if I said it didn't bother me that Courtney chased Jupiter into the house and neither has returned to the yard.

Why is this all so confusing?

"Guess I'll see you guys at school Monday?" I say to Britain and Golly.

"Later, Rae-Rae!" Britain says, and Golly adds, "Good to see you, Dr. Chin! Happy New Year!"

"You too, fellas!"

Despite having the opportunity—as Daddy predicted, Bess is reluctant to end her conversation (they're talking about the role of US history textbook modification in dismantling white supremacy)—I don't have the nerve to go looking for Jupiter and Courtney. So after thanking Troy and Emilio, we leave without me saying goodbye.

In other words, the night is a catastrophe.

Five minutes after crawling into bed, I get a text from Courtney: **R U OK?**

It totally causes a spike in my heart rate, but since old habits apparently die *very* hard, despite the fact that my pillow is drenched in tears, I reply, "I'm fine!"

Which means I totally shouldn't be upset about the **Don't**

wry about Jupe. She will b OK response I get in return. Had I been honest, he surely would've said something different.

But I am upset. Furiously upset.

In fact, I might be internally combusting with rage.

Yes, Jupiter and I being in this freakish friendship purgatory is more or less my fault. And yes, Courtney did warn me about pushing this curiosity thing, and I obviously didn't listen.

But the fact that he *knows* I'm a people-pleaser, yet didn't bother to delve a little deeper before telling me about his precious Jupiter? What is she, the queen of the frickin' universe or something?

I get it: she doesn't want to be anyone's test subject, and I shouldn't have done what I did. But *she* leapt to a repugnant conclusion about me without considering that my feelings could be genuine.

She alleged that I couldn't be interested in her because she "see[s] the way [I] look at Coop," but if she were paying attention, she'd have noticed it's the same way I look at *her* a lot of the time. Can't a person be attracted to a boy *and* a girl? Is that not allowed or something?

Even beyond the physical attraction, could it not be remotely possible that I have actual *feelings* for her? She's made me smile and blush and feel all fluttery inside just like boys have when I had crushes on *them*. Before the epic disaster that was this evening, I probably had more admiration for her than I've ever had for anyone. Yet she acted as if I were objectifying her.

My hands are shaking, I'm so angry. I've never experienced *anything* this perplexing before, and I can't even be vulnerable with the one person who could help me navigate it? I guess at the end of the day, it's all moot: she made it clear she's not interested in being more than friends.

I sigh and stare at the immobile ceiling fan. It's funny: the whole time she was shunning me, I was fixated on her charm bracelet. What the haydiddly is she even looking for in a girl? Is she into Breanna? It's pretty obvious Breanna's into her. . . .

I close my eyes and let the Jupiter butterfly flutter away.

Whatever she's looking for, it's obviously not me. I'm sure even our friendship is over.

And how ironic that my sister is leaving me again tomorrow.

Guess it's back to being alone.

So much for a happy new year.

19

SUCCIDUOUS

*(adj.) ready to or in the process
of falling*

As it turns out, my conclusions are inaccurate.

An hour after Daddy and I return from taking Bess to the airport, Jupiter shows up on my doorstep with a peace offering: a bag of kettle corn, a box of Neapolitan ice cream sandwiches, and a handmade card that says *Sorry I Low-Key Went Off on You.*

"So listen," she says when we get to my room. "I want to apologize for my behavior last night. I got a little too in-my-feelings, and . . ." She gulps and looks at the floor. "Anyway. I'm sorry I wasn't more welcoming at the party."

"Oh." Her apology is . . . discomfiting. Yes, I was fairly incensed last night, but looking back, shouldn't *I* be the one apologizing for what I did to her?

Then again, she did say she wanted to "pretend none of this happened."

175

How the heck am I supposed to respond? "Well, I'm sorry—"

"You don't have anything to apologize for," she says, waving away the very notion.

We spend most of the day watching movies.

The following day she tries to teach me how to make sofrito, and the day after that, I go with her to some social justice thing at Breanna's college.

And it continues. On and on, day after day, we're together.

And it would appear to any unsuspecting observer that she and I are thick as thieves: I go home with her after school every day, I sleep there at least twice a week (in the guest room), and I'm beside her at every single one of Courtney, Britain, and Golly's basketball games yelling my head off. People have even started that thing where they refer to us as a unit ("Chinchez"), and on a good number of days, she's the first person I see in the morning and the last person I see at night.

However.

No matter how much we hobnob, there's an air of artificiality in this reimagined best-friendship.

For one thing, outside of high fives at the guys' basketball games, we literally never touch.

Ever. Even Courtney noticed: "You and Jupes good? Y'all, like . . . never touch each other anymore," he said when he dropped me off two days ago.

Like today is the mensiversary of Friendmageddon, and I'm lying on her bed making a crossword puzzle while she sits at her desk doing homework. The music—a song called

"Spread Your Wings" that's really grown on me—cuts off as she abruptly slams her laptop shut and spins in her chair to face me. Instead of coming over to stretch out beside me like she normally would when she's frustrated (which I can see all over her face), she just crosses her arms.

I sigh and sit up. "What happened?"

"I don't know how much longer I can do this, Rae."

Gulp . . . "Do what?"

"This Shanna thing. It's getting out of control."

I'm slightly relieved she wasn't referring to the faux-ness of our friendship, but I'm also a little disappointed: I miss the way things were.

"What'd she do now?" I ask.

"She's sexting me again. Just sent me a picture of her boobs."

"Oh boy."

"I don't know what to do," she says. "We've got second-period PE together, and the other day, she made it a point to change right in front of me. Don't get me wrong, she's definitely a good-looking girl, but she won't take a hint."

"Wow." How else could I possibly respond to that? Not like I took a hint, either. Maybe she really has "forgotten" what happened between us.

"I really hate it, Rae," she goes on. "We've definitely crossed over into sexual harassment territory, but I dunno. If she were a guy, I would've punched her in the nuts or gone to the authorities by now, but because I'm supposed to be all pro-female-sexual-agency, I can't bring myself to tell anyone."

"Have you tried talking to her again?"

"It's useless. When I tell her to back off, she swears I'm playing hard to get." Jupiter looks up at the ceiling and sighs. "I just hate that thing where people assume a girl who's attracted to girls is attracted to *all* girls. I want an actual emotional connection, you know? Romance. Attachment. *Love*." She looks at me.

This is the confusing switchover: Jupiter has no problem baring her soul to me now, but it's always from across the room. Gone are the days of her lying with her head in my lap, or me playing in her hair, or her sitting with her head on my shoulder. I have this unfathomable depth of access to her insides, but her outsides are off-limits. Which should be fine and is likely for the best.

But it makes our interactions feel disingenuous.

I'm sure the physical distance is her way of making it undeniably clear that she and I are *just* friends, but I can't figure out if the tactile embargo is for my sake or for her own. I say *that* because there are instances when she'll look at me and there's a noticeable change in her eyes. They widen a bit, and the pupils dilate or something. It's that shift you see in the eyes of Disney Princesses the moment they go all twitterpated.

It's how she's looking at me right now.

"Rae, how do you think a person knows when they've found what they've been waiting for?" she asks.

Tension overtakes the room like a heavy mist, with Jupiter as the fogdog. She's all I can see. "Are you really asking *me* that?" I try to laugh it off, but I'm sure my cheeks are the color of ruby-red grapefruit innards.

178

"What do you want, Rae?" She's staring at me, and I'm staring back. The magnificent mess of curly hair, the gleaming amber eyes, the silver nose hoop, the perfectly proportioned—and super-soft—lips . . .

I apparently take too long to respond, because she says, "I mean, like, in a guy," and turns to reopen her computer.

Just like that, the moment is gone, and I'm hearing, *Let's go back to being friends.*

This is so utterly confusing.

As soon as the Jupiter ship sails into the sunset, though, Courtney comes to mind, with those eyes the color of autumn leaves. But then I see a pair of his shorts draped over the arm of the La-Z-Boy. I have a flash of the guy toiletries I saw under the sink while hunting for toilet paper in Jupiter's bathroom, and another of the *six* items of his clothing I pulled from her basket while trying to find her a shirt.

I'm obviously aware that they share a bed when he sleeps over here, but the more often *I* sleep over here, the more I get the impression that he's here on nights when I'm not. It's none of my business, but bottom line: even if he *were* what I wanted in a guy, my interest would be futile. If he sleeps with Jupiter when he has his own bed next door, he's probably not interested in *me* (though the thought of him being interested in her is also a little baffling).

For the first time since Jupiter and I "reconciled," I decide to be 100 percent honest: "I can't tell you what I want, Jupiter," I say. "I have absolutely no idea."

A few days later, everything changes.

Tuesday morning, when Jupiter arrives to pick me up

for school, she's beaming and fidgety, and her eyeballs look bedazzled.

It's unnerving.

"Is everything—?"

"Don't ask. You'll find out later," she says.

She spends the twelve minutes of our ride to school humming, and I spend the rest of the *day* peeking around corners and flinching at every unexpected sound. By the time the final bell rings, I'm exhausted and perturbed, since nothing out of the ordinary has happened.

But then I walk to the parking lot and find Courtney waiting for me instead of Jupiter.

"Is everything—?"

"Don't even ask. Get in," he says.

I don't even have the energy to object.

We ride in silence apart from the nineties hip-hop mix he's got playing, and I'm panicking a little—I hate surprises—but the smell of his cologne is definitely helping. As we exit the highway forty-six hellish minutes later, he finally looks over at me. "You all right?"

"Don't you have basketball practice today?" is the only response I can come up with.

He laughs. "Nah. No game this week, so Coach gave us a day off."

"Oh."

Pretty soon we're in downtown Atlanta, entering a parking garage. Once we're parked and headed toward our destination on foot, I feel like there are a thousand grasshoppers on speed bouncing around in my gastrointestinal tract.

"Courtney, where are we going?"

"You'll see," he says. "We're almost there."

I spend the rest of the walk taking clandestine pranayama breaths, and soon Courtney's opening the door of a place called the Shepherd's House.

"Uhh . . ."

He ushers me inside and down a short hallway to a massive room that houses what looks like some sort of clothing bank. All around us, people perceptibly in need of *new* clothes are sifting through the racks and piles of hanging and folded goods. There's even a wall of shoes.

From the look on Courtney's face, you'd think we'd arrived at the site of some long-buried treasure. "This is so much more amazing than I expected," he says.

"What is this place?"

He smiles down at me. "Look over there," he says, pointing with his chin.

There's a long line of people holding stacks of the clothes they've chosen, waiting to have them bagged by a tall, salt-and-pepper-bearded black man standing behind a long table.

"Wild, right?" Courtney says. "Talk about hiding in plain sight."

"Huh?"

He looks at me with his eyebrows raised. "Guessing you missed the sign outside the door?"

"There was a sign?"

"Come." And he pulls me into the hallway.

There is a sign. It says CARL'S CLOSET.

"Wait." I turn to Courtney. He's bouncing on the balls of his feet with his hands in his pockets. Grinning.

"There's no way," I say, peeking into the room at the bearded man. "Carousel Carl was . . . more circular."

"Look again," Courtney says. "It's in the eyes."

I step back into the room and watch the man. Tilt my head this way and that. A lady and a little boy approach the table to get their selections bagged, and when the bearded man looks down at the boy—who's probably six or so—a massive smile explodes up into his sunken cheeks, making his face shine like the moon.

Jumping Jehoshaphat.

"Oh my God," I say. "It really *is* him."

Carousel Carl.

"Mmhmm," Courtney says.

I don't even know what to do with myself. He and I have barely *talked* about Carl since the house field trip.

"But *how*?"

"Well, I know we haven't had time to investigate together, but I kept poking around on my own."

Is he serious?

"It was honestly one dead end after another, and I hate to admit it, but I was ready to give up," he says. "Jupe's the one who tipped me off. Every few months, she goes around the neighborhood collecting clothing to donate to this place. I'd never thought twice about it before, but of course hearing her say 'Carl's Closet' this time got my wheels turning. She told me the owner's name was Donovan Circuit, but when I found an old picture of Carl online for her to look at, she gasped."

"Whoa." The man smiles at the next person in line. "So it *really* is him?"

"Seems to be," Courtney says. "I popped by after a game

a couple of weeks ago to scope him out. Brought some clothes and introduced myself. He's older and way thinner, but I really do think it's him."

"Wow." I can't stop staring. Part of me wishes Bess was here. Not that I've talked to her since she left, but still.

"He introduced himself as Donovan, so my guess is he changed his name to get off the grid and dubbed the place Carl's Closet in tribute to his former glory or something."

"It's like a Mafia movie."

Courtney laughs and looks at Carl again. "I gotta hand it to you, Sprinkles: you were right about finding him . . . helping. I never really took the time to *grieve*, I don't think. And I still miss my dad, probably even more now that I've let myself admit it. But seeing our boy Carl alive and well is like . . . yeah."

"Yeah," I agree. Don't really feel the need to say any more than that.

"So you wanna meet him?"

A woman who's just gotten her clothes bagged walks away from the table, and as the next person comes up, the bearded man's eyes roam the room and land on Courtney and me. He smiles. Like there's nothing the least bit odd about two random teenagers hanging out near the door of his clothing bank.

"No," I say, smiling back at the man and then turning to look up at Courtney.

He grins down at me like that's the answer he expected.

I spend most of the drive home looking bewildered, because Courtney glances over at me every few minutes like he's not sure he did the right thing by exposing me to Carl's Closet. As we take our exit, I send Jupiter an SOS text and ask Courtney to swing by her house before he drops me at mine.

Her front door opens the moment we arrive, and I jump out of the car, sprint up the walkway, and hug-tackle her. As soon as Courtney makes it inside, I pull him into the hug and start sobbing.

This is love. For these two people who don't know me from a bar of soap to invest themselves in my semi-irrational desire to find out what happened to my childhood hero? I can smell her shampoo and his cologne, and feel her boobs on one side and his abs on the other, and I literally want to kiss her *and* him right now.

I'm squeezing them and blubbering and *Oh-my-God-thank-you-guys-SO-much-this-is-the-most-chivalrous-thing-anyone's-ever-done-for-me-and-I-have-no-idea-how-I-could-ever-repay-you*-ing when Jupiter mumbles, "Don't thank me, baby girl. This was all Coop," from where her face is buried in my clavicle.

When what she says sinks in, my heart starts racing and my vision blurs like I've been staring into fluorescent light-bulbs. The spot where Courtney's hand cups my waist feels like it's on fire, and his sinewy forearm against my lower back makes me want to melt into him, as ridiculous as that sounds. I look up at his face, and he's smiling down at me with his skin all brown and his teeth all white and his eyes all dazzly.

Now I'm even more of a mess because I am definitely falling for Courtney Cooper right in this very instant. The fact that I can picture my family's carnival photo without wanting to set things on fire or dissolve into a blubbering puddle? That the Carl Conundrum is solved? And it's thanks to him?

That he cares about me *this* much?

It's safe to say this is going to be a cataclysm.

20

SALTIGRADE

(adj.) progressing by leaps

Daddy's fiftieth birthday coincides with the Lunar New Year (aka: Bess is back for another visit sooner than I'm expressly ready for), so six days post-Carousel-Carl-closure-turned-Courtney-curveball, we host a minor *fête* at my house to celebrate both occasions. Daddy has too much to drink at dinner and thusly breaks out his Jamaican accent to regale his adult guests with tales from his childhood on the island, so after loading our plates with rice cake, me, Jupiter, Courtney, Britain, Golly, Bess, and Breanna (whom Bess asked me to invite) head down to the basement.

For a while, we stuff our faces and talk about nothing, but the moment there's a lull in the conversation, Bess sets down her ginger beer and says, "We should play Would You Rather."

At first, everything is fine. Some of the questions are gross, but all are fairly innocuous: *Would you rather spend the rest of your life a little too hot or a little too cold? Would you rather have constant BO or excessive body hair? Would you rather be uncontrollably sweaty or itchy? Would you rather fall out of an airplane or into a shark tank?*

But then Bess changes the tone. "Breanna, would you rather be completely alone for the rest of your life, or marry a guy?"

"Would I have to sleep with him?" Breanna says, and we all laugh. "'Cause nah."

"I've got a good one," Golly says. "Rae—"

When he says my name, I know I'm in trouble, so I instinctively scoot closer to Jupiter, who's sitting beside me.

"Would you rather be trapped in a car for three days with Baby Brit or with Coop?"

"Man, that's a no-brainer," Britain says. "Me, obviously."

"Don't be so sure about that, dawg." Courtney looks at me and waggles his eyebrows, and I'm sure my face is the brightest of pinks. I wish he wouldn't say or do these types of things. It ratchets up the difficulty level of keeping all these *feelings* in check.

"I'd rather be trapped with Jupiter," I say, hugging her arm and laying my head on her shoulder.

Everyone laughs again.

Except for my sister. Her eyes narrow, and I quickly look away because it gives me the type of goose pimples people get in horror films when they sense the approach of the murderous antagonist.

As the night goes on—there's lots more talking and laughing, and at one point Daddy bumbles downstairs to give each of us a red envelope with a fifty-dollar bill in it—I forget about it. But then twenty minutes or so after the last person leaves (Britain), Bess comes into my room and sits on the bed.

The moment I look at her, she says, "Rae, you need to be careful with Jupiter."

Which . . . "Huh?"

"You realize she's into you, right?"

The blood bypasses my face and rushes up into my scalp. This is exactly the type of asinine assumption Jupiter hates. "First of all, no she's not," I say. "And second, that's a little presumptuous, don't you think?"

"I see how she is with you, sis," Bess continues. "She's always smiling and touching you and gazing admiringly—"

"Just because she's gay doesn't mean she's 'into' me, Bess," I say. "If you were *really* paying attention, you'd notice she's the same way with Courtney. And she's obviously not 'into' guys. She's just affectionate with the people she cares about."

"Oh, she's totally into Courtney, too," Bess bulldozes on. "Even Breanna can see that. She's just into you more."

I roll my eyes to feign annoyance, but inside, my bodily fluids are bubbling to a boil. "Seeing as Breanna's probably bothered that Jupiter isn't into *her*, I can't say I trust her judgment."

Bess smirks at me then. There are those scary movie chills again.

I hate to admit this, but I can totally see where the witch rumors came from when we were kids. The way she's looking at me now makes me feel like my soul is getting sucked into her dark eyes, black hole–style.

"You know who else is into Courtney?" she says.

"Who?"

"You."

I don't respond.

"You try to hide your feelings for Courtney by hanging all over Jupiter—which is rude."

"Whatever, Bess," I say. But it's defensive, and we both know it.

She just sits there grinning like some mind-reading *Bess*-shire Cat, and the longer she smirks at me, the more furious I get. "You should go now."

"Rae, I'm just trying to help yo—"

"You've been around me for a sum total of eight days out of *five years*, and you think you can just barge in here all smug with your little theories? You have no idea what you're talking about, Bess."

She narrows her eyes and bites down on her lower lip, examining me. It takes maybe 1.5 seconds to make me uncomfortable. "Could you please stop looking at me like you're trying to figure out which part of my face to bite first?"

"I'll say this once, and then I'll leave you alone," she says. That's when I see the legitimate sadness tugging at the corners of her mouth. "Don't lead Jupiter on, Rae. It's not fair to her, and it's really shitty of you. If you're not into her, you should give her some space. *Especially* since you have feelings for Courtney."

The words hang there, and the air in the room goes dense with the truth of them. It's infuriating that despite her extended absence, my big sister can still read me like the Dr. Seuss books she used to recite at bedtime.

"You're using her, Rae," she goes on. "Don't give her false hope. The longer you blur the line by touching and flirting with her—"

"I don't want to talk about this."

Bess takes a deep breath and looks me in the eye. "Jupiter is watching you, Rae. There's pain in her eyes every time she catches you looking at Courtney when you think nobody's paying attention." She gets up to leave.

The glare of death Jupe shot me across the New Year's Eve doll-burning fire pops into my mind.

I gulp.

"I know you didn't ask for my advice, but I'm giving it to you anyway. For *Jupiter's* sake. You need to be up-front with her, Rae-Bee." And Bess walks out of the room, pulling the door shut behind her.

Of course I don't heed her admonition.

As a matter of fact, I spend the next month and five days doing *exactly* what Bess told me not to—rarely leaving Jupiter's side, constantly smiling and laughing and touching her . . . And just like Bess suggested, when Courtney's around my clinginess intensifies: I hold Jupiter's hand and sit super-close and play in her hair and whisper little jokes right into her ear.

What Bess didn't know, and therefore couldn't call me out on, is that Courtney and I secretly text a *lot*—first thing in the morning, during the school day, before bed at night, even sometimes while Jupiter and I are hanging out.

Does this make me feel villainously duplicitous and like the most awful person on earth? Absolutely. But the thought of Courtney figuring out how I *really* feel before I'm ready for him to know is scary enough to make me do all manner of unscrupulous, people-*not*-pleasing things to maintain my cover.

Unfortunately, whether or not I'm ready to come clean about my double life is officially irrelevant. I just got a "we need to talk" message from Jupiter.

I'm 90 percent certain it has to do with Courtney.

Reason? Last night after the guys' basketball game, the five of us were hanging out in Jupiter's room. Courtney and I were texting, but I put my phone down because Jupiter asked me to braid her hair. Once finished, I went to the bathroom, leaving said phone face-up on the bedside table, and when I came back, there was a new message from Courtney lighting up the lock screen: **Tell me how you REALLY feel, Sprinkles ;D** (I'd been ranting about some guy from the rival school catcalling me in the parking lot).

Jupiter was sitting on the bed when I returned, so if she glanced to her left at any point, there's a strong possibility she saw said message.

And now **we need to talk.**

Likely not good.

Okay, I text back. **Come on over!**

During the twenty-four minutes it takes her to arrive, I change clothes three times, put on makeup, take it off, clean my room, decide it looks too sterile, rumple the bedcovers, and lay a book open-pages-down on the pillow. I also run downstairs and make a bowl of popcorn, and grab and chug half a twenty-ounce bottle of tepid ginger ale.

When the doorbell rings, I pinch my cheeks and smile

191

big so I look excited to see her, and when she smiles back and steps inside, I hug her like it's been forever. "I made popcorn for us," I say when we pull apart. "Do you want something to drink before we head upstairs?"

She squints at me a little and shakes her head, something I have no clue how to interpret.

My legs feel heavier with each step, and I wonder if she can sense my jitters. Then we're inside my room and I'm sitting on the edge of the rumpled bed as she slowly pushes the door closed. Once it clicks shut, I see her shoulders rise and fall with the depth of an obviously preparatory breath.

And then she turns to look me in the eye. "So, umm—"

"Jupiter, I have to tell you something," I say.

Her eyebrows lift. "Okay . . ."

"Come sit." I take her hand and pull her to the bed to sit beside me.

Now *she's* the one who looks nervous.

"Okay." Gotta go for broke. "I've wanted to tell you this for a while now, but I wasn't sure how."

Her expression changes. I'd almost say there's hope in her eyes, but that wouldn't make sense, so I charge on: "Jupiter, I think I might be in love with Courtney."

Her mouth opens and then snaps shut, and then she's blinking. And blinking. And blinking.

And . . . blinking.

"I know, I know, I'm sorry." I put my face in my hands.

There's a pause full of poison-edged razor blades that I'm certain will slash me to pieces. But then she clears her throat. "What are you sorry for, Rae?"

"For not telling you sooner," I say. "For"—*using you, lying*

192

to you by omission, flirting with him behind your back, thinking about him pretty much every second that I spend with you—"not being up-front about it."

"Well . . ." She cracks her knuckles. I've never seen her do that before. Is she going to punch me? "I mean, it's not really any of my business, is it? And it's not like I didn't see the signs."

I exhale. This is going better than I expected. "Yeah, I figured you'd noticed," I say. "I thought you were mad at me."

She clears her throat again and looks down at the bedspread. "I wasn't."

Uh-oh . . . "But you are now?"

She breathes deep again before lifting her chin to look at me. "No," she says. "It's fine." Loaded pause, then: "So what are you going to do?"

"Well . . ." And I had no idea I was ready to answer this question, but: "His birthday is in a couple of weeks, right? The twenty-fourth?"

She pulls back a little and blinks some more, but nods.

"I know you celebrate together. I have zero intention of interfering with your traditions." The tension leaves her shoulders. "I was thinking maybe the week after, I'd just come right out with it, you know? Pull a little derring-do and ask if he wants to go on a date."

"Okay."

"You've taught me a lot about *agency*, so I'd really like to grab mine by the proverbial balls and just go with it."

She smiles, kind of sadly it seems, then looks me in the eye. "I think that's an excellent plan, baby girl."

"So you approve?"

She nods. "I do. You'll be good for him. Just don't ask me to get involved. You're on your own in that department." She winks.

I throw my arms around her then. "Jupiter, I'm so glad we had this talk."

She stiffens at first—must've caught her off guard—but then she says, "Me too, Rae. I'm glad, too."

Book Three

Another One Bites the Dust

JUPE'S JAMS

Save Me
Queen • The Game (Deluxe Remastered Version)

We Will Rock You
Queen • New Of The World (Deluxe Remastered V...

Good Old-Fashioned Lover Boy
Queen • A Day At The Races (Deluxe Remastered V...

Pain Is So Close to Pleasure
Queen • A Kind Of Magic (Deluxe Remastered Versi...

Jealousy - 2011 Remaster
Queen • Jazz (Deluxe Remastered Version)

Under Pressure
Queen • Hot Space (Queen 40 Limited Edition Collec...

Bohemian Rhapsody
Queen • A Night At The Opera (Deluxe Remastered...

Somebody to Love
Queen • A Day At The Races (Deluxe Remastered V...

We Are the Champions
Queen • News Of The World (Deluxe Remastered V...

Another One Bites the Dust
Queen • The Game (Deluxe Remastered Version)

Now Playing: Queen, Somebody To Love

21

"SAVE ME"

(The Game, 1980)

You are fine.

You are.

It may not feel like it right now, but you're *fine*, okay, Jupes?

Yes, the girl you came to pour your heart out to *cut you off* to tell you she thinks she might be in love with your (male) best friend.

Yes, the confession you spent weeks practicing on Freddie Mercury and working up the courage to make just detonated on the tip of your tongue. Yes, you had to swallow the bitter, smoldering, ash-flavored pieces, and yes, they burned your throat as they went down.

Yes, Breanna's warning about falling for straight girls is now ringing in your head like a fire alarm, and yes, you're wishing you listened.

Yes, Rae's hugging you now, and you can smell her

coconut shampoo, and her maybe-a-little-teenybopperish-but-totally-works-for-her perfume, and even a little bit of the sweet sweat at her hairline. And yes, these are all the scents that, until five minutes ago, made up the Fragrance of Possibility but now reek of crushed dreams.

Yes, her skinny arms around your waist and her breath on your neck and her perfect little breasts against your arm are driving you fucking crazy right now.

But you, Jupiter Yolanda Maria Charity-Sanchez, are *FINE*.

You're fine.

"I've gotta get going," you say, unlatching her arms from your midsection.

"Awww, but you just got here!" She pouts.

Her lips. You remember how they felt—

Nope. Not going there since you were right about that, too.

"Sorry, sweet pea. Duty calls," and you stand because if she asks *What duty?* you'll say *Uhhhh . . .* and she'll know you're lying.

"Community service planning?"

"Mmhmm," you reply.

She tilts her head and smiles, gazes up at you with those green eyes (*Gaaaah! Damn. It!*). "Beautiful *and* altruistic. You're some girl's dream woman, you know that?"

Is she serious right now?

She rises. "Come on, I'll walk you out." And her palm brushes the inside of your wrist as she interlaces her fingers with yours to pull you to the door.

You want to snatch away and scream at her. You really

198

do. Like, just on fucking *principle* you want to snatch your hand away and tell her not to touch you. Draw back into the NO CONTACT zone like you did after the *incident* on New Year's Eve. Because this shit is not cool. This *let me be all over you and hold your hand and act like your girlfriend* thing she does.

Especially after telling you she's into a boy—*your* boy, as a matter of fact.

But you don't pull away because the sensation of your hand in hers—which is thinner than yours, but super-soft, and cool at the palm with icy fingertips you've imagined skating over your skin—makes you feel like your veins are filled with lit gunpowder.

So you hold on tight and let her lead you down the stairs and out the front door. It's cloudy now, like even the sun is trying to spare you the embarrassment of being seen walking hand in hand with the object of your unrequited affection like some lovesick puppy. A squirrel looks up at you from the lawn, seems to shake its head, and then scampers away, and yes, you're beginning to feel a little pathetic.

You've reached the car you share with the boy this radiant girl thinks she's in love with, so she turns to face you and lets go. The feeling of loss is sharp and immediate and painful like that time said boy rolled over and crushed your boob while asleep in your bed.

"Thanks for coming by," she says, bouncing on her toes now that she's free from the burden of closeted romantic feelings—a burden you realize *you* won't be free of until you can somehow manage to get over her.

It's such bullshit.

You force a smile. "No problem, baby girl. We'll chat soon, okay?"

You turn to open the car door, now anxious to get away from her, but then her arms slip around your waist from behind and she crushes her svelte little body against yours. You wish there was an *awareness knob* you could crank down to zero because her hips against your butt and her breasts against your back and her right forearm against your belly and her left forearm up under your boobs are making you apeshit.

"I love you so much, Jupiter," she says, and she sits her chin on your shoulder. Her warm breath grazes your ear and then there's fury and fire and pleasure and pain, pulsing at Every. Point. Of. Contact.

GOD, you hate her so much right now.

"Love you, too, Rae," you say.

"I'll keep you posted on everything, okay? Promise you won't tell him?"

"I promise."

You can feel the tears build as those words leave your lips, but it's a promise you intend to keep because Rae is your friend. She's always been *only* your friend.

So you are fine.

She lets go, you get into the car, she says bye, you close the door. She's back on her porch and disappearing inside the house, and you're turning the key in the ignition.

As you put the car in reverse, it hits you that "Save Me," one of the saddest Queen songs ever, is pouring from the speakers like some kind of noxious, tear-inducing gas:

♫ *It started off so well* ♫ *they said we made a perfect pair* ♫ . . .

And now you're crying.

"Curse you and your voice made of sad rainbows, Freddie Mercury!"

You drive.

♫ *I have no heart, I'm cold inside* ♫ *I have no real intent* ♫ . . .

"No!" You look at yourself in the rearview mirror as you pull to a stop at a red light. "Absolutely NOT, Jupes! You suck this shit up *right-ass now*!"

Out of the corner of your eye, you see the young man in the next car over gesturing for you to roll your window down. He's holding up his phone with a GPS map on the screen. Must be lost. So rare is it to encounter a young man willing to put aside his ego when in need of help, your spirits actually lift a bit as you push the button to comply. "What can I do for you?" you say with a smile as the window drops.

"Yo, you're really beautiful, Mami. I seen you cryin', and just wanted you to know I'll be a shoulder if you need one."

And he *winks* at you.

"Aww, that's sweet," you say in a voice dripping with butter pecan syrup (your personal favorite). "Let me give you my number. . . ."

He's smiling now, waving his phone to show you he's been anticipating this moment.

Asshole.

"It's 1-800-I-am-not-your-*mami*-and-I'd-rather-be-water-boarded-with-my-own-tears-than-come-near-your-misogynistic-lump-of-toad-shit-shoulder."

His eyebrows draw together as if pulled by magnets, and you smile as you await the magic words—

"Man, fuck you, you stupid bitch."

And there they are. Ridiculous how predictable some of these guys can be. Friggin' patriarchy, you swear.

He peels out the moment the light turns green, and you realize you feel better.

More you.

More *me*.

"Because I'm *fine*," I say, settling back into my skin. "I. Am. Fine."

After hanging my coat downstairs and dragging myself up to my room, I open the door to find Courtney Cooper kicked back in the La-Z-Boy. He's wearing basketball shorts and a T-shirt with the sleeves and most of the sides cut off.

Just chillin'.

The only light in the room is coming from the television—if the empty VHS box on the dresser is any indication, he's watching *Dead Reckoning* again—and he's got *my* bottle of pineapple-coconut water in one hand, *my* pint of salted-caramel gelato in the other, and *my* bag of Boomchickapop kettle corn in his lap.

Bastard.

"'Sup?" he says without looking up.

I flip on the light.

"Aww, Jupe! You're killin' the vibe, dawg!" (Chugs the rest of my coconut water; eyes have not left the television screen.)

"Are you even serious right now, Coop?!"

"Shhh . . . This is the best part."

Did he really just . . . ?

Uh-uh.

I walk over and unplug the TV.

"JUUUPE!" He throws his hands—with my comestibles still in them—into the air.

"Like you're seriously sitting in *my* room eating *my* food in front of *my* TV, and you're gonna tell *me* to shush?"

Yes, I am overreacting. It's just looking at him now with that stupid rich-brown skin and those stupid copper eyes and that stupid jawline and those stupid frickin' *muscles*— all that in addition to knowing who he is and how beautiful a heart he has . . . Well, it just makes perfect sense that Rae thinks she "might be in love with" him.

If I were straight, I probably would be, too.

I glance at my closet door. Try to gather some strength from Freddie Mercury. On the poster, he's got his head down and his fist in the air, utterly in the zone.

Freddie, what would you do if you went to tell someone you think you love her, but before you can get the words out she's telling you she thinks she loves someone else? It's not like I didn't notice how she looks at him. I just chose not to look too far into it because she was always with me—

"Jupe?"

Coop has appeared in front of me and is reaching up to take my face in his hands. He's giving me that

Oh-boy-something's-up-with-my-best-friend look that makes his eyes appear to be shimmering.

He is definitely, for sure, 100 percent going to say yes once she tells him. I see how he looks at her just like I see how she looks at him.

I still remember waking up that one morning a week before Thanksgiving to find him gone. How panicked I felt before I convinced myself that he'd just needed something from home and gone to get it. How relieved when I got over there and called out to him and he came bopping down the stairs, alive and in one piece.

But then . . .

"Rae's here," he said. Like it was no big deal. "Her dad's out of town, and she kinda had a crisis in the middle of the night, so I went to get her. Can she stay with you this weekend?"

And of course I said yes. I (obviously) cared about Rae, too. So much so, I forced down the barbed lump of betrayal that'd lodged in my windpipe.

I really should've known then. That he and she would become a thing. It's actually a damn miracle they haven't gotten together already. Come to think of it, I guess *I've* always been in the way.

"Jupe, what's going on?"

His hands are cupping my face now, and he rubs his gigantic thumbs over my cheekbones (we're talking about a guy who can hold a basketball in one hand). The eyes, the wide-ish nose, the hint of a mustache . . .

I wonder how often Rae imagines kissing his plumpy lips.

Do not cry do not cry do not cry do not cry . . .

204

Definitely going to cry, so I slip my arms inside the "arm-holes" of his ruined shirt and around his waist, and I press my cheek against his chest so he won't see the tears spill over. When I slide a hand up his back to pull him super-close and squeeze him as tight as I can, his skin erupts in goose bumps.

I bet he gets those just *thinking* about Rae.

"You're starting to freak me out now, Jupes."

He tries to pull away, but I squeeze tighter. "Just hold me, you Neanderthal."

"You're being weird."

"I had a rough day. Be supportive."

He wraps his adolescent-titan arms around my neck and shoulders and kisses my forehead. "Wanna talk about it?"

Completely against my will, I sniffle . . . three times, rapid-fire—*sniff-sniff-sniff*—on the same inhale.

He tenses up. "Are you *crying*, Jupiter?"

"What? No!"

He tries to pull away again. "You're totally lying!"

"Shut up."

"If you drool on my shirt—"

"Shutuuuuuuuuuup, Courtney!"

He laughs. "All right, I won't pry."

"You better not."

"Can we sit down, at least? You're squeezing so tight, I'm losing circulation to my lower extremities."

"Doesn't seem to be affecting your pelvic region."

Looooong pause.

"You can feel that?"

"It's getting pretty well acquainted with my belly button. What'd you, tuck it in your waistband or something?"

"Well, this is embarrassing."

"You're such a *boy*. I'd be totally grossed out if I didn't need this hug so bad."

He chuckles.

After a few seconds longer, I wipe my wet face on his shirt, let go, and put a little space between us. For a minute, we just stand there staring at each other. My eyes creep their way down to his . . . what-I-felt-against-my-stomach. Sadly, his T-shirt is hiding the evidence.

I don't know what it is, but lately . . .

Nope. Never mind.

When I look back at his face, he's staring at me with an eyebrow raised.

Shit.

As my face heats, I clear my throat and turn to Freddie Mercury again. "So could we maybe start that movie over? I could use a little *noir femme fatale*."

"Wait, you're really not gonna tell me what's going on?"

"Nope."

"But I'm your best pal!" He throws his arms up in exasperation.

I roll my eyes. "I'm going to change."

Once I'm inside the closet with the door closed, I switch on the light and peel off the outfit I fussed over for the "Rae, I really like you" discussion that never did—and never will—happen. That's one way to ruin a pair of jeans.

I tug on Coop's team sweatpants and hoodie from last season, pull the hood up, and turn to look in the full-length mirror on the door. I'm now maroon from head to ankle. Like a big splat of dried blood.

How appropriate, since I feel like I got *stabbed*.

When I come out—after a very sudden, very brief burst of tears—Coop smiles at me from the La-Z-Boy. He's got the movie rewound to the beginning, and apparently made a run downstairs to get more of (my) snacks.

"Kettle corn, madam?" He holds the bag open as I approach.

"You do realize it's barbaric to go into other people's houses and eat their food, right?"

"Hush your mouth and get over here, woman."

Normally I'd balk, but right now, I'm so glad he's here, I give a forced eye roll and go climb into his lap.

"Okay, who the hell are you, and what did you do with the young lady who would've punched me for issuing such a 'flagrantly patriarchal command'?"

"Shhhhh."

"You sure you're okay, Jupes?" He puts an arm around my waist and slips the other one under my knees to readjust me so he's cradling me like a baby. It occurs to me that after Rae's confession, I should probably feel guilty about being with him like this.

But I don't.

Does that make me a shitty feminist? Shitty person, even? Probably.

But I honestly don't care. Until Rae makes her declaration, Courtney Cooper still belongs to *me*.

"I am now," I say, and I breathe him in and close my eyes.

22

"WE WILL ROCK YOU"
(News of the World, 1977)

Over the next week, I watch the two of them with my eagle eyes every chance I get. What's interesting: if Rae hadn't *told* me how she really feels about Coop, I wouldn't have picked up on it. Like, yes, I often catch her giving him goo-goo eyes, but I wouldn't assume it was anything more than a schoolgirl crush. And she's also still super-clingy with me. Which is (still) simultaneously infuriating and intoxicating.

One thing is for sure, though: the more I watch *him*, the more I understand not only what Rae sees in him, but also how much *I've* taken for granted. With the other girls he dated, part of me always knew he'd be back. He just never seemed that *into* any of them. But Rae is different. When she's around, Coop lights up like the fireballs that shoot out of a Roman candle. He laughs more. He's less guarded. There's no denying their chemistry or the fact that they *get* each other. That they share something he and I don't.

I can see how much I'm going to lose when they get together. Because they *will* get together. There's no doubt in my mind. It's making me desperate to enjoy as much of him and make as much of our friendship as possible while I still have time.

The Friday morning after Rae skewers my heart like a shish kebab, I wake up at 5:47 a.m. with Coop's *thingy* poking me in the ass. He's still very much dead to the world.

I slip out from under his arm and sit up to check my phone. There's a picture message from that dastardly temptress Shanna Wilmington (I hate her). She's dangling a cherry over her outstretched tongue while wearing this appallingly thin tank top with nothing underneath, and skimpy blush-pink lace underwear. The attached text says **waiting 4 U 2 pop dis cherry, space grl.** The idiot calls me Space Girl because (1) *Jupiter*, obviously, and (2) she swears up and down that "hooking up" with me is "guaranteed to be out of this world." She also has a boyfriend she has sex with all the time—aka that "cherry" got "popped" a long time ago.

Did I mention I hate her?

Still, though: seeing her like *that* does remind me of all the things I haven't done. Not that I'm ashamed of not having done them—I have my reasons, and I stand by them. It's just that . . . well, I kind of hoped to do at least *some* of them with Rae.

And there it is again: the memory of her hand on my hip and her fingertips on my neck. How my whole body jolted awake at the feel of her lips against mine.

I peek over my shoulder at Coop. The thought of *him*

kissing her instantly brings tears to my eyes. And since he clearly likes her, *they'll* probably wind up doing stuff even *he* hasn't done (at least he says he hasn't).

I vividly remember the day in seventh grade when Coop and I were sitting in our regular seat during the bus ride home and he turned to me and said, "Hey, Jupes, you think you and me could do it together for the first time?" In response to what was surely a wildly confused expression on my face, he went on: "You know . . . *it*." And he looked around. "Sex."

Back then I was obviously appalled, but thinking about it now, and the idea of him doing *it* with Rae, I just—

My eyes trail down his body to where his pelvic region is hidden beneath the blanket. He rolls onto his back and—

"Well, good morning to you, too."

I startle so hard, I fall off the bed.

"Uh . . . Jupes? You all right?"

"Yep! Rise and shine!" And I scramble to my feet to go shower.

Except the whole scrubbing-my-thoughts-clean thing is a fail. All morning, I find myself losing focus in classes because my mind keeps drifting off to what-ifs. Mechanically speaking, a girl wouldn't need to be *into* a boy to let a boy *into* her, would she?

This is exactly what I'm thinking about as I read the same paragraph in my history book for the fifth time at lunch—which Coop and I have alone together on Fridays—when he says, "Hey, Jupes, I know it's none of my business, but I'm a little surprised you still have all of those," and points to my charm bracelet as I'm lifting a California roll to my lips.

I freeze, mouth open.

"As much time as you and Rae spend together," he goes on, "I was *sure* she'd have one or two of them by now." Which of course throws me into a mental tailspin. Rae technically *was* my first kiss, but it wasn't consensual, so while there's no way I'd actually *give* her the charm, there is this niggling voice in the back of my head that says I'll be lying when I do finally give it away. Will I have to tell the person?

I never told Coop because I've been *trying* to act like the kiss never happened (we see how *that's* going).

But now I can't stop staring at *his* lips.

"What?" He brushes away crumbs that aren't there.

"Nothing," I say, looking away. "Just . . . uhh . . . remembered I have a history quiz this afternoon. You were saying?"

"Nothing else to say, really." He shrugs his muscle-y shoulders—which, fine, are kind of nice to look at—and shifts his gaze across the cafeteria. "Y'all just act like two people in a relationship is all."

And as Courtney Cooper's best friend of over a decade, I can see in the set of his jaw and his slightly narrowed eyes—it bothers him.

"Yeah, nothing to worry about there, Coopie," I say, even though it kills me. "Rae Chin is only into guys. *I'm* certainly not the one she wants."

For the rest of the day, I think about how *relieved* my best friend seemed when I told him Rae and I are only friends. It's like I'm losing him already, and it sets me way on edge.

Not that *Rae* notices—despite being all over me. At Coop's basketball game that night, she only has eyes for him. With every squeal and shout and gasp and "Go, Courtney, go!" that comes out of her mouth, I sink a little further into my festering pit of mingled despair and desperation.

At a time-out, "We Will Rock You" pours from the massive speakers in the gym, and for a second, I latch on to Freddie's voice and try to pull myself together. But just as Brian May's earth-shattering guitar solo kicks off, Rae leans over and whispers, "Hey, is it true that Courtney's a virgin?"

I turn to look at her and can *see* the hunger in her eyes. Green, like some famished dragon with its sights set on a delectable prince to devour.

And yeah, it pisses me off. Especially since mere moments ago, she was holding my hand.

Sure, I was letting her. Was enjoying it, even. But to know that the feeling of my palm against hers has so little of an effect on her that she's actively thinking about Coop's sexual status? She might as well have baked everything I stand to lose in a pie and smashed it in my face.

So I make a decision. And an hour or so later, as I drive Coop and me home once the game is over (we won), I decide to put my idea on the table before I lose my nerve.

"Great game tonight," I say, easing in.

He reaches over from the passenger seat and tugs on my ear. "Thanks, Big Head."

"So I've been thinking—"

"Oh shit . . . somebody sound the alarm!"

I shoot him a glare, and he laughs.

"What have you been thinking, O benevolent one?" he says.

I put both hands on the steering wheel to keep them from shaking. "Your eighteenth birthday is in a week, right?"

"That is correct. March twenty-fourth. Same as the past seventeen years, Jupe."

"Shut up."

He laughs again. "Dude, you've been hella weird the past few days."

"No, I haven't."

"Oh yes you have." His eyes are totally burning a hole in the side of my face right now.

"I've just got a lot on my mind."

"Well, spit it out."

"Maybe I don't want to."

"*You're* the one who started this conversation, you weirdo."

Man, I hate when he's right.

"So let's hear it," he says.

"Okay, fine," I reply. "So you know how we've been best friends for almost eleven years now?"

"Best years of my life, I'm telling ya." He squeezes my leg just above the knee.

Deep breath. "Well, I was thinking that since it's your *eighteenth* birthday, I'd really like to give you the best gift I can think of as you enter legal manhood and everything."

"Go on. . . ."

"Well, when we were younger, you . . . umm . . ." My cheeks are an inferno. "You told me—well, you said you pledged your . . . umm . . ."

This is one of those times I *wish* he would make fun of how dumb I sound or something.

But he doesn't.

I take another breath. "I want to give you a gift you'll always remember and treasure," I say. "Well, *hopefully* you'll treasure it." Shit, I'm rambling. "Anyway, what I'm trying to say is I was thinking that maybe my gift to you should be letting you give your . . . *self*, I guess would be the way to put it, to me."

The silence that fills the car is like smoke. I signal left to turn onto our street, and the sound of the blinker makes me feel like a friggin' bomb is about to go off.

He doesn't say *anything*.

I'm glad I'm driving because there's no way in hell I could look at him right now. I might not ever speak again.

Who would've thought Courtney's silence would be worse than hearing what Rae had to say?

I pull into my driveway and am ready to *fly* out of the car and up to my closet when he puts his hand over mine as I reach to remove the key from the ignition.

"Hold up," he says.

In almost eleven years, I've never seen the expression Courtney Aloysius Cooper IV currently has on his face. I can't even describe it. My eyes trace his cheekbones, jaw-line, neck, the bumps of his collarbone near his throat . . .

His Adam's apple bobs. "Jupes, are you saying what I think you're saying?"

"Guess that depends on what you think I'm saying."

He shakes his head. "I'm serious, Jupiter. This really isn't something to *joke* about."

My eyes drop to my hands in my lap. "I wasn't joking, Coop."

More silence.

I couldn't get out of the car right now if I tried. Actually, I won't ever be able to move again until he gives me an answer. "I get if you think it's a bad idea," I say. "I guess it was presumptuous of me to assume that something you said in seventh grade still stands after all this ti—"

"It does."

"Huh?"

Don't look at him . . . don't look at him . . .

"It definitely still stands, but . . ."

But?!

Looking at him now. "But what, Coop?"

He meets my eyes. "So you only want to because I asked when we were in middle school?"

"Huh?"

"I mean, yeah, it's a big deal because it's the one thing I've 'saved' or whatever." He stares through the windshield. "But it's kind of a big deal for you, too, Jupes. At least it *should* be."

"I mean, I'd be a willing participant—"

He turns back to me and raises an eyebrow.

"Ugh, that didn't come out right."

What am I supposed to say? That I know everything is about to change? That I know when Rae becomes his girlfriend, they'll slowly disappear from my life? That even when they do hang with me once they become an "item" or whatever the hell colloquial term old people use to refer to young couples, I'm likely to cut the interactions short because it'll be too painful to see the boy who's been the best friend I've ever known wrapped around the finger of the first girl since elementary school I've had genuine feelings for? That life as we've known it—Jupe-and-Coop—will effectively be over soon?

I can't tell him any of that. And I definitely can't tell him the *real* reason for the suggestion: despite my romantic and sexual preferences, I want what he promised *me* so she won't be able to have it. Rae Chin might eventually get the rest of Courtney Cooper, but that part of him—that "first time"? She can't have that.

It's mine.

"I really want to, Coop," I say, rotating my body toward him so he knows I'm dead serious. "I want that part of you and I want you to have that part of me."

Now we're just staring into each other's eyes and it's getting *really* intense. Like I swear the temperature in the car has gone up ten degrees.

He really is a sight to behold, Coop is. And beyond that, there are so many things I love about him: he's kind and strong and he believes in the intrinsic value of women as human beings; he's fun and deep and loyal. I really do love him so, so much, and I've been lucky to have him all this time.

He breaks the eye contact and looks back out the windshield. Adam's apple bobs again. "When?" he says.

Holy shit, what did I just get myself into?

"Uhh . . . Papi and Dad will be gone the night before your birthday. Dad has some awards dinner down in the city so they're going to stay at a hotel."

He takes the deepest breath ever, holds it in for a few seconds, and then slowly blows it out through his pursed lips.

Lips I could very well be kissing in exactly one week.

Now *I'm* gulping.

An eternity passes. And another one.

"All right," he finally says.

"All right?" *Oh. My. God. What. Did. I. Just. DO?*

We lock eyes. "Okay," he says.

"Okay." I nod. "Great."

Jesus, Mary, and Joseph.

"Jupe?"

"Yeah?"

"Do you mind if we sleep separately until then? I need to process."

Process? "Wow, that's like seven nights."

"I know."

"Okay."

"Great, thanks."

"You're welco—"

And before I can say anything else, Courtney Cooper leaps out of the car we share and speed-walks to his front door.

23

"GOOD OLD-FASHIONED LOVER BOY"

(A Day at the Races, 1976)

Behind the hanging clothes in my closet, there are three posters on the wall: on the left is the sun, on the right is the planet Mars, and in the center is a second Freddie Mercury. In this one he's shirtless and in white spandex pants with a red belt. One hand is raised in a fist, and the other is holding a microphone to his open mouth. It's from Queen's 1982 LA show, and he's looking right into the camera, so it's almost like he's staring out at me from wherever he is in the Beyond.

This is my sanctuary and these three—my birth mom, Sunnie; my twin brother, Mars; and the illustrious Freddie Mercury—are my spiritual guides. I left during the fourth quarter of Coop's game so I could come get ready for *tonight*, and now I'm in said sanctuary, freaking the flip out.

"*Shit*, you guys!" I say, looking up at the ceiling from where I'm lying on my back on the floor. "Coop will be here in less than thirty minutes!"

I look at the three of them. No one responds.

"Has it really been seven days already?" I sit up now. "Like, what the hell was I *thinking*? We've barely even seen each other since we agreed to do this!"

Which is true. Just as he said he would, Coop has slept at home since the night he said yes. As a matter of fact, he's even had Britain or Golly pick him up for school each morning—which probably isn't a bad thing: being *alone* in the car with Rae has been damn near unbearable, so I probably would've dropped dead with him in there, too. Beemer full of friends and secrets and lies.

"Things are working out a little *too* perfectly, aren't they? Like what are the odds Mama Nee would go with my dads to stay downtown? Aren't they trusting us a little too much? Would *you* leave a pair of teens alone with *TWO* empty houses, Mom Dukes?" I ask the sun poster. "And what do I even *wear* tonight? I showered and everything, but like . . . I mean, whatever I put on is probably coming off, right? Oh my God, he's totally going to see me naked." Face in hands.

I shift to my knees and lean in close so I can whisper in Freddie's ear; don't want Mom Dukes or Mars to hear this part. "Freddie, is it weird that I've been *dreaming* about Coop?" I peek over my shoulder (which is dumb, I know—there's no one else even in the house). "Remember when I told you I saw him naked awhile back and it made me feel some *strangeness* down in my secret place? Well, in these dreams, he's like . . . God, this is embarrassing!"

Not to mention I'm whispering my innermost secrets to a poster.

"Okay, so he's naked and he's coming toward me and

then he smiles and I feel his hand on my stomach and it's moving down down down, and then I always wake up right before he makes *contact*, but when I do, I've got my legs all squeezed together and my lady parts are . . . throbbing."

Ugh.

"And like, I get a little turned on sometimes when Breanna looks at me a certain way, or Rae puts her hands on my scalp, or presses herself against me, or touches me in certain totally G-rated places—like she has this thing where she likes to mess with the baby hair at the nape of my neck, and sometimes she'll slip her hands under the hem of my shirt when she hugs me, and her icy fingertips will graze the small of my back—but this throbbing thing from the dreams is a *completely* different sensation, Freddie. It honestly scares the shit out of—"

"Jupe?" There's a knock on the closet door.

SHIT!

"Coop?"

"Of course, jackhole, who else would it be? Who the hell are you talking to in there?"

This is not happening.

I look at the clock (yes, I do have a clock in my closet). "You're eighteen minutes early!"

"So?"

"So I'm not dressed yet!" I scramble to my feet, shift the clothes so they hide the posters, and slip on the orange bra and undies set I got for tonight. Did I feel like the most antifeminist woman to walk the face of the earth as I purchased underwear *solely* for the sake of appealing to Courtney Cooper's male gaze? Duh.

But the goal is to be remembered, and orange is his favorite color.

"You're not dressed?" he says.

"No!"

"Well, maybe I should just come on in, then, huh?"

"You better not, perv!"

"Heh heh heh."

Ridiculous.

"I'll be out in a second!"

What to wear? What to wear? What to wear? Wait . . .

"Coop, did you shower?"

"You did not just ask me that."

"Is it not a legitimate question?"

"What do you think I am, some kinda cave dweller? I should come in there and spank you for even *sugges*—"

"COOP!"

Now he's laughing.

I settle for gray cable-knit tights, a hunter-green turtleneck sweater dress, and my black ankle boots. I muss my hair in the mirror and . . . *Crap, I didn't bring any makeup in here!*

Okay, deeeeeeeeeeeep breath. Open the closet door. Step out.

He looks me over head to toe from the La-Z-Boy and smiles. "Are we going skiing, Jupiter?"

"I hate you so much."

He laughs again. He's slouched down in the chair wearing the pale blue button-down and khakis he wore to school today. The guys have to dress "business casual" on game days, and yes, he looks nice.

How the hell is he so chill *about this?*

He's staring at my face now. It's giving me goose bumps.

"You look amazing," he says.

"I need to throw some makeup on."

He shakes his head, stands, and comes over to me. Kisses my forehead. "You certainly do not, Miss Charity-Sanchez. You are absolutely stunning without it."

Am I dying? I think I might be dying.

He looks me in the eye. There's that smile again—

"I changed my mind," I blurt.

His smile drops away. In the silence that follows, I swear I hear it hit the floor.

He steps away. Looks at the ground and rubs the back of his neck. Takes a deep breath. "Okay. I respect tha—"

"I want to do it at your house," I say.

His head snaps up and his eyes are wide.

I can't look at him anymore. It's making my heart beat way too fast. "Would that be okay? Mama Nee is with Dad and Papi, so I figured—"

"That's fine."

Silence.

Then: "Do I need to, umm . . . bring a thingy?" I say. "Or do you already have one?"

He smirks. "Pretty sure the 'thingy' is attached to me, Jupes."

"Oh my God, that's not what I meant!" This is mortifying.

"I'm kidding, I'm kidding. Calm down."

Like that's possible . . .

"If you mean a condom, yeah. I got us covered. Well . . . *me* covered." He clears his throat and won't meet my eyes.

So he *is* nervous.

"Should we . . . uhh . . . head over, then?" he says.

I swallow suuuuuuper-hard, and then nod. Take one last peek around this room that for so long has been *ours*. I don't want to ruin the memory of it in case everything goes to shit after tonight.

"Yeah." We lock eyes, and I gulp again. "Let's go."

And then it's happening.

We step into his room, and he's asking "Lights on or off?" and I'm saying "On," and his face is lighting up like he's relieved. Then the door is clicking shut, and I'm standing against it, and he's looking at me, and I'm looking at his lips.

I'm rising to my toes and my hands are on his chest and my eyes are closing and my lips are touching his. It's my first *real* kiss—that stolen one be damned—and his lips are full and soft and nice and my heart is racing.

Then his hands are on my waist and my hands are gripping his shirt. His lips are parting and my lower lip is between his teeth and he's humming . . . Oh, wait, that's *me* humming because it feels like every inch of my *body* is humming, so it only makes sense that my mouth—which is now opening as Coop's tongue slips inside it—is humming, too.

There's the door against my back, and Coop's body against my front, and—oh!—there's that friend of his I already feel like I know so well. Both of our mouths are open now, and I'm hot and my hands are sliding up to his neck. I'm humming again—more emphatically this time—because never in my life have I been so *hungry*.

It's a shock because I had no idea there was an appetite in me for this.

Then he's pulling away, and the anguish I feel over it might be the worst thing I've ever experienced.

What the hell is happening to me?

"You okay?" he says, and he's staring at me—*into* me, it seems—with wonder in his eyes and in the lifted corners of his mouth. How, in eleven flipping years of friendship, did I miss that mouth?

How did I not know it would be like this?

I throw my arms around his neck and kiss him again, and then he's lifting me. My legs wrap around his waist, and his hands are on my thighs, then my hips, then butt, lower back, bare waist as he takes off my dress. It's dropping to the floor with a **fwoomp** and his buttons are cold against my chest and stomach. The door is cool against my back as he presses me into it, but his hands? They're blazing.

That incredible mouth is on the edge of my chin, then behind my ear, then gliding down my neck, then grazing over my collarbone, and there's the tip of a tongue making little circles just above the line of my bra and I'm groaning because every inch of me is *burning*. I'm trying to unbutton his shirt because I want it off, but the bottom half is trapped beneath my thighs, so we pull apart and he puts me down so I can finish.

Moment of clarity now that my eyes are open and I can see how much my hands are shaking: I'm standing here in an orange bra, gray tights, and black booties (trick or treat, anyone?) trying to *undress* my male best friend so we can have *actual* sex. Like, *with* each other.

I look up at him, and he's looking down at me, and now I'm shaking so bad, I can't get the next button undone.

"Here." He takes my hands and puts them at my sides, then pulls the shirt up over his head.

After he drops it on top of my discarded dress, he steps out of his shoes and kicks them aside, then kneels in front of me to take mine off, too. He's so gentle: sliding his hand from my calf to my ankle, lifting my foot by the heel, un-zipping the bootie, and slowly sliding it off. Once both shoes are set aside, he tickles the bottom of my left foot, and I totally snort.

I cover my mouth, even though I've snorted in front of him a thousand times.

Just feels a little different doing it half naked.

He puts his hands on my hips and grins up at me. "Don't get mad at me for saying this, but you are cute as hell, Jupes."

"Oh, stop it." And now I'm *blushing*?

Seriously don't know what's happening right now.

I *would* like to go back to kissing, though. And more. My mind doesn't really *get* the more, but from the urge I feel to rip the rest of his clothes off and literally jump his bone(r), my body doesn't seem the least bit confused.

"You mind if I . . . uhh . . ." He tugs at the waistband of my tights.

I shake my head.

"Is that a no, you don't mind, or no, 'do-not-take-my-tights-off-I-can-do-it-myself-you-patriarchist-swine'?" He winks.

"Shut up and take them off, Coop."

So he does. Then he looks me over head to toe again. His smile fades and his mouth snaps shut.

He drops back so he's sitting on his heels.

Okaaay . . . "Coop?"

No response. Well, besides his mouth drifting back open apparently of its own accord.

I peek down at myself. I'm definitely fleshier than the average girl he dates and have stretch marks—my tiger stripes—where my thighs and butt expanded quicker than my skin was ready for, but it can't be *that* bad, can it? Weirdest part is I usually love my body, but the notion of *him* not liking it makes me question things.

Not real sure what to do with that.

Now his gaze feels like some sort of laser beam over my bumps and dips and grooves, and it's getting a little uncomfortable. I'm cold where I was hot before, and I'd really like to put my clothes back on and go crawl into my closet, please and thank you.

I shift, and my arms rise to cover what I can, but Coop catches my wrists. "No, don't," he says. He interlaces his fingers with mine and holds my arms out at my sides as his eyes continue to roam. "Jupiter, you are—" and then he looks up into my eyes. "Can I touch you?"

I nod.

He lets go of my hands—which feel icy now—and puts his hands on my waist. Then he trails them down over my hips and thighs until he reaches my knees, which he cups and rubs his thumbs over. I swear my heart, like, trips over itself.

"It's like I knew but I didn't *know*," Coop says.

"Huh?"

"That every inch of you would be . . . immaculate."

"Oh."

"You're a damn miracle, Jupes."

Annnnnd we're done here.

I unhook my bra and let it drop to the floor, and then I grab his hands and tug so he stands. His eyes seem like they're about to burst from his face, but once he's up, I unbuckle his belt and pants and squat to push them down so he can step out of them.

The second I rise, our mouths are colliding, and he's scooping me up and carrying me to what feels like both an end and a beginning.

I can't sleep afterward. Too much in my head.

First there's the constant replay of all the things I had *no idea* Courtney Cooper could do. Trying not to think about it too much, but if he used his hands and mouth with his former girlfriends the way he just used them with me, I can't begin to fathom why they would've dumped him.

The actual *intercourse* part did hurt a little, but he was super-caring and attentive, and the one time I opened my eyes, he looked like he'd stumbled into heaven.

It didn't last long.

At least the first time it didn't.

The second time, though? Well, I think things may have gotten a little complicated.

That's another thing I can't stop thinking about. In the middle of the second time, I got a little caught up in him. His body over mine, and the sweat on his back, and his scent, and the way his skin tasted . . .

227

Bottom line, in the midst of our fervor, the words "I love you, Courtney" slipped out of my mouth when it was by his ear.

And I'm pretty sure I meant it.

Then he totally said it back.

Which is confusing?

Especially since as soon as I came back down, if you will, who popped into my head but Rae Chin. Her kissing me. Her cold little hands on my waist. Her playing in my hair. Her eyes. Her laugh. Her smile.

Her telling me she thinks *she* loves the boy I just—

Yeah.

Anyway, I can't sleep now. The wrist with my bracelet feels like it weighs a trillion pounds.

So I get up.

I pull on my tights and the button-down he was wearing, and I leave and go to my house to find the original box. I take off my charm bracelet and I put it inside, and then I write a note ("Thank you for you."), close the box, and wrap it in silver paper.

After slipping back into his room and sitting the gift on the bedside table, I lift the covers to crawl into bed next to him.

He automatically shifts and wraps an arm around my waist, tucking me into my usual spot in the cozy curve of his body.

I inhale deeply and smile. Apparently no matter what bed we're in, if I'm in little-spoon position with Courtney Cooper, I feel like I'm home.

I take all the shit swirling in my head—*youcan'tbedoing this—thisisn'tright—he'saGUY—whataboutRae?—you're*

notallowedtoLIKEbeingwithhim—you'regoingtoregretthis—
thisisgonnabeashitshow—youhavenoideawhatyou'vejust
*done—you'reaterribleperson—*and I stuff it down as deep as
I can get it to go.

Then I snuggle in deeper and let Freddie's voice fill my
head:

♫ *That's because I'm a good old-fashioned lover boy . . .* ♫

24

"PAIN IS SO CLOSE TO PLEASURE"

(A Kind of Magic, 1986)

And then you leave your body again and spend the next week looking down at yourself and wondering what the hell you're doing.

This begins the morning of Coop's birthday when you wake to him (1) squeezing you tight from behind and kissing your neck as he (2) pokes you in the ass with his "morning wood," and (3) instead of leaping out of his bed while screaming bloody murder (as you very well should because eww, *boy thingy*, helloooo?), you roll over to face him and actually kiss him on the mouth. (No, *for real*, what are you doing, Jupiter? You haven't even brushed your teeth!)

He smiles at you with his eyes looking like perfect, gently worn pennies, and your heart basically explodes as you smile back and run your fingertip over his nose. Then he wiggles down and tucks said nose in the little crook between your chin and your neck, and he just lies there and breathes.

It occurs to you that you could stay this way, not forever necessarily, but until you could no longer hold your pee.

That moment, sadly, comes much too soon, but when you tell him you need to get up or you'll wet his bed, he whimpers like a little boy and throws his big-ass leg over your body to pin you down. You should be outraged at this patriarchist attempt to override your agency, *and* disgusted by the blatant display of weakness, but you are neither because he's just so damn cute.

So you giggle. (You *giggle*?! What the frick, Jupiter?)

He eventually lets you up, and that's when, upon tossing the covers off, you notice the little bloom of crimson on Coop's light blue sheet. Your eyes widen and what you did with your best friend last night tumbles down over you like bricks falling from a crumbling wall. "Oh my God," you say, and you put your face in your hands and *almost* come back to yourself . . .

But then that wonderfully cute, deliciously sweet dream of a boy (because you *have* to be dreaming) says, "Guess it's a good thing I do my own laundry, huh?" And he kisses you on the cheek and gets out of bed to stretch like nothing happened. He's still naked, and good Lord his ass. It's like the work of some master carver.

He notices the little gift box on the bedside table then, and looks over his shoulder at you with his eyebrows raised. *"Pour moi?"*

MAN, is he cute!

(Will you snap out of it, please?! *This is going to be a disaster!*)

You smile at him and swing your legs over the edge of the bed (finally). Your body has apparently reabsorbed some of the pee or something because you don't have to go as bad, but you would like to *freshen up*, as they say.

"*Oui*," you tell him, utilizing the summation of almost three years of high school French. "But don't open it yet. I need to run to the bathroom and I want to be here when you do."

As you stand he comes around the bed and lifts your chin. "Whatever you say, boss," and he gives you a quick peck on the lips. It makes you all tingly, largely because of what you did, but also because of who he is. Courtney Cooper, best friend and the first person you ever said "I definitely wanna marry a girl" to, is kissing you on the lips while standing butt-ass naked.

Because you had sex with him.

Sex.

Sexual intercourse.

Peen in va-jay-jay.

Holy friggin' shit, Jupiter!

Again, you almost come back to yourself, but then he runs the tip of his index finger over your ear, neck, collarbone, then down the center of your chest—which is exposed, you realize, because you're still wearing his shirt, and it's unbuttoned almost to your belly button. You're missing a supportive undergarment in that area, and oh my goodness, now you're blushing—and tingling—again.

(Fool!)

You finally go, and when you come back from the bathroom—eye crud removed, face washed, teeth brushed, hair bunned—he's sitting on the bed in basketball shorts (darn!), with the gift in hand.

"Open it," you say, sitting beside him.

He sees the thank-you note first—"Awwww, Jupes!"—but when his gaze alights on the bracelet, the smile falls from his face and he looks at you. His eyeballs are moistening.

You clear your throat and fight to hold the eye contact (it's kind of burning a hole in your soul at the moment, especially since you're still conflicted about the *first kiss* sapphire. But you have to push through). "Happy birthday, Coop," you say. "You earned that," and you nod at the bracelet in the box.

One corner of his mouth quirks up. "I *earned* it, huh?"

"Oh God." You smack your forehead.

He laughs. It's like the pinging of wind chimes at dawn on the Gulf of Mexico combined with the sound of ocean waves against the shore.

"It's yours, Courtney." You tuck some stray hairs behind your ear. "Probably always has been."

(Slow your ROLL, girlfriend!)

He's staring at you when his first tears fall.

"Aww, Coop, don't *cry*!" And you look away from him because you're totally about to cry, too.

And then his hand is on your chin, and he's turning your head, and he's kissing you.

Sweet *Lord*, is he kissing you.

To your surprise—especially since you spent thirty minutes making-out-plus before hopping in the shower together—when Papi, Dad, and Mama Nee come in bearing gifts and brunch, you and Coop somehow manage to act completely normal. You pick at each other through the whole meal, even throwing a bit of food and getting yelled at here and there, and when he opens your other gift—an autographed Steph Curry poster for his Great Men with Girly Names collection—he bonks you over the head with it, and you call him foul names (though you do wonder if Papi or Dad notices your naked wrist).

As a matter of fact, this normalness carries on into dinner, which Rae and Dr. Chin attend, and then spills over into the week. You still tingle when Rae touches you a certain way—which is all the time—so the rides to and from school are a little intense, but when Coop's around, so are Britain and Golly, and nobody is the wiser. School is school, and classes drone on, and Coop gives you more noogies in the hallway, but everyone looks at you the same way they did before.

Basically, everything is as it was.

Except for at night when you and Coop are alone together. And during that week after his birthday, Mama Nee is working third shift, so that computes to just about every night. There's even a night when Rae sleeps over and you sneak out at 2:43 a.m. to go next door, but when you and Coop come in together the next morning, she doesn't even bat an eyelash. *(You're a horrifyingly shitty person, by the way.)*

Your secret is safe. No one has a clue. You're in a full-blown *liaison* with your male best friend.

You're *living in the moment* on a cloud somewhere, not

thinking, not considering costs, effects, consequences. Your conscience is on hiatus.

You're *gone* . . .

Until the morning you're putting the finishing touches on an outreach for kids from a bunch of Atlanta-area shelters, and Coop stumbles into your room, completely out of breath.

"Jupes, we gotta talk like right, *right* now," he says.

You can feel every pulse of your heart in your fingertips as you look at the calendar hanging over your desk: March 31.

Coop's birthday was exactly one week ago.

Now Rae's insistence upon staying at her own house last night to "prepare for the big day" makes sense. You had no idea what she was talking about, but you didn't want to seem like a bad friend—which you *obviously* are—so you didn't ask what she meant.

You certainly know now.

Everything you've done this past week begins to trickle down over the Real You from the cloud Dazed You's been sitting on.

First a drizzle—sleeping in Coop's bed, kissing Coop, touching Coop, Coop touching you. Then fatter, heavier drops—Coop's hands on your _____, and your hands on his _____, and his mouth on your_____, and your _____ on his _____.

Then the icy deluge that soaks you to the bone: Coop on you and over you and under you and *in* you and *I love you, Courtney* and *I love* you, *Jupiter* and *I've* always *loved you* and *I love hearing you say that.*

Down, down, down, you tumble from that cloud as Freddie Mercury croons from the speakers of your laptop: ♫ . . . *sunshine and rainy weather go hand in hand together* ♫ . . .

"Hello? Earth to Jupiter, kinda in crisis here," Coop is saying.

I blink a few times. Settle back into my skin and this time and this place. Turn to look at Coop as he drops into the La-Z-Boy and drags his hands over his cheeks. "Rae just called and asked me out."

And there. It. Is.

Holy Freddie Mercury, what the hell did I do?

"Okay . . ."

He leans forward and puts his elbows on his knees. "I don't—*shit*, Jupe!" His head drops into his hands and he groans. "How the hell do I turn her down without ruining the friendship?"

I swallow the pill of my doom and clear my throat. "Why would you turn her down, Coop?"

I don't think I've ever seen Coop's head snap up so quick. Nor have I ever seen him look so perplexed. "For real?" he says. "*Why wouldn't I turn her down?* The hell kinda question is that, Jupiter?"

"I mean, you obviously like her." I look at my computer because I can't face him anymore. The tears are welling and the throat-knot is forming and I'll cry. "I just don't see why you'd say no if you like her. And I know you do. I can tell."

He doesn't respond.

"I've seen the way you look at her, Coop." And it fucking kills me. "You even told her about your Carnival Carl thing."

I swallow the sting of those words leaving my mouth. *Suck it up, Jupiter. It's done.*

"Is *that* what this is about?"

No . . . Maybe.

Whatever. "It's not *about* anything, Coop. You like her. She likes you. One plus one is two."

"Okay, who are you and what the hell have you done with the girl I spent the past week *sleeping* with?"

Do not dare think about that, Jupiter. He's not yours anymore. Let him go. "Look, it was fun while it lasted, but you should move on now." I feel like I'm stabbing myself with every word. "You and Rae are perfect for each other. You practically belong together."

"*Excuse* me?"

"You're excused?"

Oops. Probably shouldn't've said that.

Too late, though, because now my chair is rotating and Courtney is glowering down at me. His jaw is tight, and there's a vein pulsing in his neck. It's seriously a wonder there's no steam coming out of his ears and nose. "We've been banging practically every night, and now you're telling me to go *date* someone else?"

The "banging." Of course.

"Look, you got what you wanted, right?" I get up from the desk chair and slip past him to go sit on the bed. Create a little distance. "Courtney Cooper made a pledge to save himself for his best friend, Jupiter. They've done it a few times now, so mission accomplished."

"Are you fuckin' kidding me right now?" he hollers.

"Stop *yelling*, asswipe," I say. "Papi is downstairs. You want him finding out you deflowered his daughter? Think he'll let you hang out over here once he knows?"

I swear his eyes are about to explode out of his head and shoot molten bronze goo all over the room. "Jupe, if that's what you think this whole thing was about, you've had your eyes closed for eleven years, dawg."

Dawg?!

"Coop, you don't even see me as a real girl!"

"What the hell are you *talking* about?"

"You just called me *dawg!*"

"Are you *serious* right now?"

"Whatever."

"Jupe, what do you *want* from me?"

"*Nothing*, Coop. Don't you know that by now? I don't want or need anything from you." Of course this is a bald-faced lie, and I'm pretty sure we both know it. But thinking about the implications of the truth is just . . .

No.

I *know* who/what I am and what/who I want, dammit. I like *girls*, not boys.

I look at Freddie Mercury and cross my arms. Swallow and will away the tears. There's no way I'm about to let Coop see me cry right now. Hell no.

"You should go call Rae back," I say.

He looks at me like I'm a creature from another planet. "You're impossible!" he says.

That does it.

"I know, okay? I *know* I'm 'impossible'! I'm not needy enough or sweet enough or tender enough or *straight* enough, so I—WE—are impossi—"

"What are you *talking about*, Jupiter? We just spent a WEEK doing—"

"I'm *GAY*, Courtney!" Now I'm yelling. "Don't you *get* that?"

In the silence that drops over us, the sound of my phone chiming from my desk is so loud, we both startle. Coop picks it up and looks at it. His eyes narrow.

Oh shit.

"Give me my phone, Cour—"

"You knew?" He looks at me.

Shit, shit, *shit!*

"Huh?" (Have I said *Shit* enough times yet?)

"New message from Rae: 'I did it. He said he had to run and he'd call me back, but I think he's going to say no.'"

"You've got some nerve reading my messa—"

"You fucking knew."

Shit, shit, SHIIIIIT.

"Give me my phone, Coop."

"How long?"

"How long what?"

"Don't you fucking play games with me, Ju—"

"Don't talk to me that way, *Coop.*"

He glares at me.

I glare right back.

"How long have you known, Jupiter?"

I won't break I won't break I won't break.

He closes his eyes and hangs his head then. "Please just tell me."

I break.

"Three weeks," I say under my breath.

"What?"

"I said THREE WEEKS, Coop, okay?"

I'm definitely about to cry again, and from the look on his face, so is he—

But then **click** a shutter drops over his eyes. Closes me out. Feels like what I imagine being hit by a Mack truck and shot off a cliff would feel like.

He nods. "I get it now. You storming off on New Year's Eve, how clingy you get with her when I'm around."

Wow, he's sure got *that* backward. . . .

"You were in love with her."

"What?"

"You were in love with her, but then she comes and tells you she's got a thing for me, so what do you do? You bang me behind her back."

"Excuse me?"

"Except it didn't really go according to plan, huh, Jupe? Because while we were doing what we were doing, you realized you're really in love with *me.*"

"Back the fuck up, homeboy. I am *not* in love with you." *I'm NOT, dammit!* "In case you've forgotten, I like *girls.* If us fooling around got you confused, it's your problem, not mine."

"Yet you're mad at Rae for leading *you* on." He shakes his head.

Who the hell does he think he is, reading my life like that? "First of all, I never said I was mad at Rae. Your little man-mind is just running off with its patriarchal theor—"

"Oh, don't give me that sexism bullshit, Jupiter. You can't tell me you weren't into what we were doing."

"God, here we go . . . let's fight to protect our ego. . . ."

"Just stop, all right?" He looks me in the eye. "Jupe, I might be attracted to Rae, but it's *nothing* compared to—"

"Compared to *what*, Courtney? Getting to 'bang' the gay girl?"

He draws back. Frowns. "You know what? Screw this. It's pointless." He turns to leave. "I shoulda known better."

He wipes his eyes on his sleeve, and I feel like a gigantic asshole (because I am, obviously).

"Coop—"

"Look, I know you want everyone to think you're this hard-core, out-and-proud lesbian, but you and I both know that's bullshit, Jupe. Yeah, you might be into girls, but there's no way in hell you can tell me you're not into me, too."

I cross my arms and bite the hell out of the inside of my cheek to keep from opening my mouth.

He grabs the doorknob and takes one last look at me. "It's fucked up that you're sacrificing *us* for your stupid label, but fine. You want to keep lying to yourself, feel free. Just stay the hell away from me."

The door opens, and as he disappears into the hallway and pulls it shut, I hear Freddie's forlorn falsetto float into the air.

♫ *So in love but love had a bad reaction* ♫ I was lookin' for some good ol' satisfaction ♫

"Oh, fuck off, Freddie." And I walk over and slam my laptop shut.

25

"JEALOUSY"

(*Jazz*, 1978)

Coop hasn't spoken to me in two weeks.

Actually, no, I take that back. Coop speaks to me all the time so long as other people are around. As a matter of fact, if other people are around—especially people named Rae Evelyn Chin, aka his latest girlfriend who he's always tickling and snuggling and picking up and hanging all over, the wretched bastard—Coop treats me like the best friend I've always been: he pokes at me and jokes with me and tugs my earlobe and "asks my opinion" about stuff.

He no longer answers my phone calls or responds to my text messages or gets in a car alone with me unless it's to go pick up Rae, but nobody would ever know any of that because when other people are around, he acts like nothing's wrong.

And as furious as it makes me, he knows I can't do anything about it. If I blow his cover, I blow mine, and we both know *that* can't happen. If Rae—or anyone else—gets wind of stormy skies in our Jupe-and-Coop Paradise, questions will arise and questioners will go tugging at closet doors and skeletons will clatter to the floor and the apocalypse will commence, because if anyone discovers Jupe and Coop were sleeping together, Jupe's whole world will implode.

Coop will be applauded and high-fived, *Attaboy*-ed and *Play on, playa*-ed. He'll be crowned King of Men, treated like a god, worshipped for "turning the lesbo out" . . .

Me? I'll be called a slut and a fraud and treated like days-old dog shit on the bottom of someone's shoe. My lesbian friends will likely shun me—and I've been hanging out with Breanna a *lot* since Coop and Rae got together, so *that* can't happen unless I want to be alone all the time (I don't)—and my "straight-ally" friends will treat me like some vile betrayer as if *they're* personally affected. I've seen it happen.

Not to mention that if Rae finds out what I did, she'll totally hate me just as much as Coop does. Then I'll *really* have lost them both. She and I might be interacting under false pretenses right now—it's a kick to the uterus every time she thanks me for being "so cool about this"—but I'll certainly take that over nothing. Which I know makes me pathetic because she basically led me on and then picked him over me.

It's all very ridiculous.

On the way to the craft day Rae and I (mostly *I*, but who's keeping track?) planned for the shelter kids, she, Coop, and I are in the car joking and laughing and talking about sex of *all* things. I'm sitting in the backseat, of course—the lovebirds are up front with their hands inter-linked over the cup holders—but the longer this conver-sation goes on, the more I find myself peeking over my shoulder at Brit and Golly in Golly's truck behind us. They offered to let me ride with them, but (1) I'm a masochist, obviously, and (2) the thought of Coop and Rae alone in the car *my* dads gifted to us while I rode behind them was just like uh-uh. Hell to the no.

So here we are.

"When you think about the actual *mechanics* of the whole deal, it's actually kind of hilarious, isn't it?" Rae says. "Person A takes a blood-filled appendage and sticks it into a moist orifice."

"Oh God, don't use the M-word," I say.

Rae rotates in her seat to look at me. "You have a prob-lem with the word *moist*, Jupes?"

I hate when she calls me Coop's obviously-not-so-secret-or-special-anymore-but-still-*his* nickname for me. Also hate the way she's staring at me. There's this wicked glint in her eye that gives me the willies.

I turn to the window. "It's so misogynistically porn-y. Like '*Ooh, Big Papa, you're makin' me so M-word.*' It's to-tally the kind of shit Shanna would say. Actually, I think she's texted me that before."

"Well, I mean, it's better than *wet*, isn't it?" Rae says.

"Yeah, can we *not* have this conversation?" I know my face is reddening.

"It's still hard for me to believe you've never done any-thing sexual, Jupiter."

And Courtney Aloysius Cooper IV *snorts*.

He looks at me in the rearview and his eyes go wide. If I could breathe fire, he'd be toast right now.

And of course Rae's all over it. "Wait, did I miss something?" She looks from him to me to him to me, then, "OH MY GOD, YOUR BRACELET IS GONE!"

This would be a fabulous time to asphyxiate on my own saliva, except my mouth has gone so dry, my tongue is turning to dust.

She looks down at my wrist, up at my face, down at my wrist, up at my face, covers her mouth.

"How the heck did I *miss* that?"

"Well . . ." I peek over my shoulder again. "You have been a little *preoccupied* lately."

She looks at Coop (dreamily) and giggles as her cheeks flush.

I am going to hurl.

"Did you know about this?" she says, swatting Coop's chest with the back of her hand.

Annnnnnnd the cords of muscle in his forearm look on the verge of popping through his skin.

Dear God, I know I'm not real big on prayer, but please feel free to rain down fire and brimstone to take me out like you supposedly did at that Sodom and Gomorrah place. I certainly deserve it, and not at all because I'm gay. Because I *am* still gay, dammit.

Coop clears his throat and makes eye contact with me in the mirror again. "She may have mentioned it in passing, but I don't know any details or anything."

It's a good thing she's so smitten because *anyone* else would smell the bullshit wafting off him like post-basketball-game body odor.

"She'll introduce us to the special girl eventually, right, babe?" Rae runs a finger down the side of Coop's neck.

The song changes, and once Freddie Mercury hits the first refrain, I feel like he's singing right to me: ♫ *Jealousy* ♫ *look at me now* ♫ . . .

I should really keep my mouth shut. I should bite down on my tongue until the urge to speak goes away because I know it's a terrible idea to open it after hearing "us" and "babe" and "she" come out of Rae's mouth like I'm not sitting right fucking here. The wedge between my former best friend and me is pretty deep. Loosening my lips right now is *sure* to drive it deeper.

But as I mentioned, I am a masochist. "Yeah, there's no special girl," I say.

She turns around. "Well, where's your charm bracelet, missy?"

Did she really just call me missy? *(And did it really give me a little thrill?)*

I clear my throat and look right at the back of Coop's head. "It's with a friend for safekeeping. We'll leave it at that."

I wonder if Rae can tell Coop's no longer breathing.

Things really start to crumble once the ball is rolling at the outreach, which takes place in a beautiful park. We wind up with twenty-four kids, ages five to fourteen, and despite the low-key relational upheaval, it really is a lovely sight.

The Golly Brown Giant is teaching a handful of mostly boys how to knit—if this high school basketball superstar can knit, knitting is the coolest thing ever, right?

Britain is teaching a group of eyelash-batting middle school girls how to make spiral staircase friendship bracelets—something I taught *him* just yesterday. And I have a group of eager-to-get-messy five-to-seven-year-olds at my papier-mâché station.

The most happening spot on the yard, though, is Coop and Rae's Sharpie tie-dye station. And since I—ahem—*just so happened* to set up shop diagonally from them, for the past hour, I've watched helplessly as they've made goo-goo eyes at each other and charmed the shit out of the oldest kids: the boys think Coop is liquid-nitrogen-level *cool,* and the girls think Rae is SO *pretty.*

The fact that they're *together*-together is delighting their little fan club no end.

As my group runs off to play while their globular creations dry in the early-spring sunshine, I sit at my station, staring at Coop and Rae. Every time she touches him, I want to smash all my kids' handiwork. Every time he smiles down at her, I want to flip the fucking table. Every time they share a glance, every nanosecond of incidental contact, I want to smear papier-mâché over my eyeballs and let it dry so I never have to see them again.

I'm furious with her for every time she held my hand or wrapped her arms around my waist or played in my hair. I'm furious with him for being with her after we x and y and z-ed and beyond. I'm furious with myself for . . . God, where do I even start? Ruining eleven years of friendship?

Betraying my queeple? Falling too hard too fast? (For which one of them, though?)

I'm just really frickin' furious.

"So I see your kids are done, too, huh?"

I jump.

"My bad," Golly says from where he seems to have materialized beside me like some overgrown fairy. "Didn't mean to scare you."

"No, no, it's fine," I say. "Sorry. Got a little lost in thought. Yeah, my kids are done. How'd the knitting go?"

Golly smiles. "Honestly, it went a lot better than I expected. I know a lot of people don't mess with me because I'm—" He gestures to his size. "But little kids can be relentless. Don't tell nobody, but I was nervous they would flip on me when I pulled out all the needles."

I smile. Gentle giant, this one.

"How 'bout you?" he goes on. "Things went okay with the rug rats?"

"They did. Well, for the most part. Things got messier than I expected."

He nods. "You, uhh . . . you good other than that?"

"Huh?"

"Well . . . not that I was *watching* you or anything, but you seemed—*seem*—a bit . . . preoccupied." He lifts his chin in the direction of Coop and Rae's station. I watch, my internal organs in danger of destruction from the churning volcano of rage on the verge of eruption inside me (dammit!) as she playfully shoves him and he responds by tapping her nose.

Something he used to do to me.

"I'm good," I say, ripping my eyes away and forcing them to meet Golly's.

"Yeah, okay."

I look out in the opposite direction at a group of people playing kickball. Makes me want to go join them just so I can kick the shit out of something without anyone asking questions.

"How'd that one kid react to you accidentally putting a strip of wet newspaper on his forehead?" Golly asks.

"Oh God, you saw that?" I smack *my* forehead. "You think anyone else did?"

"You sure you're good, Jupiter? I know you and I don't talk much, but . . ." He sighs. "All right, look: I *know* I'm oversteppin' here, but you can't tell me *that* isn't bothering you." He gestures to Coop and Rae again. "Frankly, I can see it all over you. Brit can, too."

I clear my throat but don't respond.

"You not answerin', so Imma keep going, even though I'll probably regret it," he continues, "but you and Coop been tight for a long time. I know he's had girlfriends before, but this is the first time he's dated someone you're close with, too, right?"

I nod. Who knew Golly was so observant? I feel kind of naked right now.

"So I mean, it stands to reason that *this* girlfriend would affect you differently, right? That's not to mention the fact that he seems to actually *like* this one—"

"Huh?"

249

"Oh. Uhh . . ." Were he a little less brown, I think I'd see some red in Golly's cheeks. "Nothin', nothin'. Forget I said that."

Mmmmm . . .

"Anyway, last year a couple of my sister's best friends started dating, and it had her messed up for a minute. They grew up as this trio, but then Tay—that's my sister—started feeling like the odd one out because Nisha and Jazmine were real affectionate with each other, and they started having all these inside jokes and memories Tay wasn't a part of." He shrugs. "The *dynamic* changed, is what I'm saying."

Part of me wants to ask if the individual friendships survived, but I'm not sure I'll be able to deal if he says anything resembling a no. So instead I say, "You're really close with your sister, huh?"

"Yeah," he replies. "I'm tight with all of them. Being the baby and the only boy means I grew up with multiple mamas."

I laugh.

"Back to the matter at hand, though," he says. "Bottom line, if the Coop-and-Rae thing is burnin' you a little bit . . . it's okay." He finally looks me in the eye.

I don't say anything, and for a minute, neither does he.

But then he rocks back on his heels and says, "It's definitely burnin' Brit."

"Really?!" I glance over at Britain, who's currently bound to a chair with friendship bracelet string while a squad of giggly preteen girls marches around him in a circle like they're about to offer him up as a sacrifice. Poor guy.

"Yeah, man. Coop basically snatched Rae right out from under him."

Huh. "Well, then."

"Yep. Anyway, I just wanted to let you know Brit and I are around if you ever need anything, aiight? We're here for you."

"Hey, Golly?"

"Yeah?"

"Are they still friends? Tay, Jazmine, and Nisha?"

"You really wanna know?" He looks down at me with his eyebrows raised.

"Nope." I sigh. "But I think I need to."

He nods. "Tay and Nisha are," he says. "When Nisha and Jazmine broke up, and Jaz started dating a guy soon after, things kinda blew up, and Tay took Nisha's side."

"Oh." Well, that's certainly not what I needed to hear, and not only because both friendships didn't survive.

"Don't worry about it, though, Jupiter," Golly says. "At least Coop's with a girl who *knows* how thick y'all are and won't trip about it. I can't really speak for Rae, but you and Coop's friendship could survive Armageddon."

That's when it hits me: it's not just Coop's *friendship* I'm upset about losing.

I'd never say it aloud, but when he got under my clothes, he got under my skin. Way down into the deepest, most vulnerable, top secret, highly protected parts of me.

And I miss him.

26

"UNDER PRESSURE"

(*Hot Space*, 1982)

Breanna and I are in her pink Jeep Wrangler with the top and doors off. Frankly, I was relieved when she asked me to hang out with her tonight. It was either that or spend an evening doing homework or sitting alone in my closet, which doesn't feel like much of a *sanctuary* right now because I get the feeling even my posters are sick of me moping. If I didn't know he was inanimate, I would swear I caught Freddie giving me side eye the other day.

I haven't taken Golly up on his offer to hang with him and Britain. I've got *way* too many secrets involving our newly coupled mutual friends, and I don't trust that they won't explode out of me with the right prodding. Breanna, though, is safe for the most part. Yes, my high school world and my other world have collided a couple of times recently, but Bre exists on a different plane from everyone else. So when she asked me to go out, I said yes.

Though I did make her give *me* control of the radio.

"Are we seriously listening to Vanilla Ice right now?" she says as the opening bars of one of my favorite Queen songs—featuring David Bowie—play.

"You did *not* just ask me that," I say. "You didn't."

"Girl, bye. This is the opening to 'Ice Ice Baby.'"

"I'll have you know that *Mr.* Ice, as he referred to himself, sampled that track from the greatest band in the history of bipedal man."

She snorts. "You so dramatic, J."

"No, for real. You need to listen." I turn the volume up as my beloved Freddie breaks out his mind-bending falsetto. Hearing it makes me feel so good, I squeeze my eyes closed and sing right along with him:

♫ *Chippin arouuuund, kick my brains 'round the floor* ♫
These are the daaaaaays it never rains but it pours ♫ . . .

Breanna is cracking up. When I open my eyes, we're stopped at a traffic light and she's looking at me with this admiringish grin on her face. "You know you're a mess, right?"

"Shut up." I face forward. Even with no roof or door on the car, the usual tension between us fills the Jeep.

There's definitely some chemistry between us—so much, in fact, it gets overwhelming at times and I have to get away from her.

Right now, though? In my present self-piteous *nobody-wants-me-and-I-have-no-clue-who-I-am-anymore* state? Let's just say this tension feels *damn* good, and her lips are looking downright delicious.

♪ . . . *sat on a fence* ♪ *but it don't work* ♪ . . .

Thanks for that, Freddie.

"So I noticed you're not wearing that bracelet anymore," Bre says out of nowhere. "It was a gift from your dads, right? What gives?"

Seriously? This *is the time she picks to notice?*

I turn my face into the breeze from my doorless side of the car. "Outgrew it, I guess."

If only she knew.

"It's strange seeing you without it. Like your arm looks mad naked."

And before I can give what I'm doing any actual thought, I turn to look at her. "Are you saying you imagine me naked, Breanna?"

Her eyes widen, but only for like a microsecond—I only catch it because I'm staring at her so hard. "Slow your roll, J," she says. "You're underage."

"That doesn't answer the question."

She glances at me. If I didn't know any better, I'd say she looks nervous. "What's gotten into *you* tonight?"

More like what hasn't *been into me in almost a month now.* "I was just asking."

We lapse into silence. Which isn't good because I can feel weeks' and weeks' worth of verbal puke surging up my esophagus.

"Do you really think you'd get in trouble if we hooked up?" I say.

Wow, zero *points for finesse, Jupe.*

Breanna just shakes her head. "Not taking that bait, J."

I look back out the open door. "When did you figure out you were into girls?"

"Okay, what's this really about, Jupiter?"

I sigh and look down at my blue toenails. I'm wearing charcoal-colored denim cutoff shorts with tattered fishnets underneath, a tight-fitting, low-cut blue shirt, and peep-toe wedge booties. While I couldn't give a shit about the male gaze, when Bre told me where she wanted to take me—the yearly Spring Sapphism Social thrown by the Pride organization she runs—I just knew I needed to look as hot as possible. Play up my assets. Attract the attention I'm admittedly desperate for.

They say *you don't know what you've got till it's gone*, and I have to confess: after being with Coop and feeling his ravenousness for me all those nights, the dearth of such a feeling is . . . yeah, it's shitty.

And then when you throw Rae in there . . . you know, the fact that she never wanted me in the first place?

"I just wanna know when and how you knew," I say.

"Same way you knew, asswipe. I just *did*. Pretty much always."

I look at her hands on the wheel, her tattooed forearms, her neck, her mouth.

I gulp. "You know I've never even kissed a girl, right?" *Well, I kind of have, but not really . . . Though I have kissed a boy, and that was—*

No, screw that. That was nothing. Just like the kiss from Rae was nothing.

Right?

Breanna laughs. "Is that what this is about?"

God, I feel like I'm *seven* right now.

"I guess I'm just sick of waiting to find out what it's like."

We exit the highway, and Bre stops at the top of the ramp and turns to me. "Who said you had to?" The tension puffs up inside the open Jeep. Almost like we've driven right into a cumulus cloud.

I need to change the subject. "So are you, umm . . . dating anyone these days?"

"Nah. I was talking to this one girl, but then she mentioned an ex-boyfriend, and I had to cut it off."

"Huh?"

"I don't mess with bisexual girls."

"Oh." The cloud in the car thickens.

"It's nothing personal, really. Enough girls leave you for dudes, and you learn to keep your distance," she goes on. "Girls who touch the peen don't touch Bre the Dream."

The light goes green and she turns left.

While it's not fun hearing my fears confirmed (again), I can't say I don't get it. No, Rae never *said* she was into me, but she sure acted like she was. And losing to *peen*-possessing Coop sucked.

"So I take it *you've* never been with a guy?" I say.

"Oh, I have."

I just about choke on my tongue. "You have?"

"I've only been out for a couple years, babe."

Babe, huh? "And before that?"

"Before that, there were boys."

"But I thought you said you always knew—"

"Not all of us have the privilege of growing up with gay parents, J. My mom is the epitome of Black Church Lady."

"Oh."

"You know what I find funny about the whole thing?"

"What?" I say.

"Heaven is supposed to be this place of no sadness, right?"

"I guess?" I know nothing about this.

"Well, when I finally came out to her, she cried and went on this whole soliloquy about *'What am I gonna do if my baby ends up in hell?'* The whole time I'm just standing there thinking: If heaven is the place people say it is, won't it be impossible to be sad about the folks who 'didn't make it' there?"

Hmm. "Valid."

"And to think I wasted all that energy on *dudes*." She shakes her head.

The wind is roaring in my ears now but it doesn't keep me from feeling the awkward silence against my skin.

"So what was it like?" I finally say. "Being with boys, I mean?"

"Nothing."

"Huh?"

"It was like nothing," she says. "Awkward friction. Lots of grunting and smelliness and sweat from them, and I played along, but it was nothing. Being poked in the pelvis from the inside. Didn't feel good. Didn't feel bad. Just nothing."

"Interesting." Certainly wasn't *nothing* for me. That can't be good. "But did you, like . . . *feel* anything for these boys? Like emotionally?"

"Nah. Thought I did, but it was all pretty forced."

"Do you think that would've made a difference?"

"These questions are pretty specific." She looks at me with an eyebrow raised. "You tryna tell me something, J?"

"What? No!" Oh God. "I just . . . wondered if that would make a difference. In general." I can't even look at her right now. "Anyway. Sorry it was bad, I guess."

"It's cool." She shrugs. "Honestly, I think it didn't really help that I like being the dominant one." She tosses me a sidelong glance and a smirk.

I'd wipe away the sweat at my hairline, but the tension has gotten so thick, I can't lift my arms.

"And being with a girl?" I ask.

She turns to me. "Oh, there's no describing *that*, J."

"Oh."

"You'll find out one of these days," she says.

And she winks.

The conversation definitely causes a . . . shift. We spend the last ten minutes of the drive sneaking *super*-loaded glances at each other, and the following four hours laughing, flirting, and touching more than we have in over a year of friendship.

She holds my hand and tugs me around the party, introducing me to all of her friends. She gets me drinks ("No more than two, though.") and constantly checks to make sure I'm having a good time. We dance so close, I can feel her breath on my neck—and boy does *that* give me a shiver—and then when I say I need a rest, she pulls me into her lap and tickles me until I squeal like a piglet.

And despite knowing I'm not in the best mental *or* emotional space, it feels good letting go. Letting this thing between us breathe and bloom. By the time we get back to my house, I'm practically drunk on it (in addition to the Sapphisticated Screwdrivers I had), and I'm ready for—I *want*—it to take me over.

"You should come up," I say as Breanna pulls into my driveway. It's just after one.

The side eye she gives me could wither flowers. "Nope. Not happenin'."

"Come onnnnn, Bre. We've been having so much fun. I don't want it to be over yet." I poke my lip out. "Please?"

She shakes her head. "Nope."

"Breeeee!"

"I don't want to wake your dads, J." She stares up at the house.

I wave her off. "They're not even . . ."

Her eyes narrow.

Okay, so if I tell the truth—they're not home—she'll definitely refuse to come up because she'll know this is a trap.

"They're not light sleepers," I say.

She's not buying it.

"Bre, please don't leave me yet." I take her hand and trace circles on her palm. When she still doesn't bite, I lean forward a little so she can see down my shirt. *Bat bat bat*, go the eyelashes. "Pretty please come up?"

It's a good thing I'm tipsy right now. If I weren't, I'd be *pretty* disgusted with myself.

Her eyes flick down to my chest before she looks me in the eye, and I know I've got her then. "Fine, but only for a few minutes," she says.

She turns off the Jeep and we both get out, and then I

make the mistake of looking at Coop's window and see that his light is still on. It sobers me up a bit—what's he doing up so late?—but then I remember the way he ignored me when I waved at him this morning, the asshole.

"Come on." I take Bre's hand and lead her to my house.

When we get to my room—which she's never been inside before—I turn on the light, and she makes a beeline for Coop's chair.

"No, don't sit there!"

"Okay . . ."

Way to wig out within the first half a minute, Jupiter.

"Sorry, it's just . . ." I take my shoes off and kick them at the closet door. I can feel Freddie Mercury eyeing me disapprovingly, and I'm tempted to give him the finger. "It's a really old chair," I say. "It's gonna fall apart any day now, and I don't want you to be the person sitting in it when it does."

She lifts an eyebrow.

Mmmm, stealth approach obviously isn't going well, so . . . "I lied."

"About what?" She shoves her hands in the pockets of her navy chinos and looks around my (messy) room.

"About my dads," I say, taking a step closer. "They're not actually here."

She raises her hands and takes a few steps back. "J, this is *not* a good idea, dawg."

"Oh, come on, Bre. What about the past four hours?" I close the gap and stare at the perfect brown skin exposed by the open buttons of her shirt. She has a spattering of moles across her chest. "You think I don't notice the way you look at me sometimes? Why'd you think I was asking you those questions earlier, huh?"

I reach for her hand, and she pulls away. "Jupiter, you have *no idea* what you're doing."

"I know. That's why I want you to teach me."

Her eyes latch on to mine. Then drop to my lips, my neck, my chest . . .

She shakes her head. "Nah," she says. "Nope. Hell to the *no.*"

I hook my index fingers into her two front belt loops and tug her closer. "Breannaaaaa . . ." Our hips crash together.

She still has her hands in her pockets, but her jaw clenches.

When I grin—because let's face it, I can't help but grin; it's nice to feel powerful again—she looks at my mouth again and licks her lips.

Almost got her.

"I know you know I like you, Bre. Don't you like me back?"

"Of course I like you, Jupiter—"

"Then show me what you were saying you can't de-scribe." *I'm so gonna regret this shit tomorrow.*

She takes a deep breath. "This isn't a game, babe."

"I know." *But do I?*

She's still watching my mouth, so I grin.

"You need to be one hundred percent sure about this, Jupiter. You get that, right? This will change things between us. That buddy-buddy shit will be *done.*"

"I get it."

"I'm serious. There's no going back."

If anybody gets that, it's me. "Mmhmm." I pull her shirt out from where it's tucked into her pants and begin to loosen the buttons. It's a lot easier than it was with Coop.

She grabs my wrists and tucks my arms behind me as she pulls me up against her.

"You better be sure, Jupiter, 'cause once I get started—"

"Oh, I'm sure."

"You *sure* you're sure?" She runs a fingertip down the center of my chest and stomach and slips a hand under the hem of my shirt. It's like a lightning bolt to the lady parts, and the shock shoots out to my fingertips and down to my electric-blue toenails.

Where Coop was gentle, tentative about every moment of contact, Breanna is confident, aggressive. It makes me want her—the full lips, the soft skin, the gentle curves . . . all the things that make her different from him—that much more.

She unbuttons my shorts, and I'm ready to explode. I smile because it's such a *relief* to feel my body confirm what I've always known I wanted.

My fingertips float up to the edges of her ears and the buzzed sides of her frohawk, and she hums. I close my eyes and my head falls back just as she slips her hands inside the back of my shorts and puts her mouth up to my neck. "Say it," she breathes against me.

Can I do it? Can I commit to this?

"I'm sure," I say.

Then her mouth is on mine and I'm gone.

27

"BOHEMIAN RHAPSODY"

(*A Night at the Opera*, 1975)

♪ *Is this the real life?* ♪ *Is this just fantas—*

"Can it, Freddie. I didn't come in here to listen to you gloat."

I'm on my back in the Sanctuary listening to "Bohemian Rhapsody" on repeat as tears run down into my hair. Breanna has called and/or texted me seventeen times.

It's been eight and a halfish hours since she woke up on my belly, climbed out of my bed to put her clothes back on, and left my house at six in the morning. I hadn't slept a wink because (1) I was still a bit electrified from all the things she did to me (holy shit), and (2) from where I was lying on the bed, I could see Coop's window; his light stayed on until the sky turned that pre-sunrise orange-pink that looks like the rind of a Texas Star Ruby grapefruit.

"I tried not to compare them, you guys," I say to my

posters. "But *that* was the most futile thing ever. Bre's lying there on top of me with her naked breasts on my naked hips, and *all* I could think about was how she was soft where he was hard. She was vocal where he was quiet. She was assertive where he was gentle."

I roll to my side to look at Freddie.

"They looked, sounded, smelled, tasted, felt *so* different. It was more *physical* with her but more *emotional* with him. I know I'm supposed to like one more than the other, but . . . Right? Isn't that how this works? *Shit!*" I collapse onto my belly and cry some more.

"Now Breanna is sending me all these messages, and I can't reply because I'm, like, drowning in *guilt*. For one, did I not do to her what Rae did to me? I mean, it wasn't *exactly* the same thing because I didn't force myself on her, but I certainly didn't take her 'no' for an answer," I continue. "*And* I basically used her *and* lied to her by omission. I *knew* she wouldn't've been down with what we did if she'd known about my contact with 'the peen.' So what does that say about *me*?" UGH! "Yeah, I *knew* I liked girls, but was this not a 'Let me see what this is like in comparison' type thing? How big of a hypocrite can I be?"

Now choking, sputtering bawls.

"And the worst part is the whole thing made me realize how much I miss Coop. Like I miss him *so* much, and I'm totally not even talking about just the friendship part. That scares the *shit* out of me because I'm not supposed to feel this way about him! He's a *boy*, y'all!"

None of them responds.

"And okay, fine: I'd never been with *anyone* before him,

so I guess I couldn't've known I'd be into it . . . ," I say. "But what I can't figure out is if I liked it because I really *liked* it—which was definitely the case with Breanna—or if I liked it because I like *him*.

"Or is it both? Can one be gay, yet heterosexually demi-sexual? Would that make me 'homoflexible'? *What the hell is happening to me?!*"

♫ *Gotta leave you all behind and face the truth* ♫ . . .

"Do NOT even sing that to me right now, Freddie. Do you have any idea of the shit people will say if I pop up all *yeah, totes in love with my best dude friend* after spending all this time going on and on about recognizing lesbianism as a legitimate sexual identity and not just a 'phase'? It'll look like every word out of my mouth has been a lie.

"Besides, I don't even know what to call myself now. I know *you* identified as bisexual, but that doesn't feel quite right. Like there's this trans guy, Toby Faletti, who comes to Iridis meetings sometimes . . . I've always felt a little some-thing when he's around, but I never gave it much thought before. Now, though? I mean, trans people fit the binary, but it got me thinking: Who's to say I won't eventually be into someone who doesn't? I looked it up, and some places say *bi*sexual implies *bi*nary, but other places say it means 'attracted to two *or more* genders.' So I, for real, don't even know.

"And then there's *queer*, but does that just mean 'not straight'? I guess there's *pansexual*, but that feels *too* broad at this point. I don't want to pick a label and then wind up going through *this* again. . . . Can't I just like who I like? Why is this so complicated, you guys?"

I roll over. Take a deep breath. Think about what would happen if I just . . . came out. About Coop, I mean. *"You're sacrificing us for your stupid label"* still stings. Would it really be that bad if people knew how I felt about him?

Of course it would, goes that other voice in my head. "I can't do it, you guys. I can already hear the imbecilic shit those patriarchist morons at school will say if they know. They'll smirk at me in the halls and be all *'We knew you just needed a taste of the D.'* The very *idea* of Coop being treated like some conquering hero for 'showing the gay girl who's boss' is enough to make me want to burn the whole goddamn place dow—"

"Jupiter?" There's a knock. "You in there?"

Dad.

"Yes, I'm in here, Daddy."

"Can you come out here for just a sec?"

"Sure." I stand and cover the posters. Wipe my face, ignore the mirror—don't wanna see myself—and pull the door open.

Judging by how puffy and red *his* eyes are, Dad's been crying, too.

"Dad? You okay?"

"Just need a hug is all," he says.

"Did something happen?" I wrap my arms around his waist and squeeze the way I used to when I was small.

He sets his chin on my head and exhales. "You could say that. It's Troy Jr.'s thirtieth birthday."

"Whoa." Dad never talks about his other two kids. "That's wild."

"Mmhmm. Made the mistake of looking him up and trying to call. He, uhh . . . wasn't real happy to hear from me."

"Really?"

"Yep. I know I don't talk about my old life much, but the divorce was . . . difficult. Definitely hit Troy Jr. the hardest."

"Wow."

"And he doesn't know it because his mom told a different story, but I had no intention of going anywhere, Jupiter. When she found out about my attraction to men—because I kept it under wraps for a *very* long time—she couldn't handle it. Whole split was her idea."

I don't respond. He was going to *stay* married to a woman? My brain can't even comprehend it.

"Anyway. Sorry for dumping that on you."

"It's fine, Daddy."

"Figured you'd say that." He kisses the top of my head. "You're the perfect reminder of everything I gained."

He lets me go, and as I look up into his beautiful brown face, I want to tell him everything. The Rae stuff, the Coop stuff, the Breanna stuff—all of it.

But I can't, can I? For one, he's my *dad*. Yeah, we've had the sex talk, and he and Papi are super-open, but still. And what if he starts asking questions I can't answer?

"I'll leave you to it," he says. "Appreciate the hug." And he turns to leave.

But as soon as he steps into the hallway, the doorbell rings.

A few seconds later, Papi calls up the stairs: "Jupiter, Cuatro and Rae are here! I told them to come in, but they said they'd rather wait outside."

It's like a shot of adrenaline.

Dad pokes his head back into the room. "Everything okay?"

I barely hear him. Too busy tripping over my feet, trying to get shoes on. If Coop and Rae are together, Coop will actually smile and talk to me, even if it's all fake. I bolt from the room and down the stairs toward the front door.

God, when did I get so pathetic?

"Hey, guys!" I say, bounding onto the porch barefoot like a kicked puppy hoping for a head scratch.

"Hi, Jupes," Rae says.

Don't look at her mouth don't look at her mouth don't look at her mouth.

And then I see they're holding hands.

Kicked again.

"'Sup, girl?" Coop looks me over, and one corner of his mouth lifts.

And shit. I'm wearing his damn clothes. Like I always do when I'm alone these days.

Now Rae is checking me out, and the corners of *her* mouth are pulling down.

Is this sticky feeling of shame my comeuppance for being so shitty to people I supposedly care about? Maybe.

Nobody's saying anything.

The first question to rise in my throat is *Why didn't you guys come up?* but maybe that's a blessing in disguise. What if they could sense that Breanna had been there?

Rae clears her throat. "So, umm . . . I don't mean to pry,

268

but . . ." She looks at Courtney, and he gives her a nod to continue.

Seriously?

Rae takes a deep breath, then charges forward: "I noticed Breanna's Jeep leaving your driveway this morning and . . . well, she agreed to help my sister write a grant for something but hasn't been returning her calls. Do you know what's going on with her?"

Is she for real? "She's got a lot going on, so I'm sure it's an oversight—"

Wait.

"You said you saw her *leaving* my driveway?"

She peeks up at Courtney again. "Mmhmm."

The sun was rising when Bre left, so if Rae saw her go, she either came to Coop's *really* early—or stayed there all fucking night.

I look him dead in the eye, and he glares right back at me.

"Rae, I need to tell you something," I say, fully intending to put Courtney Cooper's ass on *blast*—and yeah, myself, too, by default, but I don't even care right now.

I look at her. Her eyes are wide. Expectant.

Back at him. His eyes are narrowed. A silent threat.

Back at her. She's getting nervous. Her eyes dart between me and him.

Back at him. He checks to make sure she's not looking, then mouths *I will never speak to you again.*

Dammit!

"Jupiter?" Rae says.

Now what do I do? It's not like he's speaking to me anyway, right? What harm could it really do? "I . . . umm . . ."

Now his eyes are pleading, not angry.

Shit.

What to say? What to say? "Breanna and I hooked up."

Why the hell did I say THAT?!

"Oh. Uhh—"

"You *what?*" Coop shouts.

Which actually does me a favor: now Rae's looking at *him* like he's lost it instead of me.

His eyes dart between us. "I mean—"

Come on, punk-ass. Say something. I know you want to . . .

Coop clears his throat and shifts his gaze toward the street.

Rae eyes him, clearly confused. But then she looks at my bracelet-less wrist, and then her face totally changes. I'd almost say she's . . . sad. "I mean, that's a good thing, right?" she says. "Finally found a girl who's worth it?"

"Yep," I say. And I cross my arms. "It was great. *Totally* worth the wait."

Out of the corner of my eye, I see Coop's jaw clench.

That's right, asshole.

"Well, I guess that's that!" Rae forces a smile. "We're happy for you, Jupes—"

"It's *Jupiter.*"

She pulls back like I smacked her. Which, I guess, in a way I did.

"I'll talk to Bre," I say. "Was there anything else?"

Rae looks at Courtney—who's now staring at the sky— and then back at me. "No," she says. "That's all."

"Great! I'll catch you guys later."

I spin on the ball of my foot and go inside without waiting for a response.

28

"SOMEBODY TO LOVE"

(*A Day at the Races,* 1976)

At 6:59 p.m. that following Thursday, I hear the doorbell from where I'm lying on my belly in the Sanctuary. My heart takes off—*FWOOOM*—like the hooves of a dozen horses thumping against the dirt of a derby track. "Shit, you guys, they're here," I say to my posters.

My sense of triumph in lording Breanna over Coop lasted twenty-seven minutes before the guilt set in. Then I spent the next three days playing happy when other people were around, but spending all my private time crying in my closet.

No clue how Rae did the fake-joy thing long-term.

I also wasn't very good at it because when I got home from school on day four, there was a holographic gift bag on my bed. The T-shirt inside had the word "Freddie" above the box from the periodic table that contains the atomic symbol *Hg.*

It was my first time smiling in weeks.

The card, though, caught me by surprise:

Baby girl:

    *Saw this shirt and thought you'd like it. Took me
a minute to figure out the meaning, but life can be
like that sometimes, wouldn't you say? :)*
    Love you, Sweet Pea.

                Sincerely,
                Mama Nee

*P.S. Y'all think y'all slick, but ya not. "Hash tag
stained birthday sheets," or whatever the hell it
is you kids say these days. Y'all better keep it
responsible.*

Once I managed to get beyond my mortification—which
involved a day of avoiding Mama Nee like patriarchal-ass
US History homework—I decided it was time to take action.

Now it's too late to turn back.

I roll over and sit up. Stare at my legitimately petrified
face in the mirror on the inside of the closet door. "Is this a
terrible idea?" I say. "It's the right thing to do, isn't it? Tell
me it's the right thing, Freddie."

The stairs creak and groan on the other side of the wall—
though Freddie stays mum—and I imagine the two pairs of
massive feet tromping up to lead me to my doom.

"Shit, shit, *shit*." I stand and go to the Sanctuary door. Take a deep breath. "Okay, Jupes, focus. What's to gain versus what's to lose. You can do this."

I step out of the closet just as there's a knock on my bedroom door.

Deeeeeep breath.

When I open it, Britain and Golly are standing on the other side. Britain is smiling tentatively and there's a twinkle of excitement in his blue eyes, and Golly is flat-out beaming. "Madam," he says as he takes a small bow.

Me? I'm wicked nervous. Especially considering what I plan to say. The only other times they've been inside this room—inside my house, even—they were with Coop.

But Coop isn't here. He went with Rae and Dr. Chin to check out some super-elite high school called Braselton Preparatory Academy. It's why I invited Britain and Golly over tonight.

And I made them promise they wouldn't tell him they were coming.

"Hey, guys, come on in. Sit wherever you want."

Golly makes a beeline for Coop's chair. Nestles right on down into it and pulls the lever so the recliner part kicks out.

I open my mouth to say something, but Britain pipes up first. "Golly, get your big ass outta Coop's chair, brah. You're defiling a holy place right now. Jupe-and-Coop *only*."

"Whatever. Jupiter just said sit wherever we want."

I guess I did say that, huh?

"She doesn't mind if I sit here, do you, Jupiter?" He stretches back and clasps his hands over his massive, brick-like midsection.

I clear my throat and smile. This has been an excellent icebreaker. "I kind of do, Golly, and my mistake for saying 'wherever.' No offense to you, of course, but I have to go with Britain on this one."

"See?"

"Oh." Golly sits up and pushes the leg extender down. Stands. I have no doubt his chiseled brown cheeks are hot to the touch.

"Told you, fool." Britain takes a seat on the floor with his back against the bed. "Blatant disrespect."

I'm laughing now. It feels really good.

"Here, you take the desk chair, and *I'll* sit in the La-Z-Boy," I say to Golly. "I'm going to turn on some music, if you fellas don't mind."

"You go right ahead, Miss Jupiter," Britain says.

I open my laptop and put my favorite playlist on shuffle. "Somebody to Love" comes pouring out of the speakers.

"Oh, *hell* yeah," Britain says. "Freddie and the dudes be takin' 'em to *church* on this song."

Wait . . . Britain knows Queen?

"Dawg, what are you *talking* about?" Golly says.

"Of course your uncultured yeti ass wouldn't be familiar with the best music to ever come outta the UK."

"Shut your tiny ass up, fool. I know who the Beatles are."

"The *Beatles*. Pffffft." Britain looks at me like *Do you believe this guy?* and I swallow a laugh.

"This is *Queen*, brah."

"Queen?"

"Yes, dummy."

Don't know if I've mentioned it, but I absolutely adore these two.

"You see the poster on Miss Jupiter's closet? That right there is Freddie Mercury," Britain goes on. "You know, I'm ninety-eight percent sure *the* queen would've knighted that guy had he not died so young, may his soul rest in peace."

I'm floored. "You really know your stuff, huh?"

He smiles at me. "My mom was born and raised in southwest London. Burb called Twickenham. She 'Queen-doctrinated' me from the womb."

"Wait, your mom is from England?" How did I not know this?

He laughs. "Why you think my name is Britain?"

"If only your little ass knew as much about not getting played as you do about this boy band—"

"Hush up, Godzilla."

I laugh as Britain flips Golly off while Golly smiles smugly, and then I take a seat in the La-Z-Boy, and we descend into an awkward silence. They're looking at each other to avoid looking at me, and then my precious Freddie—wanting to speed things along, I guess—goes ♫ *I just gotta get out of this prison cell* ♫ *Someday I'm gonna be free* ♫ . . .

I get it, Freddie. "So, guys. First of all, thank you for coming," I say.

They both turn to me. And both look nervous now.

"I'm sure you're wondering why I asked you here today. . . ."

Britain nods vigorously.

"Well, you've both offered me your friendship in recent

months, so I decided to take you up on it. Together." *I'm also desperate*, but I don't say that.

I look back and forth between them: Golly, the lovable giant, and Britain, who might have an issue with woman worship but is really very sweet.

Sure hope I can trust them. And that they'll help me.

"Coop and I slept together," I say.

You'd think I was Medusa the way they've turned to stone while staring at me.

"You mean slept as in *sleep*, right?" Britain says. "Because we know you do that all the time."

"Brit!"

"What, brah? Coop told us that shit a long time ago—"

"But Jupe's not supposed to know we know, you idiot."

"It's fine," I say. "That's not actually what I meant." I look down at my hands. "I'm saying we . . . had sex."

Complete and utter silence.

"More than once."

Still nothing.

"I think I might be in love with him."

When I look up, they're staring at each other and doing some kind of dude telepathy or something. Golly turns to me. "Sorry, can you say that again? We're not too sure we heard you right."

"*Ugh*." I put my hands in my hair. "Okay, so I'm telling you guys this because (1) you're obviously trustworthy if Coop spends so much time with you, and (2) of the people I can even remotely consider *true friends*, you're the only two I haven't shit all over in the past month."

They look at each other again, but neither of them speaks.

"Before I go on, I need *both* of your words that you will neither mention *any* of this to Courtney Aloysius Cooper the Fourth—"

"Aloysius?" Britain says. He looks at Golly. "Coop's middle name is *Aloysius?*"

"Seriously, dawg?" Golly gestures to me.

"My bad, Miss Jupiter," Britain says. "Do go on."

"Okay . . . so I need you to promise me you won't tell Coop *anything* I'm about to tell you. Not a word of it leaves this room."

"Done," Golly says.

"I also need your word that you will neither judge me *nor* view my forthcoming confessions as support of harmful notions about the legitimacy of sapphism."

"Say *what* about sapphires?" Golly asks.

"She's asking us to promise we won't look at what she's about to say as evidence that supports negative stereotypes about lesbians." Britain looks at me.

"Exactly," I say.

"We promise." Britain smiles. "Rae taught me that word."

"And promise not to judge me," I say.

"We won't judge you, Miss Jupiter," Britain says.

"Promise?"

"We promise," Golly says.

"Okay. So, long story as short as I can make it . . ." Man, am I really going to tell them *all* of it? Guess I kinda have to, don't I? "Rae kissed me on New Year's Eve—"

"Wait, for *real?*" Britain says.

"Yes. For real. And despite knowing she probably didn't have actual *feelings* for me, I fell pretty hard for her, but just before I could tell her, she told me she was in love with Coop."

"Damn," Golly says.

"I knew Rae and Coop would wind up together once she told him how she felt, so I decided to have *sex* with Coop so that no matter what happened between the two of them, his first time would be with me."

They both draw back.

"Thing is, I enjoyed it a *little* more than I expected to."

Golly's eyebrow rises.

"As in I went back almost every night for a week."

"Well, damn, Coop," Britain says.

I shoot him a look that could wither roses.

"Ignore the tiny imbecile, Jupiter," Golly says. "Please continue."

"As I was *saying*"—I glare at Britain again—"this went on for a week. It really only stopped because Rae finally told Coop how she felt. I tried to cover my ass by being like *'That's awesome, you should date her,'* but when he found out I'd known all along, he cut me off. He acts like everything's fine when we're all together, but Coop hasn't really spoken to me in almost a month."

"A *month*?" From Golly.

"Twenty-five days, eight hours, and"—I squint at the clock—"thirty-six minutes, to be exact."

They lock eyes again, both clearly shell-shocked.

"That's the other part: the longer he cold-shoulders me, the more I realize the main reason I kept going back was because of the *feelings*," I say. "I won't pretend to know the ins and outs of human sexuality, but that whole week, I couldn't sleep or eat or think, and the only time I felt right was when I was with Coop."

"That's pretty deep," Golly says.

"Well, it freaked me out because, hello, Coop is a dude. I'm not supposed to be into those."

"Fair point."

"So I hooked up with Breanna." I cover my face.

"The *college* girl?" Brit says.

I nod.

"Damn, Jupiter. You've gotten more play in the past month than Baby Brit has in his whole high school career."

"Hey, fuck you, brah."

Golly giggles in his little baby laugh.

So do I, actually.

"Sorry about the foul language, Jupiter," from Brit. "You were saying?"

I smile. "Well, the encounter with Breanna was *fucking* mind-blowing"—I wink at Britain—"but it just, like . . . like it wasn't the same as with Coop, you know?"

"We don't but we'll certainly take your word for it." Golly grins.

I smile again. I've said it before, but it bears repeating: I really, *really* love these two.

"After she and I were done, all I could think about was how the *emotional* bond and all the friendship and attachment were missing with her. I couldn't stop thinking about Coop, you guys. If you ever tell anybody this, I'll deny it, but I spent *hours* sobbing in my closet because I was so torn up missing him."

"Aww, that's sweet." Britain's beaming like he struck gold.

"So . . . and I hope I'm allowed to ask this," Golly says. "But does this mean you're like . . . *bi* now?"

My eyes drop to my hands in my lap. "I'm, uhh—well, I'm not really sure."

"Huh?"

I sigh. "You guys know Toby Faletti?"

"Sure do," Britain says. "Had a thing for him in fourth grade when he was Talia. Good-lookin' dude, too."

Golly shakes his head. "You not supposed to use the deadname, Brit."

"Oh." Brit turns as red as Freddie Mercury's famous queenly cape. "My bad. Won't happen again, I swear." And he crosses himself.

I smile. "Well, I think he's really good-looking, too," I say. "Might even have a bit of a crush."

"Okay . . . ," Golly says.

"And I dunno. Being attracted to someone not cis makes me think I could be attracted to someone nonbinary. Which is why I'm not sure 'bisexual' is the right word, at least for me. Not that there's anything *wrong* with bisexuality. I've just seen different . . . definitions, I guess, and—I just don't know at this point. It's a weird place to be."

Golly nods. "This shit's hella interesting."

"Yeah, well . . . *identity crisis* isn't an exaggeration," I say.

"Damn, I didn't even think of that," says Brit. "Sorry, Miss Jupiter."

"Ah, it's fine. I'm working through it."

They both nod.

"I grew up with gay parents, and I've always known I like girls, so I just assumed I was a lesbian, you know?"

"Makes sense to me," Golly says.

"This Coop thing was jarring. And there's a part of me that's still uncomfortable because loving him seems too easy. My dads have only been married for a few years because before then it wasn't *legal*. How dare I fall for a boy and just *avoid* all the shit my gay friends have to deal with?"

"Wow," Brit says. "Shit's deep."

"Yeah. But I do love Coop, and I think that needs to take precedence," I go on. "I'd be lying if I said I didn't still feel something for Rae, but how dumb was I, you know? Making it seem like Coop was just some fling? We said some pretty intense stuff to each other all those nights, and of *course* he meant every word. Yes, when the whole Rae thing came up, the first words out of his mouth made it seem like he was focused on the sex, but like how much of a jackass am I for even allowing myself to latch on to that? Of *course* Courtney Cooper *loved*-me loved me."

"He's definitely been madly in love with you for as long as *we've* known him," Golly says.

"We made fun of him for it, too."

I shake my head. "I know he's with Rae now, and I wouldn't do anything to sabotage that. But I wanna make it *clear* to him that he's more important to me than my . . . reputation, I guess."

They don't respond.

"I'm sick of lying to everyone, myself most of all, and I want him to know I meant every word of what I said while we were . . . uhh . . ."

"In the *moment*?" Britain makes his eyebrows dance.

I laugh. "Yes, that. Though I also want to be perfectly

clear about who I am and how—or even *if*—I choose to identify for the sake of *me*, you know? Because isn't that really what it comes down to?" Man, it feels good to say that aloud.

Golly looks at Britain, who's looking at Golly, and they nod at each other. Then they stand, wrap their arms around each other's shoulders, and beckon me over. "Come huddle up with us, Miss Jupiter," Britain says.

Once their arms are draped over my shoulders, and mine are across their mid-backs, they both lean down low.

"So Jupiter needs a game plan," Golly says, and he starts kind of moving from left to right. When Britain joins this swaying motion, I get pulled into it, too, just because they're both so much bigger than me.

"I actually think I already have one." *Sway sway sway.*

"That's that shit I'm talkin' about," Britain says. "An *independent* woman."

I laugh. And sway. It's kinda fun.

"So hit us, Jupiter," Golly says. "What's the plan, and how can we help?"

I take a deep breath—they both smell really nice.

And I tell them exactly what I want to do.

29

"WE ARE THE CHAMPIONS"
(News of the World, 1977)

The next time the doorbell rings—6:11 Monday morning—
I'm in the Sanctuary again, but I'm ready to go this time.
I've had "We Are the Champions" on repeat since I got up,
and I can picture Freddie in his black-and-white spandex
jumpsuit with his hairy chest all exposed, pouring his heart
out of his vocal cords into the microphone on the end of his
bottomless mike stand.

It's magic.

I've got on Coop's practice jersey from ninth grade
(which fits me like a glove), these charcoal-gray ripped
jeans that he loves, and the low-top Chuck Taylors covered in Queen lyrics that he had custom-made for my last
birthday. "Well, you guys," I say to the posters, "I guess this
is goodbye." I give each of them a kiss, slide the clothes back
over them, then step out of my closet and pull the door
shut behind me.

When I open the front door, Britain and Golly look on the verge of bursting. Saturday night, the team won the state basketball tournament, and Coop was named MVP. We're definitely going into this whole thing on a good note, and nobody—Rae included—will question my choice of outfit. "Milady, your chariot awaits," Britain says, gesturing toward Golly's massive truck.

"Dawgs!"

Shit.

Golly and Britain make panicked eye contact and then look at me as Coop trots over from his house.

I pull the front door closed and we start making our way to the truck. "I *swear* he's not usually awake this early," I mumble. "Play it cool, play it cool."

Coop makes a beeline for me and hugs me around the waist with one arm. He kisses my forehead without looking me in the eye, though he does look over my outfit. "I got your message about not needing a ride," he says, "but you didn't tell me it's because *these* assholes were picking you up." I can hear the spiked barbs at the tips of his words, but I don't think Brit or Golly is any the wiser.

"And why wouldn't we be?" Golly says with indignation. "For your information, *brah*, Miss Jupiter is our friend, too."

Coop looks down at me and lifts an eyebrow.

And my heart totally melts all over the sidewalk.

"Umm . . ." *Oh my God, has it really gotten this bad?* "They're helping me set up for the Iridis meeting this morning."

Both of Coop's brows shoot up now, like *Oh, really?* And

then they pull down, and he pokes his (delicious-looking) bottom lip out. "You didn't ask *me* to help you set up for Iridis."

Is he serious right now? It's times like these I wanna smack him and smooch him simultaneously.

"Quit being a baby." Golly shoves him.

"Yeah," Britain says. "Go get your girlfriend, you tutor stealer."

Britain extends his elbow, and I drape my arm inside it and let him lead me around to the passenger side. Once he opens the door, he gives me a boost to help me up into the truck and then I slide to the center of the bench seat and set my book bag at my feet. Golly's just made it inside, but before Britain hops in, he turns to Coop. "By the way, we know Miss Jupiter's birthday is this weekend. She turned *us* down because she said it's 'tradition' to hang out with *you*." He points at Coop. "We had some dope shit planned, so you better not let her down."

Once he's got the door closed, I turn to him and laugh. "You are awful," I say as we back into the street. "I can't believe you totally lied to his face." Britain and Golly didn't plan some "dope shit" that I turned down. I called and asked if they wanted to do something because I figured Coop would shirk our tradition, since he's still pissed at me.

"He deserves it, man," Britain says. Coop's still standing in my driveway with his mouth open. "Actin' like everything's all hunky-dory. Golly, did you see his eye twitch when I said that birthday thing? Bet he won't be blowin' you off now, Miss Jupiter. There is no shutting down the competitive nature of an adolescent dude. Especially if his closest homeboys are involved."

We wind up blasting the 1981 version of *Queen's Great-est Hits* and belting "We Are the Champions"—Britain's got it on his phone—during the twelve-minute drive to school, but as we pull into the student lot, my stomach twists. "Am I really ready for this, guys?"

"You're the only one who can answer that, Jupiter," Golly says. "Just know me and Brit are with you the whole way."

"You got the peace offering and everything?" Brit asks.

I look down at my book bag. "I do." Inside there's a bag of Boomchickapop kettle corn, a bottle of pineapple-coconut water, a can of Axe body spray in Peace scent, and a card Britain and Golly helped me with. It says *I Admit That What I Did Was a Technical Foul, but Please Don't Eject Me from Your Game.* "You guys remember the plan, right?"

"Yep," Britain says. "I intercept Rae, and the Golly Brown Giant over there accompanies Coop to the locker, where he'll find your gift."

"Right."

"Everybody good?" Golly says, peeking at his watch.

I take a deep breath. Look up into the faces of these wonderful boys who have been better friends to me over the past few days than I've been to *my* friends in almost two months. "I'm ready, you guys."

"Good."

Once in the building, we head straight to the Family and Consumer Science classroom that hasn't been used—outside of our Iridis meetings—since the school was built eight years ago. It's already filling up. Usually there are about twenty-five people, but I could swear there are more this morning.

Coop and Rae come in and sit closer to the front of the

room than I'd expressly like for them to, but what can I do? Britain's beside me, and Golly's manning the door as people continue to file in. I glance at the clock—three minutes until he closes it and I have to face the music.

Rae, who's all snuggled up under Coop and holding the massive brown hand at the end of the arm wrapped around her thin shoulders (ugh!), smiles up at me and gives a little wave.

I will not lose my shit. I will not. I will *NOT* . . .

"Britain, I think I'm gonna lose my shit," I say as I turn and grab his upper arm. I squeeeeeeze.

"You won't," he whispers.

"But how do you *know*?"

He puts his hands on my shoulders and looks into my soul-ish innards, it seems, with those piercing baby blues. "I know because you are Jupiter Got-Damn Sanchez, and you *own* this shit, all right? You *do* this damn thing."

Good at pep talks, that Britain.

I hear the classroom door close, and Golly appears beside us. "It is time." He puts his hands together and bows.

"All right," I say.

"Hands in, break on three," from Britain. We stack our hands super-fast and then: "One . . . two . . . three . . ." and we all whisper "Break!"

"You *got* this, Miss Jupiter."

As Brit and Golly go to their seats to my right and left, facing the group like they're my bodyguards or something, I take a moment to close my eyes and collect myself with my back to the room. When I turn around, Courtney Cooper is staring at me.

Hard.

Rae, of course, looks like a kid on Christmas and is totally oblivious.

Won't be that way for long, though . . .

"Hi, guys! Thank you all so much for coming this morning." I want to run, but I wave instead. *Am I really about to do this?*

I clear my throat. "So today's meeting is going to be different," I say. "More . . . personal." I can't help it: I look at Coop.

For the first time in months, I've got his full attention.

I take a deep breath and charge on. "So over the course of the year, we've talked about the importance of recognizing *all* sexual identities as legitimate," I say. "We've discussed how oftentimes, when a girl comes out as lesbian, she's not taken seriously due to the notion that girls who claim to like girls are 'going through a phase' or can be swayed by 'finding the right guy.' This is especially true for girls like myself who don't take on a more masculine presentation."

There are some nods around the room.

So far so good.

"Well, over the past five weeks, a lot has *changed* in my life, and—well . . ."

I take another very deep breath, but I don't think anybody else in the room is breathing at all. It takes everything in me not to look at Coop now.

"Okay, before I go on, please note: what I'm about to say in no way diminishes what we've talked about in the past, nor does it validate that 'just a phase' thing I mentioned earlier. Life is a journey without a map, and as such, we'll *all* encounter twists and turns that force us to correct our course or change directions entirely."

I can feel the tension creep into the room and slip down over different faces and shoulders I see in the crowd.

Here goes . . .

"With all that said, I, Jupiter Charity-Sanchez, am here today to announce that . . . well, that I'm dropping my label."

The murmuring begins. Coop's eyes are burning a hole in the side of my face, just *willing* me to look at him.

But I can't. Not yet.

"Hold on, y'all," Golly says. "She's not done yet." The room goes quiet again.

"The truth is, I've been learning a lot about myself lately, and at this point, I don't feel like any of the labels really *fit* me. I thought I was a lesbian, and yes, I still like girls. But I've come to realize girls aren't *all* I like."

"So you're saying you like boys now?" someone asks.

I clear my throat, and my eyes drop. "I mean, I definitely like *a* boy—"

"So you're bi, then," from someone else. "It's fine if you *say* it, Jupiter. I'm bi, too. It's nothing to be ashamed of."

I shake my head. "It's not that cut-and-dried for me right now," I say. "I'm still figuring things out."

"What's there to *figure ou*—"

"Did you not hear her say no labels fit? If she doesn't wanna use one, she doesn't have to. It's *her* life. She can love whoever the hell she wants to."

That would be Courtney Cooper.

He and I make eye contact, and I blush and look at the ground. Between my outfit, his outburst, and my red face, I have no doubt most of the people in this room now know *exactly* which boy I "like."

So much for discretion.

Once I pull it together—and I cannot bear to look at Rae right now—I take one last breath to say my final piece. "For anyone who's interested, Britain, Golly, and I are hosting a special meeting this Thursday to talk about different sexual identities, including bisexuality"—I look at my dissenter—"and some of the negative stereotypes attached to them."

"Same time, same place," Golly says.

The ten-minute bell rings, and everyone begins to gather their things. "Thank you all so much for listening to what I had to say. We appreciate you joining us and hope you have a great day."

I turn around as everyone heads to the exit so no one will see me burst into tears. I'm crying, but I have no idea how I actually *feel*.

A pair of arms wraps around my waist from behind, and judging by how far above the floor my feet wind up, it's Golly. Britain comes to join the hug from the front. "Miss Jupiter Sandwiiiich!" he says. I exhale and laugh.

Then a throat clears, and they set me down.

Oh boy.

After taking a series of woosah-breaths, I force myself to rotate and face Courtney Aloysius Cooper IV.

He smiles.

I can't take it. Eyes drop to my shoes.

"Well played, Sanchez."

"Oh, shut up."

He laughs.

"Where's Rae?" I take the tissue Golly is holding out to me and wipe my eyes and nose.

He looks over his shoulder at the last few people trickling out the door. "I told her to go on ahead. I think she needed a minute."

"I'll go find her," Britain says, and then he looks at Golly. "Phase two, brah. Don't forget."

As he trots off, Golly shakes his head. "That guy has absolutely no concept of subterfuge."

Coop laughs again.

"Well, since it's out there now, Coop, let's go to your locker so you can 'find' Jupiter's peace offering," Golly says.

"All right, let's go," Coop replies without taking his eyes off me. He's staring at me and I want him to stop because it's burning me to the ground. I'm already a kicked-wide, open-souled mess; would prefer not to add *hot and bothered* to the mix, especially since—hello!—he still has a girlfriend. "Guess we'll catch you on the flip side, Jupes." He winks and tugs my earlobe.

Melllllltiiiiing.

He and Golly head for the exit as the five-minute bell rings, and I go and drop down into the sad, unused chair behind the teacher's desk. Highly doubt I'll make it to first period this morning.

"Hey, Jupe?" Coop is standing just inside the door.

"Yeah?"

"I'm really proud of you," he says.

And then he's gone.

30

"ANOTHER ONE BITES THE DUST"

(*The Game,* 1980)

Things with Breanna go a lot better than I anticipate. The worst thing she says during my lengthy coffee shop apology after school is "You suck, J. Really, *really* bad. Hope you know that."

Is she pissed when I tell her about Courtney? Quite. She says she suspected I had more-than-friendship feelings for him, but when I threw myself at her "like a live-ass grenade," she thought she was wrong. "You were *really* into what we were doing, J. Dunno that I've ever been with a girl as *enthusiastic* as you were." She looks me over a little lasciviously when she says this, which sets off a fireworks show worthy of Times Square on New Year's Eve below my belly button.

When I get to Rae's that evening, however, *she* doesn't say a word as she opens the door to let me in. By the time we reach her room, the silence feels rabid, like any second it'll attack and fry my central nervous system and I won't be able to speak.

So I break it. "Hi."

"Hey," she says, sitting down on the bed with her back against the headboard.

And that's it.

I take a peek around because there's a chance that after tonight, I'll never be invited into this room again. "Guess I'll jump right in, then?"

"That's probably best."

Ouch. "Mind if I sit?"

"Go ahead." She pulls her knees up to her chest to make room for me.

I ease myself down and take a deep breath. "Rae, I fell for you," I say. "Hard."

Her eyes go wide, but she doesn't respond.

"And I know there's no going back, but there's some stuff I need to tell you in order to move forward."

She nods.

"Like Thanksgiving. I know you don't remember, but after you asked to kiss me, I had to take a cold shower."

"Oh." She blushes.

"And when you *did* kiss me, although I was mad—*am* mad—because you took something I can't get back, I shoved you away because it made my feelings too real, and I didn't know how to handle it," I say. "I thought you were unattainable. I could see how you and Coop looked at each other, and when I learned that he told *you* something he never told *me*, I just . . . shut down."

She nods. "That's fair."

"I felt bad after because I overreacted. And I really didn't want to lose you as a friend—"

"You didn't overreact," she says.

"What?"

"Your reaction was perfectly reasonable, Jupiter. I shouldn't've overridden your agency, as I've heard you put it. And I'm sorry."

Oh. "Okay."

There's a loaded pause.

"Sorry for interrupting," she says. "You were saying?"

Shit, what *was* I saying? I'm so thrown by her apology, I can't even remem—

"You didn't want to ruin the friendship?"

Ah. "Yes. So I was trying to keep myself in check, but we were spending all this time together because Coop had basketball. And every time I looked at you, my mind would replay that kiss. So my feelings just took over."

Her eyes drop to her knees.

"I kept thinking about what you said the night you kissed me, and after the whole Carl's Closet thing, you got *super*-affectionate with me. So I started to wonder if we *could* be something more. That's what I planned to tell you the day *you* told *me* how you felt about Coop."

Now she won't look up at all.

Might as well go for it now . . .

"Coop and I had sex, Rae."

Her head snaps up. "You *what*?"

I sigh. "I'm not proud of what I did—and I assure you it was *me*. Coop had no idea you liked him." I gulp. "You hadn't told him yet."

She doesn't respond, but she doesn't need to: her face is so red, if I didn't know the cause, I'd be worried about her health. "It's no excuse, but I panicked when you told me how you felt about him because I *knew* you guys would wind up together. I could see it. And yeah, I was pissed at you for leading me on, so that was part of it—"

"So *this* is what dropping your label is about."

I swallow. "Yeah."

"You're into Courtney, then."

Ugh. "Yeah. I am."

"Wow."

There's that menacing silence again.

"I don't plan to *do* anything about it," I say. "I've done some shitty things, but that's a whole other level. My announcement this morning was for *me.*"

She just sits there. Blinking.

"Anyway, I wanted to tell you that I'm sorry. What I did was wrong, and I hope one day you'll be able to forgive me, but I'll give you some space."

I stand to leave, hoping against hope that she'll say *something.*

She doesn't.

"I—umm . . ." And I force myself to look at her before pulling the door open. "I know it's hard to believe considering everything I've done, but you really do mean a lot to me, Rae. Coop's lucky to have you."

I watch her chest rise and fall as she sighs, and then she shifts her gaze to her lace-curtained bedroom window.

Guess that's my cue.

I leave.

By the time I wake up on my big one-seven four days later, I feel like I've aged a decade. The fragrance of my traditional birthday breakfast hits my nose—French toast *tres leches–*style, bacon, fried plantains, and scrambled eggs smothered in sofrito—but all I can think about is how much has changed. In a few minutes Papi and Dad will call me down to eat breakfast and open presents, and I'm not sure if Coop will be there. He and I are cool again, but we haven't really seen each other or spoken a whole lot because . . . well, Rae.

Whom I haven't heard from in five days.

I sigh and sit down at my desk to open my laptop—

There's a loud bump on the stairs and somebody yells, *"Damn, brah, could you watch where you put them gargantuan-ass phalanges?!"*

Of course it makes me smile.

My bedroom door opens and Coop strides in carrying a small wood table with bowed legs and a cardboard box sitting on top of it. "Happy birthday, my little Jupey-Jupe!" he crows, stopping to smile as the room fills with the fragrance of Axe Peace body spray.

"Could you not stand *right* in front of the door?" Golly says from behind him. "This thing is heavy. Britain's tiny ass can't keep up, so this horn keeps hittin' me in the chin!"

"Yeah, brah. And that Axe you bathed in got *me* 'bout to pass out. Did you have to use the whole damn can?"

Coop rolls his eyes and carries the table and box over to the corner near my window. That's when Britain and Golly waddle in carrying—

"What even *is* that?"

Coop sets the table down, crosses his arms, and rocks back on his heels. "*That* is a Pyle Pro turntable. With horn. It looks like a vintage phonograph, but plays vinyl, cassette tapes, CDs, *and* MP3s." Britain and Golly stumble over and deposit the turntable (!!!) on the bowlegged stand. "Good ol' Freddie Mercury in every form!" Coop continues. "Speaking of which . . ." He brings over the box he was carrying and sets it on the floor beside me. Freddie and the guys look up at me from the perfectly square cardboard cover of *The Game*.

I know my eyes are as big as the Queen coasters Dad has downstairs. "Are these—"

"All originals. Some of them signed."

There's no way. "But *how*?"

"I went to donate some clothes to Carl's Closet, and he literally handed me the box. Which was kind of a *moment* for me: *the* Carousel Carl, scientist of circles and cycles, handing me a box of circular objects that work by spinning on a turntable? Man." He shakes his head. "Anyway, he told me somebody left it with a bag of men's suits, and asked if I wanted to go through it. 'I know some of you kids are getting into vinyl these days, right?' is what he said. Shit was wild."

I don't know what to say. "Wow."

"There's a card in the box that you can open later."

"Later?"

"Yep. Hey, dawgs, thanks for your help. We'll see you tomorrow, all right? Cool. Goodbye!"

Golly glares at Coop. "You better be lucky we love Jupiter, fool."

"Right, brah," Britain chimes in. "'Ol' ungrateful ass."

"Fellas, fellas," from Coop. "Can we not inundate this amazing young woman with our masculine vitriol on her birthday?"

Britain sucks his teeth, and Golly rolls his eyes. "Happy birthday, Jupiter," Golly says. "Let us know if this punk-ass steps out of line."

"Yeah, asshole," Britain says to Coop. "You better make our friend feel like she's experiencing the glory of a serein today."

"The glory of a *what?*" Coop says.

"A *serein*, brah. It's a fine tropical rain falling from a cloudless night sky." Britain closes his eyes and stretches his arms out like he's standing in the midst of one. "Rae taught me that shit."

Golly smacks his forehead and then shoves Britain toward the door. They pull it shut as they leave, and Coop drops down into the La-Z-Boy.

He's just sitting in the chair with his eyes closed and a slight smile tugging at his lips—I swallow and say, "Thanks for the gift," and he opens his eyes to look at me. And grins.

Can't even deal. I turn to face my laptop. "I'm really glad you're here," I say. "Wasn't sure how this birthday thing was gonna work with you having a girlfriend and all."

"That reminds me . . ." The La-Z-Boy groans as he shifts, and then he taps me on the shoulder and hands me a pink envelope. It smells like Rae's teenybopper perfume, and the blurred vision from my instantly wet eyes catches me off guard. I look up at Coop—who seems to be avoiding eye contact—and swallow super-hard before gently opening it.

There's a card inside. The front says *Best Friends Are*

Like Sweaty Thighs, and when I open it and read the punch line—*Thick or thin, they stick together*—I laugh and cry simultaneously.

Inside the card are a receipt for a yearly subscription to *Feminist Monthly,* a pressed violet, and a letter folded into the shape of a rabbit:

April 30

Dear Jupiter,

First, it is my genuine hope that this card isn't overtly offensive. Out of all the available options, it was the most apt expression of how I feel about our friendship.

I know we haven't spoken since your confession of sorts, but that's largely because I haven't known what to say. The things you told me . . . well, it was a lot to process, as I'm sure you can imagine.

I'm still pretty pissed at you (and Courtney, for that matter), but I do feel I need to make a series of confessions and issue an apology of my own. To keep matters brief: I really did like you, like you. I've apologized for kissing you without your consent, but I do want you to know that I meant it. It was a new thing for me, being attracted to a girl—and I truly do think I'm bisexual. While I was apprehensive because I'd never experienced anything like it, I did want our interactions to . . . blossom beyond the bounds of friendship. Yes, I was also grappling with feelings for

299

Courtney, but it wasn't until after you shut me down that I even considered him a possibility.

All that said, I was using you. After my feelings for Courtney crystallized, I clung to you for the sake of hiding from him. When you explained what you'd really come to tell me the day I professed my feelings for him, I felt culpable because you're right: I did lead you on.

I'm sorry.

I'll go ahead and tell you that things will probably be tense for a little while, but I do think we'll eventually get back to seminormal functioning. A lot's about to change (Courtney will fill you in, I'm sure), but know that you truly were the best friend I ever had, and despite this mini mutual treason (though, not that we're keeping score, yours was WAY bigger), I wouldn't be who I am today if not for your friendship. I do hope that in time, we'll get back to thick-as-thieves (or thighs, if you ask this card), but not under false pretenses from either of us this time.

Meanwhile, I hope you have a prodigiously wonderful birthday! I'll see you at dinner tonight and we can hug and all that if you're okay with it.

I love you very much (in a strictly platonic way!).

Sincerely,
Rae Evelyn Chin

My face is officially a five-spout faucet: tears pouring from both eyes, snot flowing, bit of drool running down, the whole deal.

Coop goes to grab my box of tissues from the bedside table, but he doesn't say a word, and I'm thankful. It makes me cry a little harder because the fact that he knows exactly what I need right now makes it clear that he and I are back to *us*—

And with *that* I have to leave the damn room because—hello—bittersweet much?

He's got his eyes closed and his hands clasped over his stomach when I come back. It stings to see him sitting like that and know I can't really sit with him the way I want to. "Yeah, this is gonna take some getting used to now that everything's out in the open." I plop down in my desk chair.

"Hmm?"

"You know. You and Rae being like . . . *together.*"

"Oh, that reminds me . . ." He pauses. Waits till I turn. "Since you've got your laptop open and I have no idea how to use that turntable thing . . ." He looks down at his hands, then back up at me. His eyes are shimmering. "I need you to cue the Jam, Jupes."

I turn back to the laptop and am just about to click on the little triangle icon when the *meaning* of what he said hits me. It's been eight months since the last time this happened, after all.

I spin around to face him. I'm sure my face looks like he just told me he got her pregnant.

"She called and dumped me right after you left her house on Monday," he says.

Monday?! "You mean you've been single this whole week?"

"Yep. Her dad's been driving her to school and everything."

Which *I* wouldn't've known because I've been riding with Britain and Golly to avoid causing unnecessary tension in the car with Coop and Rae.

I put my face in my hands. "Oh my God, I totally ruined another one of your relationships."

"I mean, I *did* spend the duration of said 'relationship' lying by omission."

"Fair point."

He pauses, and then: "I'm sure she was also getting sick of the fact that I wouldn't really kiss her."

Say whaaa? "Huh?"

"Well . . ." Our eyes meet, then he looks away. "Can't believe I'm telling you this."

He pauses again.

"Spit it out, Coop!"

Now he sighs. "Well, I only kissed her once. She tried to kiss *me* pretty early on, but I stopped her. Told her I didn't wanna 'move too fast' or some shit like that."

Can't help but grin. "You ass."

"But then when you hooked up with Breanna and were all *gloaty* about it—" He shakes his head. "We'll just say things mighta gotten a little hot and heavy when Rae and I were alone that night."

"Oh." *That* hurts way worse than I anticipated.

"Didn't go *too* far. I knew I was only doing it to get back at you, and I couldn't stop thinking about what your dad or mine would say if either knew. So stopped before we reached that point of no return. But yeah. Haven't really touched her at all since."

"Wow."

"We prolly only lasted *this* long because she was still under the impression I was some ultra-pure virgin."

Talk about loaded eye contact. Now *I* have to look away.

"Well, sorry another girl dumped you because of me," I say.

"Ah, it was for the best. She's going to that fancy prep school next year and will be in Nicaragua for most of the summer with her dad and sister, so we wouldn't have seen much of each other over the next couple months anyway."

"Interesting."

"So you gonna play the Jam or what?" He relaxes back into the chair.

"I need to tell you something first." I take a deep breath. "You weren't my first kiss."

His eyebrows shoot up.

And then he looks at the floor, but not before I catch the hurt all over his face. "Oh," he says.

"It was Rae."

His head lifts.

"She kissed me on New Year's Eve."

"Wow. That explains a lot."

"Yeah."

He clears his throat. "Did you like it?"

I should've known this question was coming. "I didn't like that she just *did* it," I say. "That's why you have the entire bracelet. Yours was the first kiss I actually wanted."

He gulps. "I see."

I sigh. The whole thing is still bittersweet. Not sure if that'll ever go away.

"Jupe, can I ask you something?"

"Hmm?"

"It's really none of my business, and you don't have to answer. . . ." There goes that Adam's apple. Bobbing like one of those red-and-white ball thingies on a fishing line. "I just know if I don't ask, it'll eat away at my internal organs."

I roll my eyes. "Ask the question, Coop."

"Exactly how far did you go with Breanna?"

Oh.

"You *really* wanna know?"

"No . . . Yes?" He takes a deep breath. "Mayb—"

"We went all the way, Coop."

"Ah."

"It was kind of terrible, though?" No idea why I'm saying this. It's not the least bit true.

"Mmmm, *terrible* is pretty strong for a person with your novice level of sexual experience."

"Oh, shut up."

He laughs. Stares at me.

Annnnnnnd I can't take it. "Okay, so I'm totally lying," I say. "It wasn't terrible. It was actually phenomenal. That girl *definitely* knows a thing or two about what to do with her—"

"Yeah, stop. Zero interest in hearing the ins and outs of your girl/girl sexcapades."

"Only happened once."

"Still."

"Anyway, physically, it wasn't terrible." I pause, and there's that loaded eye contact again. "But it wasn't like with you."

He smiles. "You know, this is normally where'd I'd make

304

some 'friggin' patriarchal' joke to rile you up, but I'll refrain because that might be the nicest thing you've ever said to me, Jupiter."

"I hate you."

He stares at me for a few seconds. Grinning. Eyes sparkling. "I love you, too," he says.

More staring, smirking, nonverbal communicating, a kind of magic zipping through the air between us. "I can't have a boyfriend yet," I say. "Girlfriend, either. Any kind of *partner*. I'm not ready."

He smiles. "I figured as much."

"We can't sleep together, either, Coop."

He draws back, *aghast*, it seems. "What kinda guy do you take me for, Sanchez?"

"One with a ding-a-ling," I say, and he laughs.

"Fair enough."

I smile at him.

He smiles at me.

"I want you to know you have my full support in your . . . journey. You could be anything, and it wouldn't—"

"It's SCIENCE!" I say.

His eyes go wide, and I clear my throat. "Might've looked up Carl on YouTube. Got pretty sucked in, actually. That water-cycle episode? Man."

"I really, really, *really* love you, Jupes."

I blush. Look over my shoulder at Freddie. Back at Coop. Smile again (because I can't help it). "I love you, too, loser."

"Oh, I know."

"Just don't get cocky. I'd feel the same if you had a vagina. Might love you even more then."

"You're ridiculous."

"And you love it. As you said."

"Can't argue there," he says. "So the Jam?"

I nod. Turn back to the computer. "Dance break verse two?"

"You better believe it, baby."

I press Play.

AUTHOR'S NOTE
(AND ACKNOWLEDGMENTS)

I got married to my dream man before fully accepting certain things about myself, namely my attractions to other women. And while in many ways it's not *as* taboo a thing as it was back then, being open about it is still a little nerve-racking for me after years and years of lying by omission, in a sense.

Which is why I wrote this book. It's a book I needed at twelve, when I was skittish at slumber parties and worried about playing truth-or-dare because I didn't want the other girls to know about the fire I felt below my navel when I watched them kiss each other and stuff. I needed it at fifteen, sixteen, seventeen, when I would change for cheer practice separate from the other girls because I didn't want anybody to catch me looking. (*Flee temptation!* my Bible said.) I needed it at twenty-one, when trying to navigate intense romantic feelings for a female friend. And I need it now as I *continue* to waffle between labels. (Am I bisexual? Pansexual? Queer? Heteroflexible? All of the above? None of the above?)

Bottom line: there's nothing wrong with questioning, and I personally don't think self-discovery has an expiration date. For some, labels are grounding and give a sense of identity. Others find them too narrow or restrictive. Some might be attracted to one gender identity at one point and a different gender identity at another. A guy who has only ever been attracted to men might find himself attracted to a woman. A girl who has only ever liked boys might find herself falling for her trans female best friend.

None of this is as simple as we want it to be. And I think that should be okay. Being who you are and loving who you love may not be easy, but it's always worthwhile.

I owe the existence of this book to the following people:

The first girl I ever kissed (who shall remain unnamed for the sake of her privacy); my incredible husband, Nigel, who wasn't angry at all when I came out to him a few weeks *after* our wedding; my Book Mom and editor extraordinaire, Phoebe Yeh, who encourages me to write what I want ("It just has to be *good*"); my wonderful agent, Rena Rossner, who continues to put up with my shenanigans; and my beloved friends Maggie Thrash, who encouraged me to write this book for ME; Ashley Woodfolk, who read it countless times and fueled me with her cries of "I JUST LOVE IT SO MUCH" when I was ready to throw my computer out the window and then run it over with my car; and Dede Nesbitt, who let me bounce ideas off her at all hours of the day *and* night and wouldn't let me give up on this story.

Love to all those who allowed me to ask them invasive questions for research and/or did beta/sensitivity reads: Yanata Bell, Mr. Jose and Mrs. Yolanda Perez, Dan Perez, Misty Novitch, Taina Brown, Erik Rogers, Alexandra Chen, Melissa Wilcox, Taliyah Daniels, Malcolm McAllister, Becky Albertalli, Kevin Savoie, Marcus Alexander, Tehlor Kay Mejia, Dave Connis, David Arnold, Greg Andree, Anitra Van Prooyen, Wesaun Palmer, and Ava Mortier. And Sarah Taphom, Jarred Amato, and the Amato All-Stars, Jakaylia, Rodrea, and David, for being my pinch readers.

Also: Elizabeth Stranahan for her tireless work behind the scenes, Kathy Dunn for making me seem way more appealing than I actually am (lol!), and my Random House squaddies—Adrienne, Kristin, Jules, Mary, Dominique, Sydney, Alison, and Lisa.

And thanks to Joey Tam for being Joey Tam.

I'm sure I forgot somebody because I can be very forgetful. My sincerest apologies for making you the Odd One Out.

ABOUT THE AUTHOR

Nic Stone is an Atlanta native and Spelman College graduate. *Odd One Out* is her second book and the one she wishes she had back when she was trying to figure out who it's okay to love.

Her first novel, *Dear Martin*, is a *New York Times* bestseller and is loosely based on a series of true events involving the shooting deaths of unarmed African American teenagers. It was honored as a William C. Morris finalist, an ALA-YALSA Best Fiction for Young Adults selection, an ALA-YALSA Quick Picks for Reluctant Young Adult Readers Top Ten selection, and a Teen Choice Book Awards nominee.

Before turning to write full-time, Nic worked extensively in teen mentoring and lived in Israel for several years. You can find her fangirling over her husband and sons on Twitter and Instagram at @getnicced or on her website, nicstone.info.